D0114527

THE JASMINE PROJECT

THE JASMINE PROJECT

MEREDITH IRELAND

SIMON & SCHUSTER BFYR

New York London Toronto Sydney New Delhi

SIMON & SCHUSTER BFYR

An imprint of Simon & Schuster Children's Publishing Division
1230 Avenue of the Americas, New York, New York 10020

For information about special discounts for bulk purchases, please contact Simon & Schuster
Special Sales at 1-866-506-1949 or business@simonandschuster.com.
The Simon & Schuster Speakers Bureau can bring authors to your live event.
For more information or to book an event, contact the Simon & Schuster Speakers Bureau at
1-866-248-3049 or visit our website at www.simonspeakers.com.
Interior design by Hilary Zarycky
The text for this book was set in New Caledonia.
Manufactured in the United States of America
First Edition
2 4 6 8 10 9 7 5 3 1
Library of Congress Cataloging-in-Publication Data
Names: Ireland, Meredith, author.
Title: The Jasmine Project / Meredith Ireland.
Description: First edition. | New York : Simon & Schuster Books for Young Readers, [2021] |
Audience: Ages 12 up. | Audience: Grades 7 up. | Summary: When Korean American Jasmine
Yap's long-time boyfriend, Paul, is caught cheating on her, her giant, overprotective family
secretly arranges to use her graduation party to introduce her to Orlando's most eligible men.
Identifiers: LCCN 2020050023 (print) | LCCN 2020050024 (eBook) | ISBN 9781534477025
(hardcover) | ISBN 9781534477049 (eBook)
Subjects: CYAC: Dating (Social customs—Fiction. | Family life—Florida—-Fiction. |
Self-esteem—Fiction. | Korean Americans—Fiction. | Orlando (Fla.)—Fiction.
Classification: LCC PZ7.1.I743 Jas 2021 (print) | LCC PZ7.1.I743 (eBook) |
DDC [Fic]—dc23
LC record available at https://lccn.loc.gov/2020050023
LC ebook record available at https://lccn.loc.gov/2020050024

For my heart and sunshine

CHAPTER ONE

Burrito Fridays are an institution. The cornerstone of my relationship with Paul and how we started dating. One fateful day in freshman bio he passed me a note that said, "Wanna go to Chipotle y/y?" and the rest was history.

I framed the ripped piece of paper and it rests on my dresser next to pictures of us at junior prom last year and senior prom this year. Yes, it's a little cheesy that I kept the note and bedazzled JASMINE ♥S PAUL on the frame, but that's okay. Cheese is honest.

I pull my long hair into a ponytail just as my sister knocks on my door.

"Almost ready?" she asks.

Carissa's giving me a ride to Tijuana Outpost. I'm sure Paul would've picked me up if I'd asked, but I like driving with Cari. I missed her this past year when she was away at college.

"Almost done," I say.

"You look pretty, Jaz." She smiles.

Do I? Not compared to her, but I take a last look in the mirror. I look okay—Korean and kind of plain. I wish I were comfortable wearing the tiny rompers and miniskirts that catch Paul's eye, but even this spaghetti-strapped shirt makes me uneasy. I keep moving it around hoping it'll cover more boob, and so far . . . no. No, it does not.

I fuss with it more, then give up. It's fine. Really. No one will be looking at me, anyhow.

"All set," I say.

Cari stands straight to her ridiculous five-nine height. She's the combo of our Filipino and white parents and a full eight inches taller than me. Everyone asks if she's a model. Note: no one happens to ask me that question.

"Davey's coming along for the ride," she says as we pad down the cool, tiled hall.

"Ugh, he's just trying to mooch a free burrito," I say.

"He definitely is. Stay strong, little sis," Cari says with a wink.

As we walk into the living room, Davey jumps up from lounging on the couch.

"Man, I'm so hungry," he says, patting his T-shirt-clad stomach. I swear it's like he ESPed his way into our burrito conversation. "Basketball really took it out of me today," he continues. "I wish . . . shoot, if only I could get a part-time job like you guys. Mom and Dad are being extra stingy with the allowance, and I'm starving."

He reminds me of Mrs. Hernandez's twenty-two-pound cat, Cuddles, who circles, mews, and begs for food like he'll waste away if there's not kibble in his dish, stat.

"You don't get an allowance because you don't help around the house," Cari says, folding her arms.

"Because he doesn't need an allowance," I say. "Aren't

you at least a part-time bookie at this point?" I reach up and run my hand over his brown curls.

He skews his face trying to look hard. It fails. He has the same deep dimples as when he came into our family as a toddler. Of the three Yap kids, zero of us look alike, two are adopted, two are Asian biracial, and we're 100 percent family.

"Whoa, whoa, whoa," Davey says. "Just because a man can spot some hidden financial opportunities does *not* make him a bookie."

"*Man?* What man? Where?" I arch my eyebrow.

"I don't see one." Cari puts her hand on her forehead, scanning.

Davey pushes my palm off his head, which isn't hard as he's fourteen but already six inches taller than me. He frowns. "Damn, you guys."

"Aw, we're sorry, baby," Cari says.

She does not, incidentally, sound sorry.

"I'm crushed," he says. "I gotta think this kind of offense to my manhood is worth say . . . half a burrito from each of you." He rubs his palms together and waits.

"You're pathetic," Cari says at the same time I say, "Fine."

He smiles, all white teeth against dark brown skin. He knew I'd give in. But he's my little bro and I can't help it.

We make our way over to the shoe tray and slip on our flip-flops.

"We should probably bring dinner home anyhow," Cari says. "Mom's at the hospital until eight, and she'll be hungry."

Our mother is a labor and delivery nurse at Orlando

Medical Center and works long shifts, plus overtime. Years ago I started making dinner on the four nights a week she's gone, since Dad and Cari are amazing except . . . not at cooking. And Dad's out of town today for a library conference, anyhow. I hadn't realized Mom was staying at work through dinnertime. If it weren't Burrito Friday, I'd whip something up, but I can't let Paul down.

"I'll treat to takeout from Tijuana's," I say.

"Nah, I got it, Jaz. I just got paid from the ad sponsors," Cari says.

My sister is the host of a wildly popular *The Bachelor* podcast. It's the number-one teen fancast, podblast, or whatever. Our whole family talks about it. Except me. Podcasts aren't my thing, and neither are fake romance reality shows, but it makes her happy and earns her money so I'm all for it. She'll need to save up anyhow, being prelaw.

"And, no offense, but we'll probably get Agave," she adds, opening the front door.

None taken. I know it's better.

"Sweet! Yes! Agave!" Davey says with an arm pump. "Burrito and queso and chips and guac for Daveeey."

"You're not getting queso *and* guac," Cari says.

We step into the soupy humidity of Florida in May, and she locks our wooden door behind her.

"Cari!" Davey clutches his chest. "How could I possibly choose between the smoothness of avocado and the beauty of cheesy goodness?"

"You're cheesy, all right," Cari mutters.

"I like both too," I say as we head to the carport. "I wish Paul weren't lactose intolerant and we could split queso fundido."

Cari and Davey exchange looks as she unlocks the Corolla. As I stare from one to the other, I get a distinct uncomfortable feeling. Like I farted in an elevator or something and they don't know what to say.

"What?" I look around.

"Nothing," they respond at the same time.

Yeah, that's not weird. "No. What?"

"It's just that Paul . . . ," Cari says. Then she opens the driver's-side door and slides behind the wheel.

"It's just that Paul what?" I open the passenger door but pause before getting in.

"Well . . . it's just that he sucks," Davey says, diving into the backseat.

I sigh and lower myself into the red car. It's not the first time we've had the Paul Kinda Sucks discussion, but it's been a while. My family doesn't see him the way I do, and we've accepted the impasse. Mostly.

"He has a food allergy, Davey," I say. "That's not the same as being difficult."

My seat belt clicks like it agrees with me. It's weird to sit in the passenger side of what's been my car since Cari left for college. Freshmen at Miami can't have cars on campus, so I lucked into getting the Corolla for a year. But Cari will take it with her in August. I've tried not to think about my impending car-lessness.

I've kept the Rolla immaculate for her/us. No beach sand. No food or drink inside. I make an exception for Paul, but I don't mention that.

"It's not the queso, Jaz," Cari says. She bites her lip. "It's . . . well, he . . ."

"He's an asshole," Davey says.

Cari purses her lips but doesn't contradict him.

"Language, or I'm telling Mom," I say, pointing at my brother's face.

We're all teenagers and cursing is pretty minor, but Mom still sees Davey as the toddler they adopted from the Dominican Republic and she'd give him the business about his mouth.

Davey raises his hands. "Sorry, but he is, and you deserve better. A lot better."

"Aw, look at my baby brother trying to act all grown and protective." I turn in my seat and lay a kiss on his cheek. He promptly wipes it off, because we've reached that stage.

"Knock it off, loser," Davey says, pushing me back into my seat.

"You knock it off," I say. "You know Paul is solid. He's the one who taught you how to play basketball. And he bought you those sneakers, which you need to get off our car this instant." I push his foot from the center console and wipe it with my hand. "And don't you have plans to turn my room into your gaming den when I move out? You should be thrilled that we're close to finding an apartment for August."

I have to add a little more cheer than I feel at the exag-

THE JASMINE PROJECT • 7

geration. We've been looking for a place near our future colleges . . . or I've been. All Paul's done is shoot down my top choices as being "too far" or "too expensive." The second is funny as his family practically trips and falls into piles of money.

Cari glances in the rearview mirror and exchanges another set of looks with Davey.

"That's great, Jaz," she says. "Really. Are . . . are you ready for the graduation party?"

"Um, just about," I lie.

For the record, I'm not a good liar. Between studying for finals, going to prom, and planning out my future, I haven't given it more than a passing thought. And the party isn't for another eight days, anyhow. That's a lifetime away.

"Well, Aunt Minnie, Cousin Teagan, Cousin Crystal, and Aunt Tammy all want to know if you picked out a dress yet," Cari says. "And what color, so they don't wear the same."

As Cari pulls down our street, Davey leans forward and turns on the radio. He puts on rock and moves the sound to the rear speakers to block us out like the little punk he is.

I shoot him a look and Cari gives me one right back. Oh, yeah. The dress. The one I don't have. I was supposed to get a dress but helped Paul pick out a new shirt instead.

"Um . . . it's a shade of . . . not yet," I say.

Cari raises a threaded eyebrow. She's only nineteen, but sometimes, like when she disapproves, it feels like she's thirty. "You'd better get on that before Aunt Tammy takes you shopping."

I groan.

Aunt Tammy is one of our fifteen assorted aunts and uncles (not to mention the unrelateds we call "Auntie"). She means well, but her taste is like a beauty pageant on safari— all sequins and animal prints and feathers. She's been designing her own purses lately and . . . they're *a lot*.

"The family is excited," Cari says. "Uncle Vin has special flowers ordered, and you know Aunt Jay is going to cater. Or . . . Aunt Jay is going to cook and Mom is going to question every decision she makes."

My heart still squeezes at the mention of Aunt Jay cooking, but I let it go because Cari continues.

"Also, Cousin Wesley is bringing his newest girlfriend," she says.

I move my eyes to their corners trying to recall the girl's name. "Julie?" I guess.

Cari shakes her head as we drive down Aloma Avenue. "No, that was last month. This one is Amanda."

I raise my eyebrows and purse my lips. We have twenty-six first cousins, which is enough to keep track of without one of them being the Serial Dater of Central Florida Med School. Add the five people of my nuclear family to my cousins, my aunts and uncles, and my grandparents on the Yap and Ventura sides, and we're fifty people strong.

Basically, if I sneeze in Orlando, forty-nine people say bless you.

"I know you've had exams, but you should get more into the party," Cari says. "You have all summer to look at apartments and whatever with Paul, but your graduation is special.

I can take you dress shopping this weekend, if you want."

My sister has all the taste I lack as evidenced by her looking like she stepped out of Asian *Vogue*. Plus, she won't pressure me like Mom. Mom's great, but she has *opinions*.

"That'd be awesome," I say.

She smiles. "Let's do it tomorrow. I have to prep on Sunday for the big watch party on Monday."

"Ah, yes, *Bachelor in Purgatory* is starting," I say.

"*Paradise*."

"That's what I said."

She side-eyes me, though she cracks a smile. When traffic clears, Cari takes a left into the strip mall parking lot. There are much better burritos in town (for example, Agave), but Paul likes the routine of Tijuana's. So do I.

"You sure you don't want to just have dinner with us?" Cari asks as she pulls into a spot near the entrance.

I wrinkle my brow at her and tilt my head. What a strange question. "It's Burrito Friday," I say. It's self-explanatory. We've done it for nearly four years.

"Didn't he cancel on you two weeks ago?" Davey asks.

"Oh, now you can hear us?" I aim a pointed look at the backseat.

Cari lowers the music. "We, um . . ."

"There was uh . . . ," Davey says.

We linger in the car as they utter more "ums" and "uhs." I know they're trying to tell me something, but I wish they'd hurry up. It's after six o'clock, and I don't want to keep Paul waiting.

I tap my foot and linger another minute. Sixty slow seconds grate on my skin, and I keep sighing and glancing at the storefront. He's going to be upset, and things have been off between us. I don't want to make it worse by being late.

Finally, I push open the car door. Whatever it is, we can talk when I get home.

"Guys, I have to go," I say.

Davey and Cari exchange yet another glance.

"Have fun," Davey says.

"See you later, Jaz," Cari adds.

I want to know what's so hard to say, but I get out of the car and hustle into Tijuana Outpost.

CHAPTER TWO

DAVEY'S FAMILY GROUP TEXT
MAY 17

So, that went great

Cari
Yeah, way to step up. Coward

Me??? You were all like: I'm the BIG sister, I'LL tell

🐢

Mom
Are you really texting each other when you're in the same house?

You feel that?

Cari
Feel what?

That breeze?

Mom
Did Daddy adjust the Nest thermostat again?

Dad
What am I being accused of now, mahal?

No, it's not the AC. It's def the wind from two parents hovering overhead

Cari
Lol

Mom
We are NOT helicopter parents, thank you very much . . .

Idk that's exactly what a helicopter parent would say . . .

Mom
Very funny. You included us in this chat! But you left off Jaz . . .

Cari
Because we need to talk about her

Dad
How'd she take the news? I'm sorry I couldn't be there. I'll be home tomorrow

Cari
You missed nothing. Some 'man' chickened out

You were supposed to tell her!

Mom
About the bimbo?

Cari
Momma, please, we don't know that she's a bimbo. I don't think people even use that word anymore. We just know Paul was with a girl and definitely not 'sick' when he canceled on Jaz two weeks ago

Yeah, he was studying with some girl at a concert. At night. With his arms around her, feeling on some side boob. And lying to Jaz about it. Sure sure

Cari
I'm just saying it might not be how it looks

Mom
We can't keep going round after round on this. We need the family

Cari
You don't mean the entire . . .

(Thirty-two people enter the chat.)

Aunt Minnie
What's going on?

Uncle Carlos
Hey, fam

(Thirty-two salutations.)

Mom
We have a bit of a crisis here

Aunt Tammy
Who's in jail??

Aunt Minnie
You didn't even let her finish

Aunt Tammy
Oh, my bad, but I know a good bail bondsman if you need one, Dolores

Mom
We'd just call my brother Rich at the DA's office if someone was in jail. No, it's . . .
David you tell them

Scumbag Paul is cheating on Jaz. He was tagged
on IG with a busty blonde (link)

(Outraged replies until . . .)

Cousin Madison
That's not how we describe women, Davey

Cousin Wylan
Oh here we go. You've set off the feminist bath bomb. Just
let her go until she fizzles out

Cousin Madison
Whatever Wylan. The objectification of women is a huge
problem in this country. Silence doesn't help

Cousin Wylan
🎳

Cousin Madison
Awesome comeback, bro! Shame Harvard hasn't recruited
you yet

Aunt Regina
Sidebar, both of you. I apologize for my children. They need
to go back to school

Cousin Wylan
School just ended

Aunt Regina
My point exactly

Uncle Carlos
Let's get back on track. Poor Jaz. She deserves so much better

Uncle Steve
Agreed

Cousin Joe
Are we going to talk about how this guy keeps getting such great girls?

Cousin Teagan
No

Cousin Joe
I mean he should teach a class or something. Is he wearing a fanny pack in that pic?

Cousin Teagan
Let it go, cuz

Mom

Can everyone just focus? Jaz doesn't know yet

(A full minute of silence passes—unheard of for this family.)

Nonna

It's a shame we can't take care of this like we would in the old country

Cousin Teagan

Nonna!

Cousin Joe

Lol, Nonna

Mom

I've suggested a hitman, Mama, but I've been overruled

Dad

Violence isn't the answer, mi amore. Even if it's tempting

Aunt Minnie

We have to do something

Cousin Wesley

I don't get it. Why are we triaging this? Just tell Jaz and let her dump the jerk

Cari
I think the fear is that even if Jaz knows she'll stay with
him because she's never understood she's worth more

(Another thirty seconds of silence.)

Cousin Wylan
Well, damn

CHAPTER THREE

I scan the inside of Tijuana Outpost. It's the kind of place where you order at a counter, grab your tray, and take a seat at questionably clean tables. An enormous array of hot sauces decorates the back wall, and funky-colored string lights crisscross the ceiling.

Paul sits with his headphones covering part of his wavy black hair. There's a half-eaten burrito in front of him along with a mostly drained sweet tea. I beeline for him, and I'm practically a foot in front of his face before he notices me. His hazel eyes meet mine.

"Oh, hey," he says.

I lean down and kiss his cheek. He's never been a fan of PDA, but he tolerates it. He wears the same cologne as he did in freshman year, and the scent floods me with warm memories. His neck would smell like this when he'd meet me in the high school stairwell to sneak a kiss. Or when I jumped in his arms after he won a stuffed bear at Dave & Buster's.

I linger next to him. I'm not sure if I should order, or if we're going to leave, or if maybe he got something for me, too.

"You already have your food?" I ask.

He sighs, pauses his song, and removes his Beats

headphones. He wants to be a music producer, and I know he's focused, but it'll only take a second to talk.

Paul turns all his attention to me, and it's like being bathed in sunshine. He was the first guy to really see me, to notice me. But lately his eyes don't soften when they meet mine. Not the way they used to.

"Yeah," he says. "I was hungry. And . . ." He checks his phone. "Don't we normally have dinner at six?"

I stare at the concrete floor. "Yes. I'm sorry I'm late."

It's 6:07.

"Okay," he says. He has a thing about people being punctual—people being me. He's never said a word about his friends showing up whenever. But I know waiting alone embarrasses him. I should've gotten out of the car sooner. This is on me.

"Did you order something for me, too?" I ask. "Or should I . . ." I do a weird miming gesture between me and the counter. I feel ridiculous, so I stop.

His forehead knits. "Why would I have ordered for you? I didn't know what you'd want . . . or when you'd get here." He mutters the last part.

I order the same thing every time, but okay, I *am* late. And cold burritos are nasty. It's not like there's a skillet where I could reheat it in here. I turn and step away.

"Jaz," he says.

My heart skips when he says my name. Like it did freshman year when he'd call for me in the hall and jog to catch up. Like when he'd wave me down to sit with him and his football

THE JASMINE PROJECT • 21

boys at lunch in sophomore year. Like when he'd thread his fingers in mine after he scored the winning field goal during junior year—before he quit this past fall.

"Yes?" I hold my breath.

"They have a new skinny burrito on the menu. You may want to check it out."

I stare at him, but he shrugs and takes out a twenty.

I don't know what I was waiting for, but that wasn't it. Still, I smile.

"Maybe," I say.

I leave his money on the table and walk to the counter, where a line has formed. I should've ordered when I came in. I can't remember the last time Paul got something for me I didn't specifically ask for. Maybe junior year when he brought in bagels from Panera. I was so charmed, I ate mine painfully slowly, savoring every bite. Later I found out he had two only because they'd messed up his order, but still. He could've given the extra to anyone and he chose me.

My phone chimes and I slip it out of my purse. It's a screenshot of a flight itinerary from my best friend. June Tam and I have been inseparable since her parents moved to Winter Park in the third grade. I don't know what I'm going to do when she goes to Emory this fall. It's yet another thing happening soon that I refuse to think about.

But maybe because she's moving on, or maybe because I'd had three spiked seltzers, or maybe it was that she'd been talking about spending a semester abroad, but I wound up telling her how I'd like to go to Paris. I even let it slip that I dream about cooking professionally there—the birthplace of fine cuisine. I like to blame the alcohol, but maybe dreams that big refuse to stay bottled.

I regretted it as soon as she set fare alerts on her phone—i.e., that night. And she constantly forwards them to me because she's the worst.

No matter what, I can't help but look at the info. This one is the best deal yet—$280 one-way from Orlando. I have seven times that saved from birthday money, tutoring, and slinging fro-yo at Berry Plum. I count my savings all the time, and it'll be minus this burrito dinner, but it doesn't matter since it's just a fantasy. I might as well dream of being the first astronaut on Mars or the first five-foot-tall Korean girl in the NBA. Becoming a chef and cooking in Paris takes a whole lot of things I'm not.

My phone dings again.

JT

June

Under $300! I'd chip in a hundred and Emily would too. $80 total from you.
You have to go

Not going to happen

Why not?

Bc I belong here. My life is here. Plus Paul and

I are moving in together and I start Valencia in
August

Those are all horrible reasons

?

It's your dream, Jaz

By the way: Never get drunk and tell your best friend
your secret ambition, because they'll remember it. And bring
it up later. Constantly.

I put my phone away.

A sigh escapes my chest and it's the heavy kind. I shouldn't
feel it, though. I'm blessed to have the life I do. My *real* life.
Not a useless dream. How many people have a loving family,
graduate high school with honors, get a full academic scholarship to community college, and will soon move in with the
love of their life? I need my savings for my future, not to fly
overseas for a fantasy.

Yet every time I push Paris away, this sadness rises up. I tamp
it down because it doesn't make sense. Every reason I gave June
is a great one. There's no need to throw my life into chaos with
a one-way ticket to France. Not to mention that I'd disappoint
my family, especially my mom, who expects me to follow in her
footsteps. Besides which, even the thought of leaving Central
Florida makes me want to puke. The closest I've come to a solo
adventure was driving to Winter Park High alone when Davey
had the flu this winter. Transatlantic it was not.

The bottom line is, I refuse to risk losing what I have to reach out for something I'm not.

I glance at Paul, who's texting on his phone. What I do have is a solid life ahead of me. I'll go to Valencia, then transfer to UCF's nursing program. Nursing is a good profession. It may not be my dream, but it's reliable and something I can actually do. Mom has been a nurse for twenty-five years, and she's provided us with what we need. It's good and that's good enough for me. If I'm lucky, I can vacation in Paris one day, even save enough to eat at fine-dining restaurants—eventually.

"Next," the counter person calls.

I step forward.

"Oh, hey, Jasmine," Gus says with a smile. We see him every Friday. "Don't you look pretty."

"Hey, Gus," I say. "Still trolling for tips, I see. Are you having a good night?"

He laughs. "So far. Thanks. You?"

"Great. Really great." Again, I feel like I'm acting. I force myself to smile.

"What'll it be? The usual?"

"No, I'll um . . ."

I look at Paul one more time. So many girls wanted to date him over the years, and somehow he picked me. Somehow I have one of the handsomest guys in my school as my boyfriend.

While I'm staring, Paul looks up and grins. I remember the smile on his lips when I talked to him for the very first time during the cooking club bake sale. He took a bite of my brownies and a wide smile lit his face. He looked right at me and told me they were amazing. That *I* was amazing. A burst of forgotten happiness makes me smile back.

I face Gus. "Do you guys have a skinny burrito now?"

His pierced eyebrows knit. "We do. It's chicken breast, beans, lettuce, salsa, and a low-carb tortilla. But . . . you don't want the usual?"

Solid question. "Just, you know, just in the mood to try something new," I say brightly.

"Um, okay."

He rings me up, and I can't help feeling this is wrong, but I take my cup and go to the fountain to get a Diet Coke.

I hate Diet Coke.

CHAPTER FOUR

**DAVEY'S UNWIELDY FAMILY GROUP TEXT
MAY 18**

We told her last night

Aunt Tammy
What'd she say??

Uncle Steve
How'd she take it?

Cousin Mabel
She dumped him, right?

Cousin Crystal
She didn't mention breaking up with Paul in the cousins'
group chat. . . .

Cousin Wesley
How can you even keep track of all the messages in there?

Mom
She didn't break up with him. They're still dating

Aunt Minnie
What?!

Cari
Long story, but Scumbag Paul convinced her that the IG girl was 'just a friend'

Aunt Regina
No

Cousin Joe
Man . . . I need better friends

Cari
But they're not going to be exclusive this summer.

Uncle Steve
Come again?

Cari
He got Jaz to agree to see other people because 'moving in together is such a big step and they should both be sure'

Aunt Minnie
The nerve of this damn kid

Cousin Amberlynn
Why would she buy any of that?

Cari
Because she wants to believe it

Cousin Wesley
So she's going to date other people? That's good. She can meet a better guy

Cari
Except she won't date anyone else. She said this is something he needs and that she understands. I said she should date too, but she shook her head

Which is 'absolutely not' in Jaz speak

Cousin Wylan
So he's going to be playing the field while she sits home?

Cousin Madison
I don't get it. Why wouldn't she date?

Cari
Well, she's never dated anyone other than Paul. And you know how she is with new things

Mom

And she's always thought he was the best and that she was lucky to have him. He convinced her of it

Grandpa Yap

She thinks the world of everyone else but not of herself. How can we get our Jaz to understand her worth?

Mom

That's the million dollar question, Papa

Cari

She's so much like Meghan last season—she's a gem and doesn't know it

Okay, look, you don't actually know the people on *The Bachelor*, even if you rope one onto your podcast every season. It's still just a made up show

Cari

Paid for your dinner, ingrate. And it's the perfect show. It's The OG. There's a reason it's had so many seasons and imitators. People love love and someone finding it and themselves

Aunt Regina

How is this helping, guys?

Cousin Wesley

Yeah, what do we do? Set up *The Bachelorette* starring Jaz
so she goes on dates?

(Fifteen seconds pass.)

Uncle Carlos

I mean . . .

Cousin Mabel

Wait, bro, you're on to something

Cousin Wesley

I've been up for 31 hours. I'm on to sleep deprivation

Aunt Rosey

Go to sleep, Wes. Turn your ringer off, baby

Cousin Wesley

It's okay, Ma. I'm fine

Aunt Rosey

Did you eat a good breakfast?

Cousin Wesley

Geez, I'm a doctor. I'm fine

Aunt Rosey

You're not a doctor yet. A simple yes or no will do

Cousin Wesley

Yes

Cari

Guys, wait, we could actually do this

Aunt Kim

A dating show?

Cari

Not a show, but something where guys come to her and she'd date them. She'd realize she has options, and see that she shouldn't settle for anyone

Grandpa Yap

A little Jasmine project. I like it

Uncle Steve

Exactly

Cousin Teagan

This could be really great for her . . . if she'd do it

Aunt Tammy

I love my girl but I don't see her going for a dating contest.

She's our shy, night-blooming Jasmine

Cousin Crystal
You're right, Momma. There's no way she'll say yes y'all

Cari
If we do it right, she wouldn't have to know

Uncle Steve
How could that be?

Cari
Well, we'd be the ones to find the boys—do the casting, right?
We'd be the ones inviting them to meet her. We'd just need to
set up a situation where she wouldn't know it was a contest

Aunt Regina
How would that work? Logistically

Cari
I'm not sure. We could definitely find guys, but I don't know
how we could get her to meet them. She pretty much just
works, volunteers, and goes to school and even that's over
soon

Mom
Wait, the graduation party. We already have over a hundred

people coming. She might not realize there were extra boys
there

Uncle Carlos
It's not a bad idea, Dee. Our family parties are pretty massive
with the Aunties and Uncles, and neighbors. Even Steve and
I wind up not knowing some people

Aunt Jay
That could work, but it's so soon . . .

Aunt Kim
So the plan would be to find a bunch of boys and invite them
and she'd pick?

Cari
I think the fewer options the better. Otherwise, she'd be
overwhelmed and figure it out. We could vet and weed
potentials and present her with a top five . . . or a top three

Cousin Teagan
I love this! I have a friend who's been bugging me about my
'cute cousin'

Cousin Joe
Same and it's gross

Aunt Kim
There's an adorable boy who works at our bookstore! I've wanted to set him up with Jaz forever, but she was always with her boyfriend

Aunt Minnie
Ugh. 'That boy.' He needs to go. Immediately. I'm in for whatever gets rid of him

Nonna
Jasmine, my little Bachelorette

Cari
If we do this, we'd have to start looking tonight. *The Bachelor* takes months of prep and we'll only have a week. Let's focus on finding three boys that will be great matches for her

Wait, this is all pretty half-baked. Is everyone good with this? Dad?

Dad
Well . . . I don't like the idea of lying to Jaz

Mom
Remember when we caught her doing Paul's homework two years ago and he almost broke up with her when she stopped? And she cried and begged us to let her help him with his term paper because he'd fail without her?

Dad
I'd almost forgotten

Mom
This may be our only chance to get him out of her life. If she moves in with him . . .

Dad
You're right, mahal. If it gets Scumbag Paul out of the picture . . . without murder . . . yes. I think it might be okay

Aunt Tammy
I don't know anyone offhand. . . . What should I do?

Cari
If you don't have anyone in mind, let's use social media to find contestants. Tell them we're doing a local version of *The Bachelorette*, with a twist, but don't use her name. We don't need this getting back to her

                           Cari, I don't know. She could find out

Cousin Joe
How? She has the tech skills of an 80yo woman. No offense, Nonna

Nonna
Hey, I'm on here and she's not

  Still

Cousin Wesley
I bet I can find someone before anyone else

                                    Bet? Bet what? How much?

Cari
If any of you think of a better idea, I'm all ears. Otherwise,
let's get to work!

CHAPTER FIVE

I'm in my bedroom getting ready for work, and it's hard to remember to breathe. Sometimes I can fool myself into thinking things are normal—that it's just another day—but other times I know my world has cracked in two. It's been like this since I came home from Burrito Friday and Cari and Davey told me about a post they saw on Instagram.

It was Paul with another girl.

The second Cari opened the app, it was like a sucker punch. I physically gripped my stomach. My body recognized the truth before I could even process it. Before Paul had a chance to come up with excuses.

When I confronted him that night, my boyfriend of four years, the one who'd remembered the one-month anniversary of our first kiss, looked me in the eyes and lied to me. He said the girl in the pic was just a friend, but I knew she wasn't, even though he stood there and insisted nothing had happened. Even though he said I was overreacting. Even though he accused me of being controlling, of spying on him since he hadn't posted the photo to his account and wasn't even tagged. And he was so persuasive, I started to believe him . . . until he talked about us "exploring our options" this summer and "taking time apart until August."

I knew then that even if the girl was a friend, he didn't want her to stay one. But I agreed to see other people. I agreed because he was already doing it and at least he still wanted to be with me. I agreed because I wasn't willing to toss away the future we'd planned for so long. I agreed because more heartbreak would've physically cleaved me in two. I agreed, most of all, because I love him.

I know it sounds weak. June and Emily, my two closest friends in the world, have made it clear it sounds *super* weak, but how could loving someone be weakness? And I know he loves me too. What we have is special. I know who he is when no one else is around and he lets down his guard. I see him when the stress of trying to be cool rolls off him and he becomes his real self. How he's vulnerable and kind. How he's still the boy I met at the bake sale.

And I get that all through high school we've only ever been with each other. It's normal to want to see what else is out there. Especially before we take this to the next level and move in together. I mean, that's starting our adult life and a huge step. Doubts and cold feet are to be expected, right? Not too long ago I was drunk and dreaming about Paris, so I get it. I do.

I mostly do.

Somehow, I've made it five days into this "seeing other people" thing. It's almost like a short-term breakup. We're not supposed to talk until August 1, to really have time and space to make a decision, so the majority of the past week I've been in my room listening to "Jolene" and creeping on Paul's socials. Honestly, it's turned me into an amateur cyberstalker.

But I can't stalk today. I have to work at Berry Plum.

Normally, I like my job. I enjoy watching kids fill their bowls with way too much sugar and listening to first dates discuss their favorite toppings. It's nice to be a part of something that's a special treat, that makes people happy. But I'd rather stay home and keep checking Paul's last seen on WhatsApp and refreshing his IG Stories and yeah . . . maybe I need to get out of my house and focus on something else.

Anything else.

I smooth out my plain white tee in the mirror. The manager doesn't care what we wear, and this is what I pick: nondescript jeans and a T-shirt I got on clearance at Target. I have them in four colors: black, white, gray, and beige. Katia, who I usually work with, has an array of patterned sundresses she rocks with flawless makeup. Paul used to compliment her on both when he came in. He'd flash his smile and say she looked great.

He's rarely said that to me over the past year or so.

I close my eyes and sigh: I rarely deserved it. I've never tried to look like the girl in the IG pic, and I'm not naturally model gorgeous like Cari.

I grab my phone. I can fix this. I won't be complacent anymore and if that was the problem—that I didn't put in enough effort—I can change starting today. But I stop typing the message. A shred of dignity tells me not to press send. Ever since Friday there's been a thought nettling me, telling me I shouldn't contact Paul ever again.

The doorbell rings and I startle. My heart pounds like there's a rabbit thumping in my chest, and I delete the text. I rest my phone on my dresser.

My bedroom door is closed, but a loud, lilting Georgia accent echoes through the walls of our ranch. Aunt Tammy is here. She's married to Uncle Vin, my dad's middle brother, the florist extraordinaire. Mom and Dad are the eldest of their siblings, and our house is the epicenter for both sides. Our grandparents used to host their own families, but when all the cousins were little, it was way too much energy with way too many breakable Virgin Mary statues. So my parents took over as hosts of the gathering spot—it's why the Yaps and Venturas are so close.

There's another voice in the house, and I can't tell if it's Aunt Tammy's daughter Crystal or Amberlynn, because my older cousins sound so similar. It's like they're twins—but born a year apart.

The doorbell rings again, and there's more commotion and the unmistakably raspy voice of Aunt Jay fills the house. Jay is Mom's youngest sibling, who's closer in age to Cari than she is to Mom. She used to be my favorite aunt, and I used to be her favorite niece, but that was all years ago.

The more reserved voice of Uncle Steve follows hers. Uncle Steve married Uncle Carlos, my dad's next eldest brother.

I know. It's a lot. I drew a chart for Paul in freshman year so he could keep everyone straight.

Although it's normal for family to randomly drop by, with

that many together at the same time, there's a reason. The word "graduation" floats around the house.

Ugh. I'd forgotten about my party. I rub my hands over my face and tip my head back.

Paul, of course, had been invited, but because "we're taking time apart," he won't be here Saturday night. My shoulders sink again, but I can't dwell on it. I have to go or I'll be late for work. I'm never late. Mom raised me to be punctual.

I throw my hair back in a bun and grab my employee card and step into the hall.

Aunt Jay, Aunt Tammy, Uncle Steve, Cousin Crystal, Mom, and Cari are gathered around the dining room table. There's food laid out because there's always food, but Aunt Jay must've brought this, because it doesn't smell Italian or Filipino. As a professionally trained chef, Jay can cook us all under the table. She used to have an award-winning restaurant. And I used to want to be just like her.

I shake off the memories and look up. It's like a record scratch, freeze-frame as my family notices me. They stay frozen for a second too long, and I know they were talking about me. Mom nudges Jay as if to say: Look at that mess. I told you so.

It takes me everything not to groan.

"Hey, Jaz," Aunt Jay says brightly. "I brought party dishes to sample. Come and try some. I want your feedback."

Jay has a similar face to Mom's, with wide-set blue eyes. They're both fairly tall for women, five-seven, which means they tower over me. Jay has pixie-cut hair that's dyed almost as black as mine. She also has a sleeve of tattoos my mother absolutely hates. They are total opposites. Mom looks out for everyone and has said more than once that Jay only cares about herself.

"I'm good with whatever you want to make," I say, remaining in the hall. I'm not in the mood to talk, and I have mixed feelings about eating Jay's food again. It used to be all I'd look forward to every week. But a lot of things were different then.

"Come and eat, honey," Mom says.

I can't really say no to her. Not with a growling stomach, but I push it off. "I need to go to work," I say.

"Take some to go then, baby," Aunt Tammy says, grabbing a serving spoon.

In the Venn diagram of Southern, Filipino, and Italian, they all intersect at: Baby, you need to eat more. Like Cuddles, I'm in no danger of wasting away.

"You have a few minutes still," Mom says, eyeing her watch. She knows my schedule down to the minute.

A dish materializes with a variety of delicious-smelling appetizers, paella, and thin-sliced tenderloin in gravy. My stomach gurgles in anticipation, because although my aunt stopped wanting me around, she never stopping being a great cook.

Crystal holds the plate out to me with a sad smile. There's a similar look in Uncle Steve's gray eyes.

Great, so they all know about Paul. Of course they do. Gossip is my family's extreme sport.

There's no way for me to eat standing here, and I don't

eat in the Rolla, so I walk into the dining room and perch on a chair. My mother is right, of course. I have ten minutes, maybe twelve, before I have to be out the door.

"This looks delicious, Aunt Jay," I say.

"Don't you think I should make a lasagna or two?" my mom says with a frown. By "a lasagna," she means an enormous pan of pasta that could feed twenty men.

"Dee, there will be more than enough food," Aunt Jay says. "There'll also be fruit and cheese trays, a minisandwich tray, salads, desserts, and the cake for Jaz."

"It's one hundred fifty people though. . . ."

"I catered a four-hundred-person sit-down dinner last weekend," Aunt Jay says with her hands landing on her hips. "For a very particular bride."

Mom folds her arms. Challenge accepted. "But the family will expect a pasta dish. . . ."

This will go on for a while—Mom undercutting Jay and Jay rising to the challenge. Mom acts like a minimother to Jay, who can't stand to be patronized. And they both always think they're right. Ever since Jay's restaurant closed four years ago, it's only gotten worse.

I tune them out and focus on the beef with gravy. It's the perfect medium rare and the gravy has a certain umami. It's flat-out fantastic.

Her food is so good that everyone thought Ventura's Bistro would be a huge success. And for a while it was. My parents don't talk about it, but they took out a second mortgage to invest in the restaurant. When it suddenly closed, there was no chance Aunt Jay could pay them back. Mom started working overnight shifts, and Dad's been driving for a rideshare to make the loan payments and keep a roof over our heads. I hear them whispering about it in the kitchen when they think I can't hear them or they forget I'm home. One of the reasons I'm going to community college is I know they're not like Emily's or June's parents, who can foot the bill for a university. Valencia offered me a full scholarship and I jumped at it. It was the safest option, and Paul going to UCF meant our schools would be close.

But everything that happened is why becoming a professional chef is just a fantasy. Even for those with the talent, it doesn't work out. And I don't have the talent to begin with.

The worst is hopefully behind my parents, though. This past spring Aunt Jay got her catering business off the ground, and despite the aunties (and my mom) saying she should've picked a "more worthwhile" profession, it seems to be going well. Maybe this business will succeed and Aunt Jay will be able to pay my parents back.

"Dee, I know what I'm doing," Aunt Jay says. Her voice is full of exasperation.

"You can sometimes make bad choices," Mom says.

Everyone stops eating, and silence settles on the room. Jay stares at Mom, then turns on her heels, grabs her shoes, and walks out of the house.

"What? What did I say?" Mom says. But Jay is already gone.

No one answers.

Mom makes a "hmmph" sound in her throat but sits back down at the table. She still looks troubled, but it's been like this between her and Aunt Jay for the past four years—these barbs and this tension. Mom used to just be proud of her.

I swallow hard. I would never want her to be as disappointed in me as she is in Jay.

"So what color's your dress going to be, Jaz?" Aunt Tammy asks. She's also blond like Mom, but with Texan large hair that somehow never moves.

Ugh, the dress. The very last possible thing on my mind. I'd put off Sunday dress shopping with Cari because sobbing in department stores is frowned upon.

"Uh . . ." I shove another bite in my mouth to buy time to come up with something. But I picked a lobster puff and it's distractingly good.

"It's blue," Cari says. "Almost teal."

Savior.

Aunt Tammy looks relieved as she cuts into her shrimp. "Oh, good. Mine is peach, Crystal's dress is yellow, and Amberlynn will be in rose."

I'm honest to God not sure why it matters, but I nod.

"We can't wait for the party," Crystal says. "It's so exciting!"

I knit my eyebrows at the sparkle in Crystal's eyes. I have no idea why she's so stoked about a backyard graduation party.

"It'll be nice to celebrate with you, Jaz," Steve says in his gentle tone. His manner has a way of putting everyone at ease—what you'd want in a dentist. Uncle Carlos is also a dentist, and they met at a convention five years ago. They have a practice together now.

"It'll be great," I lie. And because I can't lie, it sounds super forced. "But I have to go or I'll be late."

"Yes, get going, honey. You need to be on time," Mom says. "I love you."

"Love you too," I say. I hand my plate to Cari, who's gathering the dishes.

"We'll shop tomorrow," she whispers.

"You're the best," I say.

I say my goodbyes and head for my sneakers. As I slip them on, it's comforting to know that even though the past few days have been rough, I still have my family. And the good thing is, unlike a boyfriend, they'll never deceive me.

CHAPTER SIX

DAVEY'S PLOTTING FAMILY GROUP TEXT
MAY 22

Aunt Kim
How is Jaz handling everything?

Cousin Crystal
She seemed out of it today

Uncle Steve
She wasn't herself

Carl
At least she went to work. Getting her out of the house is important since she's low key turning into Paul's web stalker. June and Emily locked her out of her phone 'accidentally' last night, and she wasn't pleased

Aunt Minnie
Ugh, that boy. How's the search coming along?
We're getting close to the party

Cari
Lots of interviews, little agreement—same as it's been

Aunt Kim
What does everyone think of Simon from the bookstore?

(Fifteen seconds of pure silence.)

Aunt Regina
All the boys at my law firm are way too old. Ferdinand, did you say you found someone?

Dad
I did. Our old neighbor is back in town for the summer. Justin Michael has an internship at Disney. I couldn't believe the luck when he stopped at the library today. He and Jaz were so close. She'll be thrilled he's back. I think he's a great candidate

They're not running for office, Dad

Cari
For casting. You know what he means

Aunt Jay
There's a boy from one of the local restaurants I think might be perfect. His name is Eugene and he's home from

college for the summer. I can see if he wants to interview

Aunt Kim
I really think Simon is a nice boy

Cousin Teagan
What did y'all think about Mike Evans?

Cousin Joe
He has a mustache

Cousin Teagan
So?

Cousin Joe
It's as bad as a fanny pack, but it's on his face

Cousin Teagan
Some people have them. They can look cool

Cousin Joe
His looks like a lazy ferret

Cari
We have a good start, everyone, but we're running low on time. Let's really try to agree. If we keep nitpicking choices, we'll never have three before the party

Aunt Kim

So that's a no on Simon then?

Cari

Talk later. Gtg

CHAPTER SEVEN

CARISSA'S PROJECT JASMINE CASTING NOTES

We've gotten so much done this week!!! I wonder if I should do a podcast on this—anonymously, of course. It could be fun to make a show about someone I know. Switch it up and see how I do without the clout of The Bachelor. And okay, yeah, my rival podcaster is getting to me. Vanessa said I'm only number one because I had my show before hers, and I know she's just trying to get to me, but . . . it's working.

Dad found Justin Michael Simmons, who used to live next door. He moved four years ago. I don't remember much about him other than he wore glasses and sweatpants, like, every day. I'm hopeful that's changed?? Pretty nerdy, but Jaz used to spend a ton of time with him.

Okay, he came by the house. No sweatpants in sight, just a handsome, nice guy. We almost wrecked this whole thing before it even got started because Jaz came home early while we were talking to him. We had to sneak him out the back. But, anyhow, he's a definite top three.

Aunt Kim wants to set Jaz up with Simon from their

bookstore. He's . . . well, he's the definition of bland. He said his favorite food is water—tap water. I laughed, thinking he was joking. He wasn't joking.

Aunt Jay loves Eugene Matthews. He goes by Eugene—I don't know whether to respect or hate that. He's home for the summer and likes that we're in this to help Jaz find herself. He's cute and a definite maybe. Update: I met him and we all agree he's great. Top three. Just one more to go!

Aunt Tammy found someone who . . . I'm not convinced he's . . . I mean, I'm not calling him a serial killer, but if bodies turned up on his property, I wouldn't be surprised.

Teagan's friend Mike is nice, but yeah, that mustache is out of control. He looks like a Mario Brother and his hobby is hunting. No. Jaz cries when the animals at the shelter need to have blood drawn. That's not going to work.

Everyone else's choices can be boiled down to: too old, too hairy, too weird, or too into this for the wrong reasons. There was even a guy who turned out to be married????

I found Aaron Coopersmith. Friend of a friend of a friend. He's twenty and plays Minor League Base-ball, which is so cool. He's from Nashville—so he'll have a country music connection with Jaz (who seriously needs to stop listening to "Jolene"). He has three younger sis-ters and clearly loves them—they're all over his Insta. He was just traded to the Braves and their farm team plays in Kissimmee. I met him for coffee and he's gorgeous. Charming, easy to talk to, and he likes the novelty of a

Bachelorette contest—said it sounds fun. He even follows my podcast. I think I have a winner. We'll do a Skype interview with my family, but he'll round out the top three nicely—if they can actually agree on anything. Update: He aced the second interview. He's in. Thank God we're ready for Saturday!!!

CHAPTER EIGHT

DAVEY'S BOOKMAKING NOTES

Team Justin Michael: Dad, Aunt Minnie, Uncle Steve, Uncle Edward and Aunt Kim, Cousins Charlotte and Eliza, Cousin Wesley, Uncle Rich and Cousin Teagan, Cousin Clayton, Uncle Jimmie, Cousin Colton

Team Aaron: Cari, Mom, Nonna, Uncle Carlos, Cousin Joe, Cousins Mabel and Stella, Uncle Vin, Aunt Rosey, Cousin Tom, Cousins Liz and Jill, Aunt Tammy and Cousin Crystal, Cousin Grey, Cousins Max and Mai

Team Eugene: yours truly, Aunt Jay, Cousin Duncan, Cousins Wylan and Madison (who agree on this and only this), Aunt Regina, Uncle Al, Cousins Jim and Tim, Aunt Jen, Cousin Amberlynn, Cousins Diana and Caster, Grandma Yap

Team Paul: no one, literally no one

Abstainers (cowards): Grandpa, Poppy, and the youngest kids

Bets: Wesley-$2¢ on Justin Michael

Clayton-$2¢ on Justin Michael

Joe-$2¢ on Aaron

Wylan-$2¢ on Eugene

Bragging rights for everyone else-priceless

CHAPTER NINE

Work at Berry Plum was surprisingly good. For one, I put my phone away. For another, Katia was awesome. She cornered me and asked what was up since she'd covered two shifts and I've never asked for favors before. I told her my tale of woe, and turns out she dated a boy who cheated on her last year. She was all "forget him" solidarity, which shocked me. Sometimes you think you know someone and you're just wrong.

I would've talked to her more, but we were running around all shift. It's late May, a billion degrees out, and everyone's off from school. I was so busy, I didn't have time to think about Paul for eight hours. It was . . . blissful.

My busy streak continued yesterday because Cari and I had to search for a blue party dress. We finally found one that's more light blue than teal, but close enough. It's one shouldered—different from what I would normally choose, but Cari talked me into it. And what the hell. The old me wasn't working, might as well try to be someone else.

By dinnertime last night I was feeling okay, almost like a person again, but sleep was impossible. I knew today was coming.

It's Friday and my graduation day from Winter Park High

School. Where I'll definitely see Paul. And through the hours I should've been asleep, my mind played out scenario after scenario. At four a.m. I gave up and watched a Netflix documentary on David Chang.

I close my eyes for a long blink and try to shake off how I thought I'd graduate hand in hand with Paul. Instead, I wonder how I'm supposed to act today. Should I be aloof and ignore him? Throw my arms around him the way I normally would? Tell him I'm proud of him, which I am, or just do that weird head-nod acknowledgment? Because what does space even mean when we don't talk anymore?

There are moments, like now, where I almost wish he'd permanently broken up with me. Where I think this limbo is worse.

Sixty-eight more days until August 1. Two months and a week for him to realize we're meant to be.

"Hey, Jaz, you almost ready?" Mom calls.

"Just about," I say. I'm not sure how long I've been standing in my bedroom in this polyester gown. Probably a worrisome amount of time.

I rub my face then stop, remembering I have makeup on. Carissa put eye cream and foundation on me after my shower this morning, which was a very kind way of saying I look like hell. She's not wrong. But since she did my makeup, she hid all the tired sadness. She used to have a makeup tutorial channel and only stopped because her *Bachelor* podcast took off. So I know the graduation pictures will turn out okay.

There will be a lot of photos if I know my family. Winter

Park High limits graduation tickets to ten per student, and for most people that's fine. In fact, June and Emily gave me their extras. (Lol, "extras.") But my family had to have a raffle to decide which fourteen people could come, with grudges kept about Cari's graduation last year and promises made for Davey's. Listening to all my aunts argue in the kitchen when I got home on Wednesday was one of the bright spots in a bad week.

Aunt Minnie was furious at the thought Aunt Tammy would get the nod and not her. And Aunt Regina was laying out logical arguments for why she should be there, like the litigator she is. Then they all lost out because my grandparents pulled their guilt cards, and there were only six tickets left after that.

I should be so grateful that fifty people desperately wanted to come to a high school graduation on a Friday afternoon. Seriously, who actually wants to go to one? Cari's ceremony was like reading a phone book, and aside from worrying about seeing Paul, today is sure to be just as dull.

But my family is so proud of me. They love me and their love is what got me here. And they're waiting.

I force my shoulders back and stand straighter. This is my day. My family's day. I can smile and bear it for them. They've always been there for me.

I slip the gold sash over my head that marks honors students and straighten the large blue tassel for community service. Then I put on my cap. There are some people who look good in this square cardboard hat—Cari was one of them. I am not.

All in all, I look like an oversize key chain.

Awesome.

My cheeks puff out as I exhale a long breath.

It sucks, but I can do this.

I open my bedroom door and nearly trip over my parents. They were waiting in the hallway with their phones, recording a video no one unrelated to me will ever want to watch.

"There she is! There's my baby girl in her cap and gown!" Mom says.

From my parents' bright smiles, you'd think I'd come out in a Miss America crown.

Mom's phone obscures most of her face, but I know her eyes are tear filled. She's a bit of a helicopter parent, but she never takes credit for our success—it's all just pride.

My dad's light brown skin crinkles by his eyes as he smiles. His black hair has turned salt-and-pepper, which my mom calls "sexy," which makes me want to crawl into a shell and die because it's cute but so gross at the same time.

I do an awkward little wave at them.

"Winter Park's best and brightest. Are you excited for today, Jazzy?" Dad asks.

"Jazzy" is a nickname only he gets away with. It used to be Jazzy Jay, as my middle name is Josephina like my aunt, but he shortened it down to Jazzy. The petite yet still embarrassing nickname.

I widen my eyes and nod enthusiastically, but I fear it looks like I'm constipated rather than excited. I'll know tomorrow when we rewatch this moment in front of my entire extended family and whoever else can fit in our backyard.

Cari and Davey wait in the living room. My sister lounges, looking effortlessly cool. My brother . . . does not. He must've grown since Mom last bought him dress pants, because he looks like he's waiting for a flood. Yet his jacket is about three inches too long in the sleeves. Additionally, one side of his dress shirt hasn't made it into his pants.

Mess.

"Congratulations, sis," Cari says.

"We're proud of you," Davey says. He sounds like a robo-caller.

"Thanks, guys," I say.

"Davey, your shirt," Mom says. She *tsks* at him, clucking her tongue.

He stands, hastily tucks his shirt in, and somehow it looks worse.

Dad stops recording. That exchange will hit the cutting-room floor when Dad splices this together.

"Maybe a polo," Cari says.

Davey looks at her like she's pardoned him from a life sentence. His big brown eyes plead over to Mom.

She sighs. "All right, fine, just hurry. We don't want to be late."

Note: we will likely be the first car in the parking lot, arriving before whoever turns on the lights.

"Let's take some pictures. Get in with Cari," Dad says.

Oh, God.

Dad has a few vices. One, he has a treasure hoard's worth of bookmarks but brings home more seemingly every day. Two,

he does the worst impressions known to man—seriously, they're unimaginably bad. And three, he's a shutterbug. He used to look like a NatGeo photographer carting around a Nikon before iPhone came out with its fancy camera. We got him the phone and he promptly took a thousand pictures, mostly of our family. He posts the pics everywhere, completely oversharing. Who knows how many photos of me are floating around in the Philippines as the extra-extended Yaps get bombarded with updates?

I smile thinking Paul and I may be the most recognizable faces in Manila.

Then I'm hit with the same wave of sadness and doubt that's plagued me for a week. Paul and I were happy then. Weren't we? He should be here patiently taking these photos alongside my family. I apologized the first time Dad really got us with his camera, but Paul laughed and said it made him feel like a celebrity. And he looked good in every pic. He always looked good, even when he was clowning around.

I should be posing with his little sister, Gloria—the only nondistant member of the Reyes family. His parents weren't cold just to me, which I'd thought at first, they're cold to Paul too. That was why he and I were going to move in together so young. He said he wanted to live with someone who actually cared about him. He'd even offered to pay for the whole apartment, but I didn't want to freeload. I was willing to save up to pay my share.

But now what? Will that still happen? And in the meantime, where are we? What are we?

I close my eyes and wish for the eightieth time I'd never seen that post. I barely use my Instagram account. I could've stayed ignorant—it might've been nicer. Is there real value in knowing the truth when it tears your world apart? Or is it better to stay in comfortable denial and be a fool?

"Jaz?" Cari says.

I lose my stupor to find my family staring at me, including Davey, who's now in a blue polo that's remarkably wrinkle-free considering it was balled up on his floor.

"I'm sorry. Coming," I say.

Cari's worry wrinkle shows between her sculpted eyebrows. The little dent has appeared all week. It seems like she wants to say something, but she smiles and wraps her arm around me. We stand by the overgrown bird of paradise and I wait while Cari arranges her curls and adjusts my hair so it flows over my shoulders.

"Ready," she says.

"Say 'graduate,'" my dad says.

I force a smile, then a dozen more, then another dozen as I pose in every room with every family member. We go outside and repeat the process as I try not to melt in the heat. Then we pile into my mom's Explorer to go to the graduation ceremony . . . two hours early.

At least my grandparents will bring food like it's a tailgate. And who can be sad when there are meatballs and lumpia? I hope not me.

CHAPTER TEN

DAVEY'S NOT NORMAL FAMILY GROUP TEXT
MAY 24

Cari
We're all set for tomorrow. The boys will show up late to blend in. If she asks, Dad ran into Justin Michael and invited him. Mom will claim Aaron is the nephew of a work friend. And Aunt Jay will say Eugene is helping out. The boys all know what to say

Uncle Carlos
Okay, got it

Cousin Crystal
Yes!

Aunt Minnie
Okay. How was graduation?

Boring

Mom

Beautiful. Stop it, Davey

Dad

Paul stared at the back of her head all through the cere-mony, but after, he walked by Jaz like he didn't even see her. His sister said hi to her and his parents said hi to us, though

Mom

Barely. You know how those people are. But at least the bimbo wasn't there

Cousin Madison

Aunt Dee . . .

Cousin Wylan

Maddy, shouldn't you be writing your thesis or pining over that girl who doesn't like you?

Cousin Madison

I stg, Wylan. At least one of us has had a real live girlfriend. Instead of an online girlfriend who lives where? In Russia? Seems totally legit

Aunt Regina

Enough or I'll block you both from this chat

Cousin Wylan
You don't have the tech skills for that, Mom

Aunt Regina
I will email IT

Cousin Madison
Uh-oh

Cousin Wylan
Oh shit

Cari
ANYHOW, I know we're all excited, but it's important everyone be normal tomorrow

Cousin Wesley
Good luck with getting this family to act normal. And why bother with this? Justin Michael wins. Period

Cousin Joe
I think tf not. Do you not know Aaron is a professional baseball player

Cousin Wesley
Because she knows so much about baseball? Oh, yeah, right. She doesn't care at all

Cousin Wylan
No. She'll go for a local boy

Cousin Joe
Maybe, but his name is Eugene. Least attractive name in history

Cari
ANYHOW

Nonna
Everyone will behave or so help me I will get out my wooden spoon. Will there be pasta, Jay?

Mom
Told you

Aunt Jay
There will be paella

Nonna
Okay. I'll bring some spaghetti and meatballs

Aunt Jay
Mom, you really . . .

Nonna
I still have some from yesterday. It's no problem

Mom
I'll make lasagna too

Aunt Jay
. . . you know what? I'm going to go check on the food I was
hired to make

Nonna
Sounds good, sweetheart

Cousin Wesley
I rest my case

Cari
Stick to med school, Wes. See you all tomorrow!

CHAPTER ELEVEN

It's five o'clock on the day of my party, and I'm outside working like a mule. You might think that because it's a soiree being thrown in my honor, I would get out of manual labor. Nope. Not in this family.

The rental company set up tables and chairs in the back-yard this morning, but then it rained—the way it rains every summer day around three o'clock—and Mom freaked out like she's never seen water falling from the sky.

Note: She grew up here. In Orlando. Florida.

It's now sunny, the air has the consistency of chowder, and I'm sweating through my shirt as I wipe down chairs and tables . . . again. We had to rearrange everything earlier to avoid the muddy grass and Mom's freak-out.

At least the lasagna smells really good.

Cari has been more of a housekeeper, cleaning and help-ing Mom do whatever inside, but Davey's so sweaty, he looks like he just got off Splash Mountain as he moves furniture from the house to the outside.

"Present table," he says, breathing hard. He had to carry the antique oak table down the deck steps and all the way across our giant yard.

Cari comes out of the screen door and has a box of something. Decorations. More decorations. There are already balloons, garlands, and flowers everywhere, courtesy of Uncle Vin's flower shop. I can't imagine the tables need anything other than the plates Aunt Jay is bringing, but Cari places lantern candles between the vases and it looks even better.

The whole place will be magical in a few hours when it's not so frigging hot.

Mom appears on the deck looking frazzled. She puts one hand on her hip and one finger to her lips.

Uh-oh. *Nothing* good comes from that pose.

"Should we do something else with the tables instead of the U shape?" she says.

Davey and I exchange horrified glances. My parents rented farm-style tables and wrought iron chairs. Everything looks amazing but is heavy as hell.

"No, I think this is best because everyone will be focused on Jaz in the center," Cari says.

I'll be impossible to miss sitting with a hundred balloons tied to my seat. I'm surprised the chair isn't floating away.

"And it leaves room for dancing later," Cari adds.

"Hmm, I guess that's true," Mom says.

I have no idea what we'd do without Cari. Actually, I do—we'd be moving all these effing tables around again.

"But where's the dance floor?" Mom says. "I'm going to call them again. This is ridiculous! They said it would be installed between four and five and it's almost five!"

Mom turns and heads back into the house and I exhale.

Better she go harass whatever poor soul works at the party rental place. We, the family who loves her, have borne the brunt of this all day. Well, not Dad. He's been conspicuously absent "running errands" this afternoon.

He's the smartest one of us.

Davey sighs dramatically. "That was a close one."

"You're telling me," I say.

"She just gets worked up with so much to do," Cari says. She tilts her head, frowns at a lantern, turns it about thirty degrees, then moves on to the next. "You know entertaining is important to her. They've spent a lot of time and money on this, and she wants to make sure everything is perfect for your big day."

Cari, as per usual, is right. Mom is stressed out because she wants the best for me. And despite my protests that I didn't need it, they did spend a lot of money. Money they worked overtime for, that should've gone to paying down their loan. I'm going to try to be less of an ungrateful shit about it.

"You should go get showered and changed, Jaz," Cari says. "I'll finish up then do your hair and makeup."

Everything is pretty much done outside now that we don't have to move every single piece of furniture again. Still, knowing Mom, there's more to do. She's never idle. It makes her a great nurse because she's always checking on patients, restocking, or doing paperwork when she's at the hospital. But it kicks into overdrive with parties like this. Probably because, with the exception of Cari, we're all useless.

"Won't Mom freak if there's more to do and I'm not out here?" I say. We've been all hands on deck since nine this morning.

"She'll be more frazzled about you not being ready soon. Trust me." Cari waves me inside. She's right, again. That happened with her graduation party last year. Mom had a meltdown because Cari's hair was in curlers an hour and a half before people were supposed to arrive.

I head toward the house, slide open the glass door, and take off my disgustingly damp sandals. The air-conditioning and the cold tile floor revive me. My skin prickles in goose bumps, and I can't wait for a shower.

Mom's in the kitchen, cradling her phone between her ear and shoulder as she stands with both her hands on her hips. The "annoyed sugar bowl" pose, as we call it. Mom looks at me, and I point in the direction of the bathroom. She nods, then resumes talking loudly to whoever is on the line.

I run into the bathroom, peel off my sticky clothes, and finally have a minute to breathe. The work is done and the party should be fun. My friends and family will all be here. Everyone, except Paul.

I've thought about him way too many times today. I missed being able to message him little things I know would amuse him. Inside jokes and memories just aren't the same without someone to share them with.

Cari took him out of my iPhotos, but I still have pics on WhatsApp. And it wouldn't hurt to look.

Okay, it'll hurt. But I can't seem to stop myself. I just . . . I want to be reminded of what it was like to feel happy.

I unlock my phone and there are text notifications. June. Emily. And Paul.

Wait, what?

I do a double take, but I was right. I have a message from Paul Reyes.

PR

♥Paul ♥

Hope you have a good party

I nearly drop my phone. I hadn't expected to hear from him today. What does this mean? Why would he message after ignoring me yesterday?

My thoughts spin in a million directions. Is he done needing time and space? He remembered it's my party and he's reaching out and that means something. Paul grew up so rejected that he doesn't put himself out there much. Nothing he does is ever good enough for his parents. He poured himself into sports, the one thing his dad noticed, and took it hard when the football coach started an all-star freshman kicker over him this year. That was why he quit the team he loved. And why this past year has been hard for us. So him texting definitely means something, but what?

Does he wish he were here? Does he regret asking to see other people?

June and Emily would say to ignore him, but I have read

receipts on. I shouldn't leave him waiting for too long for a response, because I wouldn't want that done to me. Plus, I could spend a year debating what to reply, so I type out what's in my heart.

Thanks. I miss you

And maybe that's not the right thing to say. Maybe I should've blocked his number like June, Emily, and Cari said to, but that's not how I am.

I stare at the words—I miss you.

They're true.

I hit send, then dunk myself in a cold shower. I'll leave my phone in the bathroom for the rest of today; otherwise, I'll check it every two minutes waiting for a reply.

CHAPTER TWELVE

It's evening, there are approximately one million people in our backyard, and it's my job to welcome all of them. My cheeks hurt from smiling, but I can't let up any time soon. The party has been going for nearly an hour, and I've yet to finish my rounds as I kiss aunties on the cheek and take envelopes they generously though weirdly stick in my palm.

I'm formulating how to write a thank-you note for this, like:

> *Dear Auntie,*
> *Thanks for the unmarked bills. I will add*
> *each one to my shoebox stash. Cheers.*
> *—Jaz*

But Cari will know what to actually say. She always does. She's patiently telling people about her first year of college over and over again. Davey is supposedly welcoming guests too, although it's with begrudging "hi"s when prompted. Punk.

Everyone compliments my dress, and I'll admit it makes me feel different. Confident. Like I'm a mini–Korean Greek

74 • MEREDITH IRELAND

goddess in a gauzy blue gown. I even catch myself standing with perfect posture in my five-inch heels. The statue pose is more my inability to move in these stilts than newfound grace, but hey, I'll take it.

"You're really filling out, honey," Auntie Lynn says. She's a friend of the family who's been in our orbit for as long as I can remember. She could be anything from fifty to eighty years old, and has bright orange hair that's in that short, permed, AARP style.

"Um, thank you, Auntie Lynn," I say.

I look up and around, not sure it's a compliment, and that's when I see him. It can't be. I blink hard to lose the mirage, yet he stays in my line of sight. And then I'm positive: Justin Michael Simmons is in my backyard.

My mouth suddenly feels dry, my breath too fast.

"Will you . . . will you excuse me?" I say.

"Yes, yes, go mingle, you beautiful young thing," Auntie Lynn says.

"Please let me know if I can bring you anything," I say. But I'm not looking at her.

I try to walk quickly in my heels (spoiler: I can't), as if he'll disappear if I don't make it in time. But I mean . . . he might. My heart pounds. Each beat says: Is my old friend here?

He's different from what I remember. He's filled out— that's actually a compliment. Instead of being a very lanky boy, he looks like a man, in khaki pants and a button-down. And he's gotten taller, which is unfair as he was tall four years ago—he's just showing off now. His blond hair is still short, but his thick glasses are nowhere to be seen. And he actually has a beard! But with or without a beard, I'd know that face anywhere.

I close the space between us.

"Is it really you?" I say, tapping him on the shoulder.

Justin Michael turns and looks down at me. His smile lights up the backyard better than a box full of candles.

"Candy!" he says.

Happiness bursts through my chest at the nickname he gave me when we used to play Pokémon Go together.

"Stardust!" I say, using his.

He leans down to hug me, and I wrap my arms around him. He picks me up and my feet leave the ground. He must be six feet tall now. I smile so wide into his neck that my face hurts. But he's here. He's really here with me. I didn't think I'd ever see him again.

Justin Michael gently places me back on earth.

"What are you doing here?" I ask, slapping his bicep. I can't believe this is happening. Too many old feelings and memories rush through me—it's overwhelming in the best way.

"I'm in town for the summer," he says. He's picked up a slight Texan accent from his four years in Houston. It's good on him.

"The whole summer? Really?" I ask. "How?"

"I got an internship with Disney! They're normally college-level positions, but I had enough credits to land a spot before I start Georgia Tech. And you know there's no one better to work for than the Mouse." He smiles and his formerly braced teeth are perfectly straight. "It's good to be home."

A warmth fills me because he still considers Winter Park his home. He used to live right next door. I can't even count how many times we played as kids, but right before freshman year of high school, his mom got a huge promotion. The downside: they had to relocate to the company headquarters in Texas.

On his last day in Florida, we carved "C + S" into the weeping willow tree in his backyard. It's probably still there. After that, I quit playing Pokémon Go because it wasn't the same without him.

We're still smiling when June wanders over. Her brown skin is offset by a white dress. She's around Davey's height, with a curtain of long, thick black hair that's nearly to her waist and bangs that somehow look good despite my warnings she'd regret them.

I smile at June as she takes my hand. I talked to her when she got here, but as she's practically family, she was roped into helping with the party and I haven't seen her since. Emily will be here later. Her dad insisted on taking her to dinner tonight for graduation. She doesn't see him much since her parents divorced, so she couldn't get out of it.

"Jaz," June says.

"June Bug." I tilt my head toward her and she does the same. We're finally similar heights since I'm in stilts. "Do you remember Justin Michael?"

Her face breaks into a smile. "Oh my God. I do, but wow, you've changed so much!"

"Wait. . . ." He squints at her, his brown eyes moving rapidly. "June Bug? June Tam? No way!"

His eyes expand with surprise, and suddenly it's a minireunion. The three of us were inseparable in elementary school, running around playing tag and red light green light, and whatever else we came up with that day. Or, in bad weather, we'd sit and read books in companionable silence.

Things changed in middle school, though. June and Justin didn't see each other much because he played basketball and she played tennis. Sports became front and center in both their lives, and when one was free, the other was busy, so they drifted apart long before he moved away. I, the unathletic, stayed tight with both of them.

She glances over at me with her eyes wide to say, Wow, he's gotten hot, and believe me, the change was not lost on me. I telegraph it back to her. She laughs and her laugh is sweet like a wind chime.

Note: Mine is not. Mine is more of an asthmatic trombone.

We stand around for a while, smiling like cheeseballs. It's weird and wonderful for the three of us to be in my yard. But June shakes her head as if to return to reality. "I'm sorry to interrupt, Jaz, but your mom asked me to get you."

"Oh. She probably needs help. Okay," I say. I turn to Justin Michael. "Are you staying for the whole party?"

"I am, but I know your family parties are . . . busy." He laughs, and I remember how we used to hide under the tables together when the parties would run long. We'd lie on our backs talking as my aunties would cackle well into the night. More often than not, one or both of us would fall asleep on the cool grass.

"Can we catch up over some boba soon?" he asks.

"I'd love that," I say. I know I'm smiling like a fool. But, like Pokémon Go, getting bubble tea wasn't the same after he left. Paul thought tapioca was gross, so we never went, and June doesn't like tea.

Justin Michael smiles back. "I'll text you."

I start walking in the direction June points, and it feels like I'm floating on air. Then I realize this is the first genuine happiness I've felt in . . . a while. Much longer than a week if I'm honest.

As I'm halfway across the dance floor, I realize the surprise of seeing Justin again made me forget why he and I stopped talking in the first place. The memory of his words physically hurts, but I continue toward the house. People can say things they don't mean and mean things they don't say. And I hope that's what happened, because it feels so good to see him again.

CHAPTER THIRTEEN

DAVEY'S BICKERING FAMILY GROUP TEXT
MAY 25

Cousin Wesley
Game. Set. Match. Why don't you all admit defeat now?
Team Justin Michael or Team Looooooosers

Cousin Teagan
Seriously. Did you see that smile? It's game over

Cousin Joe
She hasn't even met the other two yet
Slow your roll

Aunt Kim
That's pretty hard to beat. What do the kids say: Take that, L?

Anyone want to double down?

Cousin Wesley
I'm in

Cousin Teagan
You shouldn't be betting money on this. We're here to support Jaz

> Man, there's paella and steak, but somehow I smell chicken

Cousin Wylan
Well, I mean the Ventura side can be a little . . . KFC

Cousin Teagan
$50 on Justin Michael. Put up or shut up, both of you. Preferably shut up

> You're on. She's headed for Eugene right now

It's twilight when I look for my mom outside. I didn't find her in the kitchen or rest of the house, so she must be in the yard.

The string lights cast a warm glow on the party as I walk down the deck stairs to the dance floor. (The floor was, fortunately for everyone, installed while I was in the shower.)

Music plays as Blaze, a friend of the family, mixes the tracks. Even though no one is supposed to dance until after dinner, this group is not the type that holds back. So Blaze upped the volume and tempo as some people dance and others cruise the appetizers.

I make my way through some good and some very, very bad moves. And I do mean *bad*, because Uncle Jimmie is doing the Sprinkler without a hint of irony. Aunt Regina loves him so much, she's just smiling and dancing like he's not doing . . . that.

June and Justin Michael remain where I left them on the other side of the yard, still talking. With June and Emily here and Justin back home, it might just turn out to be a good summer after all. A last hurrah before they all move on without me.

I'm so absorbed with thoughts of the past and future

that I stop paying attention to the present. And that's when it happens: I round the gift table too closely and my left heel catches on the bowed leg. I notice this a millisecond too late, because I'm already falling forward.

It's like slow motion. I emit a high-pitched squeal as my arms flail out. Somehow, I know everyone here is looking at me. And since it rained earlier and the gift table is at the edge of the yard, I'm about to land in the mud. I know in my bones that no one will forget the time Jaz face-planted while wearing a fancy dress. Because who could forget that?

I close my eyes and brace myself, but before I hit the ground, the air yanks me upright. Only the air is warm and smells like boy. I yelp again, open my eyes, and find myself in the arms of someone I've never seen before. His features are both South Asian and white—like Cari, but also not. His hair is black, he looks about my age, and his blue eyes are focused solely on me.

"I got you," he says.

I hear him, but it's like I'm underwater. My heart pounds and blood roars in my ears. I must be having an out-of-body experience. I'm actually dead in the mud and an attractive boy ghost is tethered to my spirit.

But, no, pretty sure this is actually happening.

"Um," I say.

He leans his head down, studying my face. It's light enough to see that his eyes aren't just blue . . . they're teal, like my dress is supposed to be. His arms link around me, and he smells amazing.

I inhale and my eyes drift closed. I want to sniff his neck.

So there it is: the weirdest thought I could have at this moment.

"Are you okay?" he asks.

For all that's holy, do NOT say: You smell good.

"Uh . . . ," I say. The sound lingers in the air, and I wince at myself. Scholarship material right there.

"Let me get you over to a chair," he says. "You may have twisted your ankle."

Oh, good. He thinks I'm in physical pain.

"No. No," I say. "I'm fine. I . . . I wasn't looking where I was going. And I'm . . . I'm just surprised I'm not rolling around in the mud."

He smiles. "I was pretty sure it was about to happen."

"But I'm okay, thanks to you. So . . . um, thank you . . ."

"Eugene." His arms leave me as he gestures to his black T-shirt. He's a few inches taller than I am in my heels, so that makes him five-eight-ish, but with broad shoulders and tattoos that peek out from his short sleeves. He's not exactly dressed for the party, but I must know him somehow.

"Are you family?" I say.

Yes, there it is, the second most ridiculous thing I can say after: Can I smell you. I know who my family is. I meant to ask why he's at the party, but there's no going back now. I stand and wait for his obvious answer while trying not to shrivel and die inside.

He smiles like I'm amusing and not a train wreck. He has one part-time dimple on his right cheek, and I'm staring at it when he says, "No, I'm positive we're not related."

The fire of a thousand suns hits my cheeks. "I meant . . ."

The dimple shows again. "I'm helping Jay."

"Oh!" I yell. I don't know why I'm shouting. I swear I'm not normally this . . . me. But this boy is shorting out all my defenses. "You're a caterer?"

"Not exactly," he says. "I delivered desserts from my family's restaurant."

I nod because I want to see his dimple again. But then his words sink in. The desserts are from the best restaurant in Florida.

"Wait, your family is Lantern & Jacks?" I say.

He rubs the back of his neck. "Um, yeah."

I manage to stifle a squeal. Barely. I've read so many reviews of L&Js and profiles of its chef/owner Jack Matthews that I know way too much about a restaurant I've never been to. I figured Jay still had connections, but I was shocked to see the signature black-and-white dessert boxes on the table since they don't cater.

People say Chef Matthews is the next Thomas Keller. Which is to say: he's well on his way to becoming the best chef in the country. And that makes Eugene, Jack's only child, heir apparent, and, I guess, delivery boy. I already know a stalkery amount about him. For example, he's Indian on his mom's side, German/English on his dad's. I want to ask what it was like to spend a year in Tuscany making bread and pasta with his father, but there's no way to do that without sounding worthy of a restraining order. And the poor guy is already trapped in the world's longest awkward silence with me.

"There you are," Mom says.

I've never been so grateful to have my mom interrupt a conversation with a boy. But she looks a little irritated, and I remember I was supposed to find her fifteen minutes ago. She's been annoyed since Jay showed up late (which, in fairness to my mom, was likely on purpose).

"Oh, I'm sorry, Mom. I was looking for you but then . . ." I gesture wildly to the side like I lost my voice and I'm trying to mime out what happened.

Eugene laughs and it's warm. He's not laughing at me. Well, he is, but it's more like an inside joke than making fun of me. Thanks to middle school, I'm well aware of the difference.

Mom looks at me, bewildered, her left eyebrow rising.

"She ran into me," Eugene says. "Sorry about that."

"Oh, hello," Mom says, ever polite. "You're here helping Jay, right?"

"I am," he says. "And actually . . . I should be going."

Of course this guy who's making me . . . I don't even know what, can't get away from me fast enough.

"Really?" Mom sounds surprised, like she planned on him sleeping over or something.

He looks at his wrist, which has an old-fashioned watch on it. Something about that charms me. It's not an Apple Watch or a fitness tracker. It's a real tick-tock watch and probably an heirloom, by the looks of it. Maybe he's old school and a little antitech, like me.

"Well . . ." He hesitates.

"You're more than welcome to stay and enjoy the party,"

Mom says. "Jay cooked some amazing entrées, and you *have to* try my lasagna. We're going to sit down to dinner soon."

Mom is a food bully. There's no way Eugene is getting out of here now without taking a plate or two. Luckily for him, my mom's lasagna is the best in the world. I'd even put it up against his father's, if he made one.

"Really! You should stay!" I say, and it's like I've lost total control of my voice because it's both loud and scratchy. My mom looks at me like I'm possessed. Eugene seems slightly confused but smiles.

"It did all smell pretty awesome," he says.

"Good. It's settled then," Mom says, looking particularly pleased. "Stay for at least a plate."

She takes a step away with Eugene.

"Wait," I say. "Did you need something, Mom?"

"Yes. Nonna wants to see you," she says.

"Nonna sent you and you sent June to send for me?" I say.

"That's correct. We're all messengers for the grand dame. She's at the table over there." Mom points to the back corner of the U shape. "Come on, Eugene, let's get you something to eat."

"It was nice to meet you, Jasmine," he says.

I head toward my grandmother, and I'm five steps away before I realize I didn't tell him my name and I didn't tell my mom Eugene's name. I shake it off. Jay must've told them both, and I've unwittingly kept Nonna waiting for too long.

CHAPTER FIFTEEN

**DAVEY'S GLOATING FAMILY GROUP TEXT
MAY 25**

Aunt Regina
My, how the tables have turned. Eugene FTW

Aunt Jay
I told y'all she'd love my boy

Uncle Carlos
Oh, come on. He caught her before she fell in the mud. Of course she was seeing stars

Cousin Madison
Did you see how her expression changed when he stopped holding her? They had real chemistry. She was giving all the flirtation signs

Cousin Wesley
Way to make that sound clinical. You're forgetting the long

history she has with Justin Michael. Girls will always pick the friend

Cousin Charlotte
Date someone for more than a month before you certify yourself as a relationship expert, Wes

Cousin Wesley
Amanda and I have been together for six weeks, thanks

Aunt Regina
Oh, okay, we'll start planning the wedding

Cousin Wylan
Burn!

Cousin Teagan
Lol, dead

Cari
Put your phones away! At some point she's going to notice this whole party staring at their screens
Oh, great, now all look up like lemurs

Cousin Joe
Cari is right. And Aaron is up last. We need to all watch him score the winning homerun

You mean get shut out

Cousin Joe
Doubling down, Davey. Easiest money I'll make this year

Yeah, I just had the same thought

CHAPTER SIXTEEN

I find Nonna holding court at the main table, surrounded by a slew of aunties. Poppy, her husband, is on the opposite side with the older uncles and Grandpa Yap. This happens at every family party. Aunties to the right, uncles to the left. Grandma Yap is off playing with the youngest grandchildren, as per usual.

I walk up to Nonna and kiss her on the cheek. Best believe I greeted all my grandparents when they arrived, but I do it again anyhow.

Nonna sits in a chair with perfect posture, and somehow she's not having a heatstroke despite wearing a long-sleeved suit. My grandmother recently turned seventy-eight, and raised six children, but she looks better than I do most days. Nonna's blond hair is short, and diamonds drip from her ears and neck. She smells like Shalimar and garlic, a combination I've loved since I was little.

"There's my Jasmine," Nonna says, cupping my cheek. Eight aunties pause their conversations to watch us. Two are still talking, so consumed by their church gossip that they don't even notice the silence. But they are low in the auntie pecking order, anyhow.

"You wanted to see me, Nonna?" I say.

"Yes, baby. I was hoping you could make some of your famous punch," she says. "It goes so well with my meatballs."

She brought more than a hundred meatballs—slightly more than had been at graduation—but they'll be gone by the end of the night. They're the best meatballs I've ever had. I know everyone thinks that about their grandmother's cooking, but Nonna's are even better than Jay's.

"Of course, Nonna," I say.

"That's my girl," she says.

It's a strange request, but when you have a craving, you have a craving, I guess.

The aunties don't even wait until I'm out of earshot to talk about me. First the comments are about me following in my mom's footsteps and becoming a nurse, but then it quickly turns to my relationship—because that's the juicer topic. Someone mentions a contest, but they must mean my scholarship.

I let out a long exhale and block them out as I walk to the beverage table. It's just more stuff I can't think about right now. I've become an expert at tuning out as my mom gets increasingly excited about me choosing my nursing courses.

My punch isn't famous, but it is good. It's several juices, some squeezed fruit, and a splash of club soda. It tastes better spiked, but this isn't the place to say that.

I start mixing pineapple and cranberry juice. I'm halfway through juicing a second orange when I'm interrupted.

"Wow, the bartenders here have amazing uniforms," a voice says.

I turn and look into the eyes of a startlingly hot guy. He's so hot, my fingers stop working and I drop the orange into the punch bowl. I recover in time to just barely move out of the way of the juice splatter. I fumble for a mixing spoon and fail twice before fishing the orange out.

Good times.

"Oh, I'm . . . I'm not a bartender," I say.

Note: it definitely looks like I'm a bartender as I stand here fixing a punch bowl. But please ignore that fact, super-hot random guy.

He smiles. He's slightly taller than Justin Michael, with brown skin like Davey and a low fade. "I know. I was just . . . that was a bad line, wasn't it?" He wrinkles his perfect nose and looks down at the ground.

Wait . . . a line?

"You're trying to talk to me?" I look around like there's someone much more attractive behind me, and he laughs.

"Um, yeah. This is your party, right?" he says.

It appears I've forgotten.

All my life I didn't think looks mattered much, but here I am made speechless by his bone structure. He'd fit in with the guys who model prom tuxedos, but no one really looks like that without airbrushing . . . except this dude. I nod slowly.

"I'm Aaron," he says.

"Jasmine." I move to shake hands, but mine are covered in orange juice. I ball them in fists at my side. Why am I so gross and awkward?

"Here," he says.

He reaches across the table and grabs a cloth. I, of course, use the moment he turns to check him out. It's a creeper move, but it's worth it. He's built like Captain America. Where did this guy even come from?

He pours water from the ice bucket onto the towel and extends it. I think he's going to hand it to me, but instead he says, "May I?"

I nod, and he wipes off my palms, then fingers. The cold water and pressure from his hands is so refreshing. There's a small smile on his lips and utter concentration on his face. I want to look around to see if other people are seeing this or if it's just a heat mirage, but I don't want to lose the moment. This might be the sexiest thing to ever happen to me.

"There ya go," he says. He has a bit of a country accent that sounds familiar even though he's definitely a stranger.

I remain standing with my arms out like a zombie. When I drop them, they slap loudly at my sides. I cringe at myself.

"Have we met before?" I ask. I mentally pat myself on the back for asking a reasonable question and not: Are we blood relations?

He smiles. "No, I'd definitely remember you."

He's flirting with me? Is this flirting? It is, right? Or maybe he's just being nice. Either way, I should respond with witty repartee.

"Oh," I say.

Yeah . . . nailed it.

"I've only been in Orlando a month now," he says. "I was excited to score an invite to a party. Even if it was out of pity."

I cannot picture this guy needing any kind of social charity. "Are you in college nearby?"

"No, I work around here."

"You're a caterer?" I ask.

He laughs. He's in a button-down shirt and doesn't look any more like a caterer than I do. "No, I meant my job brought me to this area. I play baseball."

"Like the game?" I say. I bite the inside of my lip. Is there another definition of baseball?

"Yes, the game. I'm a Minor League pitcher," he says. "I was traded to the Braves, and their farm team is in Kissimmee."

"Oh, wow," I say. He doesn't look much older than me, but I guess most baseball players aren't. Suddenly, I feel like a wild underachiever.

"It's great," he says, "but sometimes I feel like I should be in community college in Nashville—if I were a normal twenty-year-old, ya know?"

I widen my eyes. "That's where your accent is from? Nashville?"

"Yes, ma'am." He smiles, and it's wide and genuine.

"So country music . . ."

"Is in my blood," he says. "I could listen to Dolly or Johnny Cash every day for the rest of my life. But I'm a terrible singer. Like people would run and duck for cover."

I laugh, then notice Nonna and the aunties looking over. Crap. I'm completely neglecting the punch. I grab for the rest of the ingredients, and Aaron begins to fill glasses with ice.

"Can you sing?" he asks.

"No, I'm . . . okay."

I add a splash of club soda and ladle in the punch as Aaron switches out glasses. We wordlessly flow together like I've known him forever, and it's amazing since I always had to explicitly ask Paul for help.

I finish pouring and gather some drinks in my hands. I'll make two trips.

"Hmm, yeah, that's a humble, great singer type answer," he says.

I shrug. I've been complimented on my voice, but I'm nothing special. "No, I'm totally average in every way."

He pauses in front of me and looks me in the eyes. "You're anything but. It was nice to meet you, Jasmine. Hope to see you again sometime soon."

My face tingles at the compliment. I'm so charmed that I'm smiling like a fool when I hand off the punch to my Nonna and aunties. I ignore their stares and go back for the rest of the glasses.

CHAPTER SEVENTEEN

**DAVEY'S INTOLERABLE FAMILY GROUP TEXT
MAY 25**

Cousin Joe
DID YOU ALL SEE THOSE MOVES
Forget the fanny-pack loser. Aaron should teach the pickup
class

Cari
Aaron was the smoothest by far

Cousin Mabel
And the hottest. Where did you even find him, Cari? He's like
Prince Naveen

Cousin Wesley
Who, sis?

Cousin Wylan
Is that *Star Wars*?

Cousin Joe
Star Trek?

Cousin Mabel
I hate y'all

Cousin Teagan
I'm still confident in Justin Michael. He's the only one who planned out the next date

Cousin Wylan
Oh, come on. He knows her. It would've been a lot for Eugene to ask her out

Cousin Mai
Didn't he want to leave? What was that about, Cari?

Cari
I'm not sure. But overall it went well

Aunt Tammy
So well! I can't believe she doesn't know

Cousin Mabel
OMG shhhhh

Aunt Kim
No!

Cousin Joe

Not cool

Aunt Tammy

What? I'm just saying it's a good thing she's still in the dark

Cousin Wylan

Welp, now we're fully cursed

Cari

I have to . . . it's time for cake

CHAPTER EIGHTEEN

CARISSA'S PROJECT JASMINE NOTES
MAY 26

The party was great and our secret setup has begun! Two of the aunties almost ruined it by talking about the contest directly in front of her, but Jasmine didn't seem to hear them. Thank God.

Our meet-cutes went off without a hitch. Aaron really wowed her. She, of course, recognized Justin Michael, and Eugene just happened to be there when she was clumsy. Eugene was having second thoughts about doing this, but Mom persuaded him to stay in. She also slipped by already knowing his name. So I guess that's a wash.

I swear, trying to keep this family from spoiling this will be like trying to herd a bunch of rabid cats.

Last night we decided the "winner" of the competition will be the one Jaz invites to our family's big Fourth of July party—at Grandpa and Grandma Yap's on the sixth of July. The Fourth is obviously Independence Day, but we celebrate on the sixth because that's when Grandma Yap emigrated here from Manila. Plus, for contest purposes, the sixth gives the boys exactly six weeks to date her. We'll make it clear to Jaz that it's a plus-one situation, and whoever she brings will be the winner.

At this point I have no idea who it'll be, but I decided to do a podcast on this because it's so exciting! I think people will really respond to it.

CHAPTER NINETEEN

The party lasted well past midnight, with everyone danc-
ing and laughing and eating great food.

My family, of course, overdid it. The second time the
whole party burst out singing "That's Amore," I thought today
would be a rough wake-up. After Auntie Lynn started a kick
line and Aunt Tammy was carried out, I was certain of it.

All in all it was a pretty standard Yap/Ventura get-
together.

There's a suspicious lack of noise in the house this morning, and I wonder how much wine my parents drank during
the sing-alongs. The quiet of the house tells me they had
more than a glass.

The reason I'm up and moving is somehow I lost my
phone during the party. I've looked through the house and
my room to the extent that I could without waking June or
Emily, but nothing.

I slip on flip-flops and check outside. Holding the curtain of
my hair aside, I look on and under the tables, but there's no sign
of it. Then I realize searching is pointless. Someone would've
told me if they saw my phone last night. The whole clan stayed
to help clean up—it's not like someone took it. It was all family.

Well . . . not all family. Justin Michael was here. And Aaron, the baseball player. And Eugene Matthews. And meeting them made the night so . . . different. Special. I know all the attention was only because it was my party, but I've never had that many boys notice me before. I couldn't help but whisper gossip about them to Emily and June before we fell asleep.

"Did you just giggle?" June asked.

"No . . . I mean, yes," I said. I could feel blood rushing into my cheeks, and I was glad for the dark of my bedroom.

"Who even is this girl?" Emily said as she put her braids into a hair wrap. "Giggling and talking about boys, plural?"

"Jaz is single and ready to mingle," June said. "Like that old dating show."

"Who will it be?" Emily said, like a game-show announcer. "Bachelor number one, bachelor number two, or bachelor number three?"

June snickered and Emily laughed until she snorted.

I hit them both with pillows.

Those two lazy jerks are still passed out. I woke up between Emily with her nose ring glinting in the sun and June looking like a murder victim on her stomach. The three of us are kind of like Charlie's Angels, if the angels were Black, adopted Korean, and snoring Chinese.

June and I didn't meet Emily until high school. It wasn't the way June and I chose each other as kids; it was more grown personalities meshing, and that was just as valuable.

I'm glad we were able to be there for Emily last year

when her parents were separating and it was stressing her out. Her sister was already in college, so she took the brunt of the drama by herself. But Emily was always welcome to stay at my house or June's.

It sucks that Emily's mom and dad split up, but she says they're happier, better people now. That you can love someone and still not be right for them. Or maybe you were right for each other at one point, but you grew in different directions and trying to stay together won't work. Once you let go, all that strain fades and you're lighter.

I think about that as I walk around the grass—the idea that two people can just grow apart. My mom and dad have been together for more than thirty years, through ups and downs and overtime, but they're the exception, not the rule. I'd figured Paul and I would also be exceptions, but now . . . I'm not sure.

I missed him before the party, but my night was so much fun without him. Lately, it felt like I expended a ton of energy trying to make him happy, and most of the time I failed. Without him, I just enjoyed the night and didn't worry.

Wait, I'd texted him. Before my shower.

My phone must still be in the bathroom.

I slide open the patio door, kick off my shoes, and race-walk to the bathroom vanity. Next to the diffuser thing only Cari knows how to use sits my phone.

Phew. Thank goodness I found it.

I check the notifications: Emily apologizing for being late. She came at nine, which was totally fine. June texting me about my mother looking for me. And Paul texting back at 11:05 p.m.

I hold my breath and click on his message.

♥ Paul ♥

Thanks. I miss you.

I know. But right now we still need time and space.

I stare at his text. I stare at it for a good long time, getting stuck on different parts of his eleven-word message.

First: "I know." Not: "I miss you too." Just . . . yeah, of course.

Second: "right now." It leaves the door open, doesn't it? Earlier this week I would've jumped on that, analyzed it to death, and clung to the hope of him changing his mind before August 1. But now it seems cruel. Like he's trying to bait me into hoping he decides sooner.

Third: "we need." Who's "we"? What he means is "I need." Because I never said I needed to be apart. And isn't saying "we" pushing it back on me?

Last: "time and space." Not only did he want to "explore our options," but it was also his idea that we shouldn't talk or spend time together this summer. Because it "wouldn't be real."

Anger courses through me and suddenly things are crystal clear. I don't know how I missed this before, but I get it now: he wanted to date other girls but keep me as a safety net. And I was just going to sit here waiting to catch him with my eyes closed.

I stare at my screen for so long with my lip curled that my face hurts when I stop. And for the first time ever, I don't reply. I slip my phone into the pocket of my pajama pants and go into the kitchen to make a pot of coffee for everyone.

CHAPTER TWENTY

It's Sunday night, which means I'm pretty much alone. I wasn't scheduled to work at Berry Plum this weekend, and the animal shelter is long closed. We spent the day with family, but now we're all on our own. Davey is off playing basketball or a hideous war video game at a friend's house. Mom left for work a few minutes ago to make that overnight holiday money, since tomorrow is Memorial Day, and Dad is doing his rideshare thing. He has a five-star rating and says he loves talking to new people and catching up on audiobooks in the car, but I still wish he didn't have to do it.

Cari is here, but she's locked in her soundproof closet recording something. Seriously, it's soundproof. She moved her clothes into a wardrobe and installed those egg-crate foam things once she got ad sponsors in order to "up her production value"—that was an actual thing she said. She even has a sign on her bedroom door for quiet when she's recording. At U Miami, where it's too noisy in the dorms, she uses the campus radio space. She negotiated time in their booth in exchange for shouting them out on her podcast and Instagram.

My sister is driven, laser focused, and always gets what she wants. She's everything I'm not.

Anyhow, everyone is busy but me, and for the first time since before Burrito Friday, I'm in the mood to cook. Maybe it was the amazing food at the party. Maybe it's something else entirely. But before the feeling fades, I take the keys to the Rolla and drive to Publix.

Publix, in case you didn't recognize, is the World's Best Grocery Store. It's decently priced, always clean, and quiet on a Sunday night when I pull into the parking lot.

I grab my reusable shopping bag and a cart that was left between cars, and I walk to the store entrance. I pause at the automatic doors. Grocery stores in Florida are always ridiculously cold, so I slip on my sweatshirt.

Instead of the Korean Greek goddess of yesterday, I look like Winnie-the-Pooh in a red cropped sweatshirt over a crop top, and yellow shorts that are a little snug. I hadn't thought to change from what I'd been wearing around the house, and luckily, it's deserted in here.

I head straight to the meat and seafood counters. Starting with proteins is the easiest way to find inspiration when you don't know what to make. I scan the glass cases. The beef looks picked over. Not surprising since it's such a big grilling weekend. The shrimp have seen better days. But they have PEI Mussels on sale, and they're fresh and clean, so that's what I go with.

Mussels are all about the broth. People complain they're a lot of work for little payoff, and while that's true protein-wise, a bowl of mussels is an excuse to dip a loaf of bread in deliciousness. The shellfish is a bonus to an already complete dish.

I can do the mussels in a white wine broth—there's still some chardonnay left over from the party. I'll add blue cheese, bacon, Vidalia onion, and some brightening green. Maybe parsley.

I love this part of cooking—the brainstorming, where my mind pulls together a dish. My parents and siblings know I like to cook, but they think of it as a hobby. Only Aunt Jay ever knew I was serious about it. And she's the reason I haven't wanted to become a chef since I was fourteen. Because whether it was mean or not, she was right: I'm not good enough.

But here, alone in the grocery store, it's different. Here I can dream. I grab bacon like I'm on *Top Chef*, then spin my cart for the cheese section. I'm so overly focused on getting to their blue cheese that I don't see another cart peeking out of an aisle.

It's too late to stop.

My cart crashes into the other one. With the clang of metal, I'm jostled forward and right back to reality. I make a lovely "oof" sound when my chest hits the cart handle.

"Oh my God, I'm so—" I begin.

"I'm sorry, I—" he says.

Then we stare at each other. Because when I look down the aisle, the cart I crashed into belongs to Eugene Matthews. Because of course it does.

He's in a white T-shirt and jeans, and unlike me and my plain outfits for work, he makes it look good. Tattooed Sanskrit scrolls on his biceps, his light brown skin perfect even under the crappy store lighting.

I immediately regret everything about the way I look and kind of hope he doesn't recognize me. But we just met last night, and we're staring too long for this to be casual.

"Jasmine?" he says.

Great.

"Um, yeah."

Did I mention I'm also wearing *Tangled* flip-flops I bought at Disney and my hair is in a messy bun? Because all these things are sadly true. If I could evaporate into a nearby drain, that'd be great.

"I'm sorry I hit you. I was just . . . in my head," he says. His eyes take on a far-off look before refocusing. "I wasn't paying attention."

"No, no. It's my fault," I say. "I really wanted cheese."

Kill me.

I grit my teeth so hard, the tension radiates in my skull and down my neck. Who even says that? And why?

He laughs, his expression amused. "Well, cheese *is* really important. What kind?"

"Blue. Maybe Roquefort, depending on what they have," I say.

"Blue cheese and mussels?" he says, peering into my cart.

I nod.

"Interesting," he says.

He gestures for me to go, then rolls up beside me. I inhale, and he smells just as good as he did last night. I can't put my finger on the exact scent. It's a combination of soap, deodorant, cologne, and just boy, I guess. But it fills me with warmth, and I can't inhale deeply enough.

I'm moving closer without thinking about it and accidentally knock my cart into his again. I jerk it away. He has the grace to pretend like that didn't happen.

"Bacon too, huh?" Eugene says. "Bold."

"I'm going to do it in a white wine base," I say.

"You may want to sauté in some cherry tomatoes for brightness. Depending on what you're going for."

"I was thinking parsley," I say.

He nods, and just like that, we're grocery shopping together.

"Are you making frites, too?" he asks.

"Well . . . now I am," I say, and that part-time dimple of his appears. "I got an air fryer for graduation and I'm dying to try it. But I didn't know I was making mussels until I got here."

"You shop proteins first, huh?" He smiles. "Interesting. So, you love to cook?"

I startle and turn toward him. "What makes you say that?" I say.

He looks away, then shrugs. "Just a hunch."

An awkward silence blankets us, and I'm not sure what I did. I just want to return to our fun banter.

"Well, good hunch," I say. "I do love to cook."

I don't know why it's so easy to admit it to him. I normally downplay the fact that I love it by saying something like "a girl's gotta eat." But he is a chef, so he'll understand, and there's something about him that makes me unable to hide.

He smiles as we arrive at the cheese section. His gaze roams over the array, and he plucks out a French bleu with a lighter rind.

"You want one that won't overpower the dish," he says. "Traditional Roquefort will be too strong for what you're going for. I think this or even Gorgonzola will be better. At least, it would be my pick."

He hands the cheese to me like he wants me to inspect and approve it. I was sold the second he touched it, but I look over the marbling and light-blue rind and place it in my cart.

"Do you love to cook?" I ask. I already know the answer. I've seen a picture of him on the line with his dad. I just hadn't realized it was Eugene at the time.

One side of his lips quirks up and that dimple deepens. "That's a complicated question."

"Is it?" I ask, genuinely surprised.

He shoves his hands in his pockets. "It can be when you're the son of a famous chef and everyone wants you to follow in his footsteps. And you're not sure if you want to."

I pause and blink at his words and tone. I . . . wasn't expecting that.

"That was *way* more of an answer than you were looking for." He smiles at the ground and rubs the back of his neck. His teal eyes peer up at me, a little shy. "Sorry to lay it out there like that. It was one of the things I was thinking about when I ran into you. Um, yeah, I do love to cook.

That's how I should've responded on the first take."

I vigorously shake my head. "No. No . . . I . . . it was honest," I say. "I get it. It's complicated because it holds more weight for you."

And I do understand, because although I love to cook, anytime I think about actually becoming a chef, I remember the little office Jay used to have at Ventura's Bistro. I remember the red past-due bills on her desk. I recall the fallout on my parents, on Mom's relationship with Jay, and I remember that I can't be a chef. And even though Eugene has what it takes, following in his dad's footsteps can't be easy.

Eugene's eyes meet mine, and his shoulders drop away from his ears. And for some reason, seeing him relax makes me feel like my chest is on fire.

"That's *exactly* it," he says.

Now I'm fully blushing. Heat speeds up my neck and into my cheeks. And I really wouldn't mind the floor opening up and delivering me from my own awkward.

We start moving toward the produce, and I'm thankful for the distraction, even though I want him to say more. He talks with an openness that's rare. People in school wanted to play it cool—even June and Emily. They couldn't be too into something or they'd get made fun of. Pretending like they were above it all was the rule. But there's none of that in Eugene. He's intense and I like it.

We're both eyeing the vegetables as we pass. For him it's probably a reflex. I love the smell of celery and pick up a bundle. I discretely sniff it. He grabs red potatoes and bags them. I can't glean from the ingredients what he's making, but he may be normal food shopping.

"So, do you work with your dad part-time or full-time?" I ask.

"How'd you know I work for him?" he says, putting the potatoes in his cart.

Shit. "Oh, the delivery yesterday . . . or were you just doing a favor?" I ask.

Thank God I actually covered that.

"Oh, right. Plus all my foodie knowledge," he says with a smile. "I'm full-time in the summer and winter break. I go to Marist in New York, so I'm up there the rest of the year."

"Oh."

For some reason, it hits me hard that he's in college. I don't know why—most people our age are. But, it's not like he's in Miami or even Gainesville. New York is just so far away. That means he'll be leaving in August, September at the latest. I deflate like a balloon. It doesn't make sense for his college to impact me at all. I don't even know him. But feelings don't have to make sense.

"I've worked for him almost all my life," Eugene says. "When I was young, it wasn't even a second thought that I wanted to be a chef. I couldn't wait to be old enough to help in the kitchen. There's video of me as a toddler and I'm in my dad's arms stirring a pot. At five I was carrying ingredients. Ten and I'd learned knife skills. Sixteen and on the line when one of the cooks called out sick."

"That's pretty amazing," I say. I feel a prick of jealousy,

but not because I begrudge him anything. More that I wanted that too. I desperately wanted to work on the line with Aunt Jay, but I never got the chance.

He nods. "It was. My dad loved that I wanted to learn. His family disowned him when he was young, and my mom's family disowned her too, so it's been just the three of us since I can remember."

"That must've been . . . I can't imagine," I say.

And I can't. My huge family is a lot, and sometimes way too much, but I can't fathom being separated from them. It's part of the reason Paris could never be real—I'd never want to be that far from my family. Or, well, I'd want to, but it's not realistic.

I wonder why both of Eugene's parents were disowned, but it's deeply none of my business.

His eyes take a far-off look before refocusing on me. "They got through it and put their lives into opening the restaurant three years ago, and I do love it. I know they're proud of me, but . . . I don't want to take a path just because it's expected, you know?"

I don't know. I don't know at all. But I nod because I like the way he talks about things. I like that he's okay with uncertainty, with making his own path. That he confronts everything that scares the bejesus out of me.

"And your parents are . . . good with that?" I venture, while inspecting the parsley.

My mom was thrilled when I said I might want to be a nurse. The day after my chef dreams had gone down in flames, she'd casually asked what I wanted to be. I said I didn't know but nursing seemed steady, and somehow that morphed into following in her footsteps. Between her excitement and my simply not having a better idea, I started down this path. I haven't been able to get off it since.

"Oh, they want me to want it," Eugene says. "They encouraged me to go to college and try things out and see what else interests me. I think because of what happened with their families, they don't want me to feel trapped. The pressure is there anyhow, though."

"Why's that?" I ask.

Eugene opens his mouth but looks past me. I turn to see what caught his eye, and it's Amberlynn and Crystal walking in with their baskets. For the first time I kind of don't want to talk to my family. I want to continue in this private conversation with Eugene. But that's not a good thought, so I smile.

"Hi, cuz," Amberlynn says. She looks from me to Eugene and back again with her brown eyes wide. Splendid. She's not going to attempt to play this cool.

"Look who it is!" Crystal says loudly, walking toward me. Then she notices Eugene and stops dead in her tracks. She eyes my outfit, which frankly I'd forgotten about, but now I painfully remember, then looks at Eugene again.

"Hi, Eugene. I'm Crystal Yap. We met at the party last night," she says. "And you met my sister, Amberlynn, too."

I quirk an eyebrow. I don't know why she sounds like a bad stage actress.

"Hi!" Amberlynn says with a little wave.

Crystal and Amberlynn both wear stylish jeans and tanks, with perfect hair. They are how I would've wanted to look if I'd thought anyone would see me.

Eugene offers a polite smile. "Yes, I remember. Nice to see you guys again."

"Are you two shopping together?" Amberlynn says. Amberlynn is twenty-one and Crystal is twenty-two. But they seem like they're twelve from their barely contained glee, and it's weirding me out.

"No," I say at the same time Eugene says, "Kinda."

Amberlynn and Crystal exchange glances and look like they're about to burst.

"Well, we should go get the limes mom wanted. She's been taking a Thai cooking class, and yeah . . ." Crystal shudders.

"Let's pick up emergency chicken tenders too," Amberlynn says. "I don't have a lot of faith that Ms. Tammy's Pad Thai will go according to plan."

"Good idea," Crystal says. She turns to me. "Great party last night. You two have *fun*."

They walk away whispering to each other and taking out their phones. Crystal says either "winning" or "twinning," and neither makes sense.

I stare at them until they're out of sight. That was strange, but I guess they haven't seen me with anyone except for Paul and it must be weird for them, too. Plus, I don't normally leave the house looking like this. They're too polite to tell me I look ridiculous to my face, but they're not above gossiping about it.

Ugh, they're going to light up the cousins' chat. I can only hope they didn't take sneaky pics. I don't need this one floating around Manila.

I turn and find Eugene staring at me. But he's not looking at my outfit. He's looking at my face, and it seems like he's forming some kind of opinion.

"Was one of us just saying something?" I ask. I grab Vidalias and shallots, trying to bury my shame in onions.

"Do you run into family a lot?" Eugene asks.

"Constantly," I sigh.

I smile, but there's a wistful look on his face and I remember he grew up essentially alone. I was somewhat on my own in eighth grade after Cari started high school and June and Justin Michael were busy with sports, and it was the worst year of my life.

I shake off the memories and look over at him.

"Um, I think I have everything," I say.

"Me too. Checkout?" He gestures toward the front of the store.

It's eight p.m., so there's only self-checkout, which takes forever with produce, and one lane with a cashier, so we get in line. The old lady in front of us is buying enough cat food to keep Cuddles happy, so this will take a minute.

"What are you making with all that?" I ask, looking in Eugene's cart.

"Oh, I'm not sure yet. I was just picking up staples," he says.

He helps me empty my cart, then puts the divider down

and loads his groceries onto the belt. No proteins, but I know his father breaks down whole animals, so he probably gets his meat through Lantern & Jacks. I can't even imagine having that kind of quality at my disposal.

Eugene is buying brussels sprouts, potatoes, cauliflower, Brie and Camembert, Pocky Sticks, Israeli couscous, and . . . Cap'n Crunch.

"Big Cap'n Crunch fan?" I ask.

He glances at the box and then into my eyes. "It's the best cereal in the world," he says.

I must make a face. Actually, I'm totally scrunching my nose.

"What?" he says.

"You're cute. Wrong, but cute," I say.

"Name the best one. I'll wait," he says. He folds his arms across his chest.

"Raisin bran." I even take a step closer and stand on my toes to say it. Without my heels on, his five-eight height is tall.

I know it's going to be an unpopular opinion—it always is. But I'm ready. I'm versed in this argument from the infinity war with Cari and Davey.

Eugene stares at my lips and then my words must register because he makes a face and throws his hands up. "What? You can't be serious. No one on earth thinks that's true."

The cashier greets us and we both stop to say hello. Eugene asks about her night and if she has plans for Memorial Day. Paul never did that because . . . well, he didn't care and small talk bothered him. But Eugene maintains eye contact until she starts scanning my items, then he turns back to me.

"Still waiting for an explanation," he says in a lower voice.

Something about it radiates through me, and I try to hold it together. Raisin bran. Right. Cereal. The least sexy discussion we could be having.

"Raisin bran is the perfect balance of sweet and not," I say. "Especially when it's soggy."

He gives me a horrified stare, widening his eyes and opening his mouth. "I've spent my night grocery shopping with a girl who likes soggy cereal?"

I point to my chest. "I will even let it sit on the counter and marinate in milk."

He shakes his head. "Monster."

I pay for my groceries, then wait while the cashier rings him up. She's pretending not to listen in, but she definitely is, given the smirk on her face.

"Raisin bran," he mutters. And it's cute. It's so cute.

But wait . . . how can I be into a new boy when I'm still . . . whatever with Paul? Then again, I'm not doing anything wrong. This is just a friendly shopping trip, right? I mean . . . look at me. It's definitely not a date of any sort.

Eugene pays, thanks the cashier, and we return the carts to the indoor corral since we only have one bag each. He extends his hand and takes my grocery bag from me as we walk to the automatic doors. Our fingers graze each other's and we lock eyes for a second.

"I got it," he says.

I eventually let go, too stunned to respond in a proper amount of time. Paul would've already been four steps ahead of me with just his bag.

We go outside and the lingering warmth of the summer night feels good on my chilled legs.

"Fine," I say, feeling generous. "I like Corn Pops too, but they take too long to get soggy."

"Which is why it's the second-best cereal out there—the shape and coating resists sogginess," he says. "But the taste of Cap'n is superior."

I stop at the Corolla and unlock it. "Did we just end the cold cereal war?"

He opens the back of the car and places the grocery bag on the floor. After shutting the door, we linger by the driver's side. It feels like there's a magnetic field between us, both compelling me closer but keeping me stuck in place.

"I mean . . . I could consider a truce," he says. "But I feel like the person who admits to liking raisin bran is just hiding more horrific preferences."

"Only one way to find out." I shrug.

"You're right. Dinner this week?"

We freeze and stare at each other. I part my lips but don't say a word. I can't believe he said that. He can't seem to believe it either, judging from the rapid movements of his eyes. Is he asking me out? Or maybe he means getting dinner as foodie friends? Yes, that must be it. Just friends.

We stand silently next to the Corolla. The quiet lingers for way too long as I wait for him to ask for my number or elaborate. I brace myself for both hope and disappointment, but neither happens. So he must've been joking. Why would a guy as cute and talented as Eugene have asked me out, anyhow?

"Where's your car?" I finally say.

He lets out a loud exhale. I can't tell if he's relieved or disappointed.

"My ride is right there." He points to a vintage black and gray motorcycle parked in the lane across from mine.

"You're not serious," I say.

"Do people joke about motorcycles? Raisin bran maybe, but not Triumphs."

"I . . . but . . . they're unsafe," I blurt out.

Yes, what a sexy, cool thing to say.

He shrugs a shoulder. "Bikes can be unsafe when people are reckless. So can skateboards, or cars, and just about everything else. It depends on the driver. Have you ever been on one?"

"No. Never. Not once. Nope. No." I shake my head, my bun tilting around and now probably tragic instead of cute messy. I take my hair down. He watches as I shake out my now wavy hair and toss it over my head.

"So . . . that's a no then?" He smiles slowly.

I wince.

"All right," he says. He shifts his groceries to his other shoulder. "If you change your mind, call me and we'll go for a ride."

"I won't, but I mean, is there a Bat-Signal I should use?" I say.

He tilts his head.

"I don't have your number," I say.

"Oh." He looks genuinely surprised.

He gives me his number, and I text him my name so he has mine. As I hit send, my heart races like I ran here from my house.

"Thanks for the, uh . . . company," I say.

Note: it comes out as awkward as humanly possible.

"It was a really pleasant surprise," he says. He pauses, lips parted.

I lean forward on the balls of my *Tangled* flip-flops waiting for him to say more. He glances at my lips again, but looks away. He smiles and crosses the quiet parking lot.

"Make sure to let that Cap'n Crunch sit in milk for a while," I yell after him.

"I'm going to eat it dry with a spoon at this point," he yells back.

I laugh my weirdly deep laugh.

He opens up a saddlebag, takes out a helmet, and puts his groceries in. Then he straddles the bike and kick-starts it. He gives me a small wave before driving off into the night.

I'm left standing there with my heart pounding, trying to figure out why he makes it race. Why do I feel this way when I'm around him? Why is there this draw to him? Is it just because he has the life I dream about? Or is it more than that?

I open the driver's side of the Corolla, and I still smell him as I put on my seat belt. When I plug in my phone, I save him as Captain Eugene Crunch Matthews and smile to myself. Oddly, I want to text him already, even though he just left. Even though I don't really understand any of this.

The thing is: if he'd actually asked me on a real date, despite everything going on with Paul, I would've said yes. And the thought shakes me so hard, I hide my phone in my bag and start the Rolla.

CHAPTER TWENTY-ONE

**DAVEY'S EXTREMELY NOSY FAMILY GROUP TEXT
MAY 26**

Cousin Amberlynn
OMG YOU GUYZZZZZ

Mom
What? What happened? Is everything okay?

Cousin Crystal
OMG I can't believe you're already on the group chat!
Snitch!

Cousin Amberlynn
You're just jelly I beat you here. I saw them first

Aunt Minnie
What is going on?

Cousin Joe
Saw who?

Cousin Amberlynn
Jaz and Eugene were grocery shopping together at Publix ♥

Aunt Tammy
What?!

Wait, isn't she home, Cari?

Cousin Crystal
Hand to God. We talked to them

Aunt Regina
Was there a run-in scheduled for tonight, Cari??

Cari
No. At last check he wasn't even sure if he was still in. And I thought she was here. I'm as surprised as everyone else

Nonna
So our girl is going off script

Aunt Jay
I kind of love that. Plus, it's my boy. I knew he was into her

Cousin Amberlynn
Well, it looked like he was alllll in

Cousin Crystal

And she looked MESSY. What was with those shorts?

Cousin Amberlynn

Maybe they did happen to just run into each other.
How weird would that be?

Cousin Wesley

Wow, gossip much? You all need more to do on a holiday
weekend

Cousin Wylan

Worried Eugene will win, huh?

Cousin Wesley

Not even a little. She has her first run-in with Justin Michael
tomorrow at Uncle Ed and Aunt Kim's store

Aunt Kim

We can't wait!

Cousin Crystal

Well, I'm changing to Team Eugene

Aunt Jay

Wow, really?

Cousin Crystal
She was a grade A mess and he looked at her like she hung the moon. They were so cute, shopping together like a little married couple

Cousin Amberlynn
Told ya from the start, sis

Cousin Joe
This isn't over. Aaron is a natural favorite and he's never wavered in wanting in

Mom
OMG go to bed everyone

It's 8:15, Ma

Mom
I stand by my point

Aunt Tammy
Good night! I made the best pad thai. Y'all should stop in for leftovers!

Cari
Um, let's regroup after she meets with Justin Michael tomorrow

CHAPTER TWENTY-TWO

JASMINE'S IPHONE
MAY 26

PR

♥ Paul ♥

Did you get my text yesterday?

CHAPTER TWENTY-THREE

It's Memorial Day, but there's no rest for the wicked (or teenagers off for the summer). Because normal people have a vacation day, I have a double shift.

This morning is unpaid labor—part of my family's involuntary volunteering program. The "oh, Jaz can help with that" enlistment from my mom. I'm going to Uncle Ed and Aunt Kim's bookstore, Books & Other Adventures. They recently added a small tea and scone bar, and that's what I'll be manning before an evening shift at Berry Plum.

I pull into the parking lot of B&OA and get out of the car with more care than usual. I decided to mix things up and wear a dress today. My family looked at me like I had three heads when I came out of my room this morning. My mom, who was just home from her overnight shift, stopped, said "I must be overtired," rubbed her eyes, and looked at me again. But I don't know. I woke up feeling good.

Or . . . actually, I do know: I cooked last night for the first time since before Burrito Friday and the mussels turned out amazing.

As I was in the kitchen, I was just . . . content. Standing by the stove feels like coming home again. There's a sense of peace in doing knife work and getting my hands dirty. There's a joy in the moment ingredients come together to form something better than the separate parts. Something I made, something I knew just how to tweak to be its best.

The greatest thing for me, though, was watching Cari and Dad dig in and fight over the French bread I bought to go with the mussels. Dad got the last piece and used it to sop up the rest of the broth. Then he rubbed his stomach while Cari gave him a stink eye. Even Davey, who won't try mussels, had some bread dipped in broth and gave me a thumbs-up while trying to talk with his mouth full. And that's what it's all about for me: making people happy. It makes me feel good and, okay, yes, special. Davey is great at basketball, Cari is good at everything, but this is mine.

And yes, I admit Eugene had an effect on me. It makes no sense since I barely know him, but I sang a love song rather than "Jolene" (again) while I was cooking. And I replayed our entire Publix conversation in my head before I fell asleep. The feeling, the magnetism that runs through me when I'm near him is something I've never felt before. And that's odd to say after dating someone else for four years.

But I don't have time to think about him right now. Or why he hasn't texted. Or why I couldn't come up with something clever or funny enough to text him. It's time for my shift.

I pull open the glass door and walk into the bookshop. As I pass the register, I wave at Simon. He never talks to me, but he shifts his glasses and I take that as a hello. Uncle Ed walks toward me. He's Mom's youngest brother.

"Hey, kiddo," Uncle Ed says. "Thanks for helping out. We're already busier than a normal Monday."

"No problem at all," I say.

"You know the drill," he says.

I nod. I've helped out a dozen times. He offered to officially hire me for the summer, but Berry Plum has always been good to me. I didn't want to leave them shorthanded, even though it would've been nicer to work here.

Uncle Ed points at me. "Keep any tips you make this time."

I usually shove them into the little cashbox. "Mm-mm," I hum.

He stares at me. "As stubborn as Dee," he sighs. "The apron's behind the counter. And help yourself to some scones. Jay brought them in earlier and they're still warm."

"Ooh. There go your profits for today." I raise my eyebrows.

"A risk I'm willing to take." He smiles and gently squeezes my chin so my face returns to normal. I slide behind the small bar.

The tea bar is just four seats and a varnished wood counter with a glass cloche for the scones. We have a few different kinds of loose tea and a milk steamer for lattes. It's not exactly Starbucks, but it's perfect for B&OA.

It's not long before I have my first customer. Although it's an obscure little counter, on a decent morning the store can move well over a hundred scones, because Aunt Jay's baking skills are top-notch. Plus, Uncle Ed's daughter Charlotte did an amazing sandwich board outside highlighting the tea bar inside. Her art is so good, she has an Instagram fan account devoted to her signs and everything.

Today's choices are: raisin, cranberry orange, and bacon cheddar. I know which ones I'll be trying: all of them. Whatever my feelings are about my aunt, my feelings on baked goods are stronger.

But I'm kept too busy to eat. I smile, chat with customers, and move scones in and out of the warming drawer for hours. It's noon when things slow down. The morning went by in a blink of friendly conversation and a few people camping out with their tea as they started their books.

"I think you're just about done, Jaz, but could you give us a hand upstairs?" Uncle Ed asks. "We could use more chairs in the reading room. Big middle-grade author coming in later."

"Absolutely."

I try to talk like I don't have a mouth full of bacon cheddar scone. It . . . doesn't work. He laughs, and I finish chewing as I make my way to the award-winning children's section.

The upstairs is a wonderland. There's a literary forest, a book castle kids can climb into, a pirate ship surrounded by swirling stars, a minizoo with stuffed animals for sale, and my personal favorite: a reading room that's accessed by moving a book marked Books & Other AdVenturas.

Uncle Al, another of Mom's brothers, said designing and installing the children's floor was the best and worst project of his life, but this space was featured in enough magazines for all to have been forgiven.

I pull the red book and the reading-room door springs open. Inside is a miniature theater—dark, with a little stage and overhead spotlights. There are already thirty chairs set up, so a dozen more should do it. I take some wooden folding chairs out of the storage room and I'm walking back when I notice a shadow of someone in the room. New customers love to explore, but usually, when they see nothing is going on in here, they turn around.

"Hey, the reading isn't until later if you—" I say, then I look up.

Justin Michael steps into the light and smiles at me. The lighting makes his blond hair glow like a halo.

"Oh my God!" I screech.

"Candy," he says. He opens his arms and I launch myself into them.

"Twice in a week!" I say, squeezing him. He's far more muscular now, and he smells like spearmint and cologne instead of Cocoa Puffs and crossword-puzzle newsprint.

"What are you doing here?" I ask. I mean . . . it's a bookstore, but still.

"I came in to pick up a couple of novels, but your uncle said you were upstairs," he says. We disentangle from each other. "You look so pretty."

I immediately fuss with my hair, and I'm glad for my green-and-white-striped dress. Better than looking like a Winnie-the-Pooh cosplayer, that's for sure.

"What are you doing?" he asks. "Can I help?"

He springs into action, and in seconds we get the extra

chairs set up. We walk out of the reading room and the faux bookcase closes behind us. The book castle lies directly ahead of us.

"We used to spend hours in there," I say. "Remember?"

I point to the small house encased in real books.

"How could I forget?" he says.

"You were a lot shorter then," I say, frowning. I reach up and place my hand on his soft hair, mock measuring.

He smiles. "I know. I used to love lying with my head in your lap as you read Percy Jackson books to me. Sometimes you'd sneak strawberry laces in there. You always shared."

As he says it, I picture us in the book castle. Like there's a ten-year-old Korean girl and a same-age blond boy with glasses quietly reading instead of what appears to be a mob of kindergartners storming the castle. The artificial strawberry and sugar scent fills my nose and brings peace in this chaos.

"I can't believe you remember it that clearly," I say.

He smiles slowly. "It was the most content I've felt in my life. It's nice when things are as good as you remember them."

Our eyes meet, and it's like I've been hit with a melting serum. Me. He's talking about me. My shoulders drop, my knees get weaker. Words bubble up inside me. I should tell him that those days meant a lot to me. I should say that even though things ended badly all those years ago that I don't care. It feels like he never left. I should be a different kind of person entirely and stand on my tiptoes and kiss him for saying something so sweet. And maybe I'd linger. And maybe it would be a real kiss.

Wait, what? No. He's my friend. My friend since we were literally babies. He'd be grossed out. And I am definitely *not* that kind of person. I'm still dating Paul . . . sort of. Maybe? Ugh. And I've never kissed anyone else. I've never wanted to kiss anyone else. Something weird is happening to me.

"Do you . . . can I make you some tea?" I ask.

"I'd love some," Justin Michael says.

We head down the stairs. His hand grazes my back as we leave behind the memories of who we used to be in the children's section.

CHAPTER TWENTY-FOUR

JASMINE'S IPHONE
MAY 27

♥ Paul ♥

Are you okay, Jaz?

CHAPTER TWENTY-FIVE

The secret, if there is one, to making good tea is to
leave it alone. Follow the instructions, go a pinch heavy on
the leaves, and keep your hands off.

While the Darjeeling steeps, I serve Justin Michael a raisin scone. He perches across from me at the counter—the
only customer at the moment. I liked the bacon-cheddar flavor the best, but he always had more of a sweet tooth so I
chose raisin for him.

"Your aunt Jay is incredible," he says, admiring the scone.
"These are so light and fluffy."

Jay was the one who taught me how to properly measure
flour, to not overwork dough, and the importance of letting
it rest. She and I used to taste test new baking combina-
tions, and nothing was better than something right out of
her oven.

Laughter rings in my ears, hers and mine, from when
we'd had a flour fight after I'd pointed out how she'd gotten some on her cheek. Mom was annoyed that I'd gotten
my black shirt dirty, but Jay had just rolled her eyes and said
she'd get me a chef's jacket. She did.

The little egg timer goes off behind me, stirring me from

my memories. I pour a cup of tea for Justin and one for me. We both use sugar. He takes milk.

He washes down another bite of scone while I warm my air-conditioning-chilled fingers on my cup.

"I'm glad I ran into you," Justin Michael says. "I was going to text you about getting tea, and here we are."

We clink our mugs.

"Cheers," I say. I lift my tea and blow on the fragrant brew. It's too hot to drink right now. "I'm glad too."

"I probably would've botched asking you," he says. "Like when I tried to ask you out."

His words register, and instead of blowing on my tea, I slurp it up. I don't have time to regret it. It's like I swallowed a comet. The back of my throat catches fire. Tears flood my eyes as I cough.

I try to respond and yep . . . that's worse.

Flailing, I slosh the tea in my mug. The hot liquid rises and burns my left hand. I shake off the tea, stumble forward, and drop my cup on the counter. It spills before Justin sets it right, but at least I didn't burn him, too.

While still coughing, I turn on the sink and run my hand under cool water until it feels better. It's not a bad burn. Only the awkward stings. There are napkins on the bar, but I dry my palms on my apron. Finally, I catch my breath. Some shoppers have turned to stare, but since I haven't spontaneously combusted yet, they're back to browsing.

Instead of noting the day's scones, Charlotte should've

written that there's a clown serving tea who's available for children's parties.

"I'm really, really sorry," Justin says, his brown eyes full of concern. "Are you okay?"

"I'm fine," I croak out. I grab my bottle of water from the fridge. I take a sip and cool my mouth and throat.

"My timing is awful. That was my fault," he says.

I tilt my head. Why is he sorry? Paul would've walked away from me for making an embarrassing scene, like he did when we got snacks at a concession stand and I tripped and spilled popcorn everywhere, but Justin Michael is apologizing? Like he's the one who hasn't mastered drinking?

"No, no. I'm just . . . I was caught off guard," I say. Because Justin Michael claimed he asked me out. Either that or he's really learned how to deadpan a joke.

"I can tell," he laughs.

His chuckle makes me laugh too, then we're both laughing hard. At least I don't snort like Emily.

"For the record, though," I say, "you never asked me out."

"No, seriously, I did," he says.

"Never happened." I shake my head, my ponytail swishing.

"I asked you to go to a movie with me," he says. "It was a Pixar film and you turned me down cold."

I'm still laughing, but he's . . . serious? It can't be, but those are too many details to be made up. Plus, his face is sincere. I rack my mind trying to think of when this could've been. If it happened, I do know one thing: I didn't realize he was asking me out.

"Did I know it was supposed to be a date?" I ask.

He shakes his head. "In hindsight, no. I was so nervous and you said you were busy so I kinda walked away. It took a while for me to realize you just had plans. But I felt rejected— listened to angsty breakup songs in my room and everything."

He laughs at himself and runs his hand over his beard. His jawline has changed so much from the boy I knew to the man in front of me.

"I didn't work up the courage again," he says. "My mom got that VP position, and with the move and all, I lost my chance."

I'm stunned, just stunned. I can't even process it because my mind gets stuck on when he ever asked me to go to the movies. We usually played games, read books, or had tea. But wait . . . there was one time.

He was pushing me on the rope swing that hung off the weeping willow tree in his backyard. It was before yet another Yap/Ventura party. He said his parents could drop us off at the movie theater, and he seemed oddly nervous about it. I didn't understand why he'd stopped pushing me or why he was swaying like a metronome and shifting his glasses again and again.

Now it all makes sense.

"Wait, this was the summer before ninth grade?" I say.

He nods.

Right before he moved away.

Pieces come together, and I finally realize why we had a falling-out. In the two weeks after Justin moved to Texas, we messaged all the time. Things were great and we were scheming on how to see each other again—flights, trains, hitchhiking across the country. Then high school started, and thinking he was just my close friend, I told him all about meeting Paul. That was when Justin got cold. I kept messaging like always, but he'd barely respond. I missed one FaceTime chat because I was busy with a group project, and we got into a fight. He said he was sorry he wasn't more convenient. I said he'd never been convenient, which didn't come out the way I meant it. That was when he said he didn't want to bother with me anymore, that I wasn't worth it. I was crushed. I was certain he was going to apologize, and I kept waiting, but instead he never messaged again.

People said I shouldn't have expected to stay in contact with someone who'd moved so far away. That most childhood friendships don't last. But I knew there was more to the story. I just never knew what. Eventually, I had to let it go. But it turns out he'd liked me and I'd hurt him.

A million apologies get dammed up at my lips. I want to tell Justin I'm sorry he felt rejected even if he can laugh about it now. Because I know all too well what rejection feels like. That I would've liked to have gone on my first date with him. And I wonder what would've happened if he'd been my first boyfriend instead of Paul. But I can't change any of that, and saying it four years later doesn't seem right. It's too little, too late.

Instead, I say, "I would've liked to have seen that movie with you."

He smiles warmly and sips his tea. At least one of us doesn't fling it around like a malfunctioning robot.

"Funny enough, it's on Netflix now," he says.

He and I could watch it together—pretend like we went on the date. But it's different, more intimate streaming a movie on a couch. The thought makes me rub my palms against my apron even though they're dry. But really, there's no need to be nervous. Justin is my friend. Even if he asked me out, we were kids four years ago. It doesn't mean he wants this to be anything other than a friendly hang.

Right?

I put my hands on my hips, imitating my mom. "Justin Michael Simmons, are you inviting me to Netflix and chill?"

"No," he says, his eyes wide, the picture of innocence. "It sounds like you are, though. Maybe we should say 'movie night'—there are children present." He waggles his eyebrows and waits with a smile on his face.

I laugh. "My house? Thursday night?"

"Sounds good," he says. "I'll swing by after work. Popcorn and strawberry laces?"

"Definitely," I say. "I'll get some other snacks too because you know Davey is a human vacuum cleaner now."

He laughs, then digs in his pocket and pulls out a twenty.

"Your money is no good here," I say, pushing it back. I fully intended on covering his tea and scone from my tips.

He reaches out and covers my hand and the money, pressing them down on the counter with his palm. Our hands are so different, compared to when we were kids. And the feeling of his hand on mine makes my stomach flip.

We lock eyes and he smiles slowly. I stare at him, forgetting to breathe.

"Please," he says. "Keep the change."

He takes his hand off mine, and it's a few seconds before I shake off my stupor.

"No. Here," I say. I have to try twice to pick up the money.

He looks me dead in the eyes then turns and bolts. He runs out of the store with his comical, small-step run, then peers at me from the store window before taking off again. I stand at the counter, laughing and shaking my head.

But all I can think about is how it felt to look in his eyes with his hand over mine. I can't explain it, but it felt like someone handing me an umbrella after I walked in the rain. That kind of easy comfort just flowed through us.

It's not until I've rung up the order that I realize: I just made a date with Justin Michael Simmons. And there's a possibility it could be a *date* date.

What do I do now?

CHAPTER TWENTY-SIX

It's Tuesday night and I'm in another dress. I felt fancy coming in to work at Berry Plum, but Katia has an honest-to-God orchid behind her ear.

What can ya do? Can't compete with that.

It's quieter than yesterday evening's shift. There's only an older couple who came in a few minutes ago, two college-aged friends who have been debating a philosopher for like an hour, and a family with young children who are up pretty late for this much sugar. I think they're on vacation since the kids were shrieking about Magic Kingdom while doing laps around the table.

Winter Park is somewhere between twenty-five and ten thousand minutes from the Mouse, depending on I-4 traffic, so we don't get a ton of tourists here. Justin Michael said his commute to Disney isn't great, but Houston is worse any day of the week.

He's staying with a cousin in Baldwin Park—another suburb of Orlando. He took me on a virtual tour of the very sleek bachelor pad when we FaceTimed last night. He showed me his bed and I couldn't help but blush.

I hate my face.

"Let's start closing so we can get outta here on time," Katia says. "I have a date." She does a little twirl.

"Ooh. With?" I ask. I've never seen her this excited.

"Lee. I met them at a concert this weekend and we went out last night," she says. She rattles off some group I've never heard of. Orlando is cool that way—it's a big mix of musical tastes, including a country presence, which I love, and a techno side Paul was all about and I couldn't understand.

Katia takes off from behind the counter. People don't normally come in late on a Tuesday, so she dismantles one of the less popular machines. We take one apart a night for cleaning and the day shift puts it together. I wipe down the other machines, essentially closing them for the night.

The family takes the hint. They get up, throw out their trash, and leave. The older couple is still working on their dessert. The college friends were done with theirs long ago.

Since we're nearly finished, I grab my phone and text Cari, asking her to come get me in fifteen.

There's another message from Justin that I look at quickly. It's a picture of him holding a very hard to identify fruit he found in his cousin's refrigerator. It's hard to ID because it's growing colorful mold, and Justin is making a funny scared face next to it.

I laugh. It's been great to talk to him again—even if I still don't know if movie night is a date or not. Or if I want it to be. Or if he does.

I feel a little weird messaging with boys (well, one boy, still nothing with Eugene) when I'm still sort of with Paul, but he was the one who asked to see other people, so this is fine. Right? No reason to feel guilty.

Note: I still feel totally guilty.

Paul has messaged too. He asked if his previous message went through and he wanted to know if I was okay. I said I was fine, just busy with work, and he said, "Good, I was worried." I have no idea why he was concerned, and honestly, I've been too busy to think about him much.

The front door chimes, and I drop my phone into my bag with a sigh. I'm going to have to wipe down the yogurt machines again. I knew I did it too early. I try to plaster a smile on my face, but when I look up, my mouth falls open because Aaron the baseball player stands in front of me.

"He . . . hey," I say.

His perfect face breaks into a warm smile. "Jasmine."

Butterflies alight and flutter through me as his eyes focus on me. I'm not the only one a little starstruck. He's in a plain T-shirt and shorts, but everyone in the place has stopped what they're doing to look at this man. Even the college girls ceased their endless debate. And there's a new feeling associated with being around him. Like I feel important. It's stardom, maybe.

"Wha . . . what are you doing here?" I say. Apparently, I've developed a hotness malfunction. Great—just what I needed.

"Your family mentioned you work here and that I should try it out," he says. "We had a home game today, so I figured I'd swing by. It's cute. Real cute."

I bless and curse my family for their meddling. A little

heads-up would've been nice. Cousin Teagan and Cousin Joe were in here earlier for a while—they could've told me, if they knew. But who knows which of my value-pack-sized family mentioned it.

At least Berry Plum *is* cute. It's aimed at kids, but it's streamlined enough for adults to like it too.

"Um, yeah, yes, you should try it out. Definitely," I say. Then I shut my mouth so suddenly, my teeth click. Seriously, Jasmine, stop talking forever.

"Do I just help myself to what I want?" he asks, leaning forward slightly.

I feel a blush starting and . . . yogurt. He's asking about yogurt, you mess.

"Yes, yes, please," I gesture toward the large cups and waffle bowls stacked to the right. He walks that way.

"Let me know if you want a taste," I say.

The second the words are out of my mouth, I realize how they sound. We lock eyes and I spin away from him because I cannot.

"Jasmine," he says.

Nope.

Reluctantly, and with the deepest internal cringe at myself, I turn.

"I will," he adds with a sly smile.

A high pitched *eep* forms in my throat. Luckily, I don't think he can hear it over the radio Katia put on too loud to make people leave. Right on cue, she comes back from the storage room. She stops and gawks at the gorgeous, muscular man who's evaluating our yogurt choices.

"Which is your favorite, Jaz?" he asks, glancing over his shoulder.

Katia does a double take between me and him, her large eyes getting even wider.

"I like espresso the best," I say. "But I also do the plain if I'm in a toppings mood."

"Great choices," he says. He pours a bit of each into his cup and wanders over to the toppings.

There's a variety of candy, nuts, and cereal in little bins at our dry toppings bar. Then there's a refrigerated section with fresh fruit, whipped cream, boba, and dessert pieces. Last, there are hot toppings with warm sauces.

Katia slinks up to my side and whispers sharply. "Who is *that*?"

"Aaron. He's a . . . friend of the family."

"You have better family than I do," she says. "That would be an *amazing* rebound."

She goes to refill the M&M's before I can argue.

"Excuse me," she says, stepping around Aaron and giggling.

He gets out of her way and gestures toward the bins. "All yours," he says.

His Nashville accent is more pronounced, or maybe I'm just prepared for it.

I'm watching him evaluate the toppings when my phone dings. I look down and it's a message from Cari.

CY

Cari

So sorry! I can't get you right now. Can you take Lyft? I'll pay for it.

I groan and it's loud. Much louder than intended. Aaron turns, so does Katia.

"What happened?" she asks. Her doe eyes are filled with concern. We were never close until we bonded over Paul wanting to see other girls, and now I'm sure she thinks my groan has something to do with him.

"Oh, it's nothing," I say. "Just that my ride bagged."

"Man, I'd drive you, but I'm being picked up," Katia says. "I can ask Lee . . ."

"Nah, it's not a big deal. I'll call Lyft," I say. There's no way I'm going to third-wheel her date.

Aaron places his yogurt on the counter. I eye the toppings he picked: chocolate candies on the espresso fro-yo, with some almonds and pretzels. Maraschino cherry sauce and chocolate brownies on the vanilla side. Classic.

"I can give you a ride home if you want," Aaron says. His voice is deep and reverberates through me.

"It's okay," I say, being polite.

I stare at him and it's like his skin doesn't even have pores. He's just so perfect. He stares back and raises his eyebrows, and I realize I forgot to tell him the total—my only job right now. He hands over a credit card and I remember (barely) to ring him up. I flip the screen toward him. He leaves a huge tip on six dollars of fro-yo. There's nothing I can do to stop him because it's already processed.

"You really didn't have to do that," I say.

"Not a problem," he says. "And dropping you off is no big deal."

"Is it on your way home?" I ask.

He smiles. "No. But it's not far. I live downtown."

"Oh. I don't want you to have to go out of your way," I say.

I can feel Katia's eyes on me like: Wtf, take the ride with the smoking-hot guy who knows you somehow. But I hate inconveniencing people. Even if he looks like he's been sculpted and I just want to find out how his nose is that straight. Paul had to get his nose fixed after breaking it playing soccer, but I doubt Aaron's had surgery. He has the easy confidence of someone born perfect. Cari is that way too. Like they have never once tripped down the stairs . . . or over a gift table.

"No pressure," he says, "but I'd feel better if one of my sisters was driven home by someone she knew rather than by a rideshare." He shrugs and picks up his yogurt.

My dad drives for them, but even he says I need to be careful. Just commonsense things like not ignoring a gut feeling on a driver and paying attention to the route. My gut feeling on Aaron is he's a nice guy who is unreal hot.

He takes a bite as he stands in front of me. "You were right about the espresso. It's really good."

"How many sisters do you have?" I ask.

"Three. All younger," he says. "We're like steps: twenty . . ." He points to himself. "Eighteen, sixteen, and a real bratty fourteen."

He swipes his phone and shows me an incredibly beautiful family standing by a lake. He's in a blue button-down and his sisters are in light blue dresses, and there's an older woman with them who must be his mom.

"What a gorgeous family," I say. "Did your dad take the picture?"

"No. He was deployed. My mom really raised us. And she'd have more than a word with me if I didn't offer to drive you or at least wait with you to make sure the driver looks okay."

And I'm charmed. He's almost offensively charming.

"Well, I wouldn't want to upset your mom . . . ," I say.

"You shouldn't." He smiles. "She's one tough lady."

"She must be so proud of you," I say.

He smiles and looks down at the counter. "She's glad I made it."

There's something off about the way he says it. It feels like there's more, that I got a glimpse under his surface, but I don't know him well enough to ask. He smiles again and his expression shifts back to unaffected and pleasant.

The older couple leaves and now it's just the college students left.

"Eff this," Katia says under her breath. She walks away and suddenly it gets darker in the store as she turns off the lights.

The girls get the very subtle hint and leave.

"Excuse me for a minute," I say to Aaron. "We need to shut everything down, but . . . stay right there."

"Sure. Take your time," he says.

Katia and I run through the remainder of closing the store, from putting away the refrigerated toppings to tallying the register. I'm not sure who wants to get out of here more—me or her.

I keep glancing at Aaron, certain I imagined someone that good looking who's content to sit and wait for me. Paul flipped if I wasn't ready to go when he came to get me. Not in the store, of course, but in the car afterward. I used to text him after we finished closing just to make sure I wouldn't keep him waiting. I'd sit outside alone and that never bothered him. And it never occurred to me to mind because he was going out of his way to drive me.

Maybe I should've expected more.

I lock the back door of the shop and we all go out the front. We stand in the muggy air, the three of us facing each other.

"Thanks for lettin' me hang out, ladies," Aaron says.

"Anytime," I say.

"You should come by again," Katia says, giving me the world's most obvious stare.

And I thought my family was bad.

A second later, and not a moment too soon, a Jetta pulls into the parking lot.

"Well, there's my ride," Katia says. "You two have fun. Don't do anything I wouldn't do."

She departs with a wink and gets in the car. She leans across the console and kisses the person I assume to be Lee. So, yeah, I'm trying not to be uncomfortable with the make-out session in front of me and Aaron next to me. But where am I even supposed to look?

A very long minute later, the Jetta reverses and drives away with a honk.

"So what did you decide?" Aaron asks. "Lyft, or can I bring you home? I'm good with either. I don't want you to feel pressured to get in the car with me. No make-out session required."

I laugh and my phone dings.

I fish around in my purse, but now I'm totally thinking about making out with Aaron. I miss my phone several times.

"Sorry, let me just see if this is Cari," I say.

His eyebrows knit. "Who?"

"My sister," I say.

"Oh. Carissa. You call her Cari?" He smiles. "You guys are cute."

"Maybe, but she's the one who bagged on driving me home. So I don't exactly find her cute right now." I finally locate my phone and unlock it.

It's not Cari. It's June. Emily is upset and June wants to go over there tomorrow. I'm volunteering at the animal shelter, but I'm sure I can fit it in. I'll text them back as soon as I get home.

I drop my phone into my bag.

"Is she busy with her boyfriend?" he asks.

"Cari?" I say. "No, she doesn't have one. I don't think she's ever had one."

For all her obsession with romance, my sister has never had a real relationship.

He raises his eyebrows. "How's that possible? Even my youngest sister has one. I don't like that Cam the Snot Monster has a boyfriend, but I've accepted it. Kind of."

He makes a face and I laugh. There's something sweet about the way he talks about his sisters, even the one he's calling a mucus goblin. It's protective without being overbearing.

"Um, if your offer still stands . . . ," I say.

"No, sorry, it expired. . . ." He looks at his wrist, which doesn't have a watch. "Five seconds ago. Darn. You were so close."

He smiles slowly and hits a button. The lights of a fancy red Audi flash. He gestures toward the car.

I follow him to the passenger door. It has all the sleek lines of a car that costs too much. "Nice spaceship," I say.

"We haven't even blasted off yet." He raises his eyebrows once and I look away, shyly. He opens the passenger door and closes it behind me. I half fall, half sit in the seat, but let's pretend that didn't happen.

The interior is all leather and space age. I feel cool just for being inside it. And for the first time in my life, I *want* people to notice me. I *want* people to see that I'm in this hot car with this gorgeous guy. I *want* attention. I want kids who were at that bonfire in middle school to walk by right now. Especially the one who said, "Not you, never you." Because even though Aaron's just being nice, they wouldn't know that.

Aaron syncs his phone and loads directions to my house. I wonder how he knows where I live, then I remember he was at my party.

My stomach knots at being alone with him and this close. He smells like an October day—the moment when the humidity suddenly drops and the air is crisp. And he seems to be leaning a little farther toward me than necessary, but then he sits up straight once the directions start.

"Seriously, thanks for the ride," I say.

"No problem. I was hoping to see you anyhow," he says.

"You were?" I ask. "Why?"

I sound as shocked as I am. Nervousness tingles up my spine.

He laughs, reverses, and follows the turn-by-turn. "Well, I was thinking if you were free Saturday night, you and your family could come out to a game."

"Oh," I say. We've never been to a Minor League game, and I don't really watch baseball, but it could be fun.

"I'm pitching on Saturday," he adds.

"Oh!" I say. It's way, way too loud.

His eyes dart over to me.

"I'd love to," I say at normal volume. "I don't know what my parents are up to, but I'm sure Davey or Cari will want to come."

"Great. I'll have three comped tickets waiting at the window. Just say you're my guests."

"That's really sweet, but we can pay for them."

"I get family tickets and mine is in Nashville. It'd be nice to see some familiar faces in the crowd." He glances over at me. "Especially when they're so pretty."

I'm grateful for the dark because I'm sure I'm blushing redder than the car as we blast off to my house. But going to his game wouldn't be a date. Not when we won't even talk to each other. He's just being kind and he needs friends in town.

I think.

CHAPTER TWENTY-SEVEN

The next morning June shows up at my door right on time. She's going to take me to see Emily, then give me a ride to the shelter. Cari promised she'd pick me up after my shift . . . this time.

Turns out, she'd accidentally scheduled an hour-long *Bachelor* Reddit AMA for last night rather than tonight. I can't believe so many people have things to ask my sister, but I've seen her accounts explode with notifications, so it's just something I don't understand.

Her abandoning me didn't turn out badly, though, because Aaron was there. He and I listened to old country the whole way home, and we exchanged numbers. I have no idea why someone like him would be interested in me, but I'm trying not to overthink it. The same way I'm trying to not overthink hanging out with Justin tomorrow. It's not possible that two boys would ask me out in one week, so I'm rolling with it.

I crash into the passenger seat of June's silver Ford Mustang, and she hands me a Dunkin' iced coffee. There's also a hazelnut cappuccino in the cup holder, which must be for Emily.

"Have you been able to get in touch with her?" I ask.

June shakes her head. "Not today. She said yesterday that everything was a mess and didn't text back, hence the drop-in."

"What do you think is up?" I ask.

"I don't know," June says. "Maybe something with her sister or her mom? Can't be a boy because she hasn't dated anyone since Shawn—thank God."

I purse my lips. That disaster was kind of on me.

Paul and I had introduced Emily and Shawn. They hit it off right away but quickly became the most dramatic teen couple. Screaming, crying breakups, passionate makeups, jealous outbursts, all of it kind of a miniversion of her parents—which we could never point out because she would've lost it.

It was a long senior year.

But it's a short drive to Emily's house. She lives around the block from Paul. I don't like the idea of being in his neighborhood, but at least we're in June's new Mustang and not my borrowed Corolla.

The Reyes family, like a lot of people in Winter Park, has a ton of money. I'm not sure what Paul's parents do other than be rich and flaunt it. I used to be super self-conscious about parking the Rolla beside a Bentley and a winged Mercedes. Before that, I'd be embarrassed when my mom came to get me in her beat-up old Honda. And I hated thinking that way. I don't care about flashy things, and I was grateful for the ride. I'm proud of my mom and dad for working so hard. But . . . I noticed.

Paul never tried to make me feel better or worse about it. But he would make little comments about eating in my car, saying it was "just" a Corolla. Maybe he didn't know those comments hurt.

He messaged again this morning, asking if we could talk, and I haven't answered yet because, for one, Emily comes first, and two, I don't know what to say. We're not supposed to talk until August, and against all odds, I'm enjoying this break. Something tells me seeing him won't do me any good.

I push the thoughts away as we pull up to Emily's circular driveway. June grabs the cappuccino and we ring the bell. Elaborate chimes echo through the interior, and after almost a minute, Emily finally answers.

Her hazel eyes are red rimmed and she's still in pajama pants and a tank. She has the same complexion as Cari and is nearly as tall, but she's slouching right now.

"We brought you a cappuccino," June says, holding it out like a peace offering. Emily looks her way but doesn't take it.

"Come in, I guess," she says.

"Are you okay? What's going on?" I ask, after we close the door. June and I linger in the enormous entryway.

"Parent drama," Emily sighs. She paces around on the marble floors like she's trying to warm the tiles with her feet.

"Are they . . . not getting along again?" June asks, diplomatically.

"Not getting along" is the understatement of the year. One day when we came to pick up Emily, her mom was tossing her dad's stuff . . . off the second-floor balcony.

Emily finally stops pacing. "No. It's worse. They want to try one more time."

I wrinkle my brow. I thought her parents getting back together would be a good thing. For a while that was all Emily wanted—just to have her family whole again.

"And you don't want that anymore?" I venture.

Her eyes become glossy. "No! They collapsed my whole world because they couldn't 'make it work.' And I accepted it. I accepted that 'adults change' and that 'we all needed to let go.' And now they want to try? Now they're all second honeymoon because they're 'ready'? Seriously? It's such bullshit."

I don't know what to say. My family and June's family never went through anything like this. The best we can probably do is let Emily vent and be here to listen.

Emily finally takes the cappuccino but pauses before she takes a sip. "You know, some people don't need a second chance when things ended for a reason."

She stares at me, and her words sink in and sting. But she's not talking about me, right? Things didn't end with Paul—not exactly.

"Last night they had me sit with them at Lantern & Jacks and gave me the 'why are you upset, honey' faces, and I can't take it," she says. "I'm not going through this again. They're the exact same people they were a year ago, and if they're going to do this, I'm going to move out. Jaz, are you still getting a place in August? Would you want to move now?"

Both June and Emily turn their heads toward me. Put on the spot, I say what comes naturally.

"Uh."

Brilliant. But I'm spinning on the fact that she randomly went to Lantern & Jacks, a place booked solid for months. My mind turns to Eugene, who I've determined is never going to text me. But now is *not* the time for that.

Moving. Right. I don't know. I don't know a thing. I put the whole situation on pause until August 1. It doesn't make sense for me to move if I'm not with Paul, since living at home would save me a lot of money. I could even help with my parents' second mortgage if I didn't owe any rent.

"I don't know . . . ," I say. "I . . . so much is going on. . . . I haven't really thought about moving since before the party."

And it's true. I stopped searching rental websites every day. I even ignore the Apartments.com new-listing emails. I wanted to move for Paul, not for me, and this break has made that clear.

Emily and June exchange glances, but I can't understand their meaning. And it's strange because I've been able to read June since we were eight.

"What?" I say.

"Nothing," Emily says.

"Nothing," June says.

Sure.

Maybe they don't like that I'm unsure about my future. Maybe they think I'm weak for waiting on Paul. We've had more than one discussion where they've questioned my desire to stay local at a community college instead of going to a university. But it feels like I'm missing something bigger this time.

It feels almost like they know something I don't. But what?

"Something is up," I say. "What?"

Emily's lips part, but June shakes her head. They stare at each other and it looks like they're in a silent war, and that's so weird. Finally, Emily sighs.

"I'm probably being a little overdramatic with wanting to move," Emily says. "But I can't believe my parents."

Note: Emily has never once admitted to being overdramatic. Even when she spent half the day crying because Shawn liked a pic of a girl's dog on Instagram, Emily felt justified. What fresh nonsense is this? How did Emily switch gears so quickly? Why is June oddly quiet?

"Have you eaten breakfast?" June asks.

"No," Emily says. "Well, unless you count the coffee. Thanks, by the way."

"Anytime," June says. "But maybe Jaz will make us real breakfast. Pancakes?"

June stares at me and her eyes shoot over to Emily like, Offer to make her pancakes now, you donkey.

I'm slow on the uptake because I'm still trying to figure out why they're acting off, but I didn't have breakfast either and pancakes do sound really good. Also, the Underwoods have an amazing gourmet kitchen.

"We can help," Emily says.

I squint one eye. Neither knows how to cook, and Emily started a small fire in her microwave . . . twice.

"By 'help,' I mean we'll talk to you while you cook," she says.

"And we'll do some dishes," June adds. Emily nods her agreement.

"All right," I say. "All the dishes."

"Done," Emily says.

We head to the kitchen, and even though I can't shake the thought that I'm missing something, it's not like they'd ever keep anything important from me, so I focus on what kind of pancakes to make. Blueberry sounds perfect.

CHAPTER TWENTY-EIGHT

June pulls into the parking lot of the animal shelter a few minutes before noon. After spilling batter on my shirt and a lot of badgering from Emily, I agreed to take a shirt from her. I'm not sure why she was so adamant I change, but the sleeveless shirt is much nicer than anything I'd normally wear. I think it's silk and probably cost as much as my graduation dress, but Emily said it was too small on her and to keep it. I'm afraid to get dirty, but I'll be at the desk today, so I shouldn't get anything on me.

Famous last words.

I thank June for the ride, get out of the Mustang, and face the squat beige building.

With a deep breath, I pull open the door and walk in. I take my seat at the empty front desk and get to work.

Over the past two years I've done just about every volunteer job here, from walking dogs to sorting paperwork, but lately I've focused on upgrading the website to help get more animals adopted.

It's a little after three o'clock when I've finished updates to the website, social media, and answering emails. The door chimes open and it's my job to greet people. I always hope it's a family who'll adopt, but usually on a Wednesday it's deliveries and sometimes it's a surrender. Pets wind up here when they get lost, when their owners die, or commonly when they're just not wanted anymore.

I look up from my paperwork. It's one person bringing in a box so large, it obscures half their body. It doesn't appear to be FedEx so it must be donations, which is great. We can always use more.

But the box lowers to the floor revealing Eugene across from me.

"What?" I say.

Note: of the million things I've thought to say to him since Publix, "what" was not one of them.

"Oh my God. Hey," he says. He blinks a few times.

We stare at each other, and I really wish we could start over. Maybe from the second he saved me from falling in the mud, but definitely today.

"Why . . . uh . . . I mean, what are you doing here?" I ask. My heart pounds like it's trying to break out of my chest and run away. There's a terror in being around a boy you kind of like.

"I'm dropping off some donations," he says. "Delivery boy extraordinaire, at your service. Well, at my dad's service." He bows gracefully.

"Oh, that's really kind," I say.

"Do you work here?" he asks. "Or did you hijack the desk?"

I laugh. "I volunteer."

"That's cool," he says.

Suddenly, I'm extra grateful to Emily for the shirt, because I could *not* have let him see me in Winnie-the-Pooh gear and a stained five-dollar tank back to back. When he's not looking, I run my tongue over my teeth, praying I don't have blueberries in them.

"It's my first time here," Eugene says, looking around. "My parents do a charity each month and this one was animals, so we're donating to a couple of rescues, here, and the Humane Society."

"That's really nice of you," I say. "We're not nearly as well funded as the Humane Society. They get a ton of support and charge higher fees, but we stretch our budget as far as we can, so I'm sure whatever you brought will be appreciated. I can give you a sheet for taxes, but just know we'll use everything. And . . ."

I pause, realizing he's staring at me.

"And . . . now I'll step off my soapbox," I say.

His dimple shows. "You'd be taller on a soapbox."

I narrow my eyes at him. "Did you bring some raisin bran?"

"Ha," he says. He opens the box and rummages through it. "We have leashes, collars, elaborate poop-bag systems, some fancy dog beds from a very overpriced pet boutique, a cat tree, and a bunch of treats courtesy of Lantern & Jacks."

"Lantern & Jacks makes animal treats?" I say, knitting my eyebrows.

"Not officially. This is just for the shelter," Eugene says.

"Do they say Lantern & Jacks?" I come around the desk and peer into the box. There must be three dozen containers. My mind works overtime. This could all be very useful.

"Yeah, they're in our dessert boxes," Eugene says as he looks at the containers. "Our sous-chef's German shepherd loves them, so I assume they're great. Collins is obsessed with making his dog's food."

"Would you mind if I put these into raffle baskets?" I say. "It could be a good way to raise money. Or we could do them as adoption incentives—adopt a pet and get gourmet treats and maybe be registered to win a grand prize gift basket that has an overpriced dog bed. I'll have to ask my boss which she thinks will be better."

"They're both great ideas," Eugene says. "Whatever helps more."

We nod, then fall into silence.

"You didn't text," I say—blurt out is more accurate.

I stare at the floor like it's intensely interesting, then finally find the nerve to look up. He's gazing down at me.

"I was hoping you'd message, honestly," he says. "Which, now that I've said it out loud, sounds weird. I could've texted first, right?"

"I . . . I don't know."

We stare at each other for a second before we start laughing. It isn't funny, but also, it is. We were both checking our phones, hoping the other would break the ice.

"I overthought it." He rubs his neck and smiles shyly. "I drafted a bunch of texts but never hit send."

"Oh, God, I did too." Many, many, many messages, but we don't need to get into numbers.

"I'd really like to hang out sometime," he says. "Are you free this week?"

I think about my schedule, and all of a sudden I have a . . . life. Justin Michael is coming over tomorrow evening for a movie, I'm working Friday, going to Aaron's baseball game Saturday night, and Sunday is Cousin Mabel's birthday. How did this even happen? Normally, I just have Burrito Friday with Paul, hanging out with June and Emily on Saturday, and family time on Sunday.

"I'm free tonight," I say. I glance at the clock and it's after two thirty. I was scheduled to finish around three anyhow. "I can leave now, if you're not busy."

Note: I sound next-level eager. I try not to sigh at myself.

"Um, I told my dad I'd go back and finish prep," he says, glancing at his watch.

My hopes deflate, but I force a smile. "Oh, okay."

"I am free afterward, though. Do you . . . would you be okay with hanging out at the restaurant while I prep? It should take about two hours, but I could feed you if you're hungry."

Excuse me, what? What even?

"Yes," I say. I break the land-speed record for overeager, because holy crap! I'm going to "hang out" at Lantern & Jacks. No reservation, maybe in the kitchen, and Eugene is going to cook for me? How did this even happen?

"And you're in luck," he says. I stare at him like he read my mind. "I don't have my bike because I had to run around with deliveries today. So you won't have to try riding on a motorcycle . . . yet."

I hadn't even thought of that, too focused on seeing Jack Matthews's kitchen in action. Suddenly, I'm a little disappointed I won't be putting my arms around Eugene. Even if it was to hang on for dear life on his motorcycle. But that word "yet" contains so much hope.

Wait, what kind of thought is that? There's no way I'd get on his death mobile. I shake off the thought.

"Oh, unless you have your car," he says. "Then you can follow me."

I smile brightly. "No, my friend dropped me off, so a ride would be great. Perfect. I need a ride. With you. In a truck. Not on a bike."

Oh, dear God. Take a vow of silence, Jasmine.

He laughs. "Okay. Do you have to clock out or something?"

"No, but can you help me take the box to the office? By 'help,' I mean carry the whole thing."

He laughs again. "Sure."

He heaves the box up, and I stare at his muscles as we walk to the office. It's a small, windowless room with walls covered, and I mean covered, with photos of adopted dogs and cats. If there was a dog and cat conspiracy room, it would look like this.

Eugene sets the box on the floor. I write a note about using the donations to raise money or awareness, then close the door.

We walk back to the front desk, I grab a tax form, stamp it, and hand it to Eugene. Then I take a placard and put it on the counter. It tells visitors to go down the hall for assistance.

"Ready when you are," I say.

"Great."

We walk out of the shelter, and as soon as I step outside, I feel relieved. I always do. It's a heavy thing, volunteering at a place that can't save every animal. I take a cleansing breath and square my shoulders. Even the muggy heat feels good on my bare arms. I close my eyes for a second and let go of everything. Then I open my eyes. Eugene is looking at me.

"Can I ask you something?" he says.

"Sure," I say.

"I'm over this way." He points to a blue F-150. I don't know what I expected him to drive, but a pickup truck wasn't it.

"Why do you volunteer here?" he says.

"What do you mean?"

"You could've picked anyplace, and the Humane Society is right across the parking lot. This seems . . . hard." He unlocks the truck and opens the door on my side. I hoist myself in.

I inhale because the whole cab smells like him, and that's so much better than the flea powder/bleach scent of the shelter. He gets in on the other side.

"It is difficult," I say. "There are more challenges with a shelter, but I can do more good here."

He pauses with his keys in the ignition. He stares at me, his teal eyes scanning before he nods. "Makes sense."

"Can I ask you something?" I say.

"Sure."

"Why do you drive a pickup?"

His brow wrinkles, then clears. "I learned how to drive in one and I've always had a truck. They're handy and I like being useful. Plus, my bike fits in the bed, so it's easy to take it up to New York."

"Oh."

He starts the truck and shifts into drive. I feel the same stomach-churning sadness about him leaving. It still doesn't make any sense. I barely know him.

"Both will stay here for the rest of the year, though." He pulls out of the parking lot.

"Really? Why's that?" I perk up. Maybe he's decided to transfer to UCF or work full-time at the restaurant and date me forever. Even though I'm still dating someone . . . kind of.

Ugh, I can't even think about that.

"Because there isn't a good way to get them to Spain."

I stare at him. "What?"

"I've looked into shipping my bike," he says, "but I can buy a used one for less. It won't be the same, but it'll get me around."

"What?" I turn in my seat. "Spain? You're going to Spain— like the country?" I draw a little box in the air with my fingers that has absolutely nothing to do with the nation of Spain.

He laughs. "Yes. I'll be at the University of Madrid start-ing in September, but my program will take me all over. I'll probably spend my weekends exploring."

Sure, he'll see Valencia the city, and I'm going to Valencia the community college. Same thing.

"Why Spain?" I ask.

He looks me in the eyes as we stop at a light. "Why not?"

A million reasons—it's a foreign country on another continent that's so far away, filled with new people, new customs, and a language barrier—just to name a few. I sputter, but nothing comes out.

"They're doing some amazing things food-wise, and I'll be getting international business credits toward my degree," he says. "But the real reason is, I went to Barcelona five years ago and I loved it. I've wanted to go back to Spain. This is a good excuse for an adventure."

"Are you going with your girlfriend?" I ask.

I can't believe I came right out and asked, but please say no.

It's occurred to me more than once that the reason he didn't text is because he's dating someone. Maybe someone in New York.

He looks at me funny. "Of course I don't have a girlfriend. I figure I'll make some friends over there. But even if it's just me, this is my chance to live in Europe." He shrugs. "I may spend the whole year there. We'll see how it goes."

I'm so relieved he's not dating anyone, but a year? Just like that? Is he serious? The way he can say it so casually . . .

"We're so different," I think. Unfortunately, I also say it aloud.

I put my hand over my mouth. What happens to me

when I'm around him? It's like I'm *trying* to make him run away from me.

He laughs. "Different?"

"Yes."

"How?"

"There's no way I'd be able to take off to Europe alone for half a year, maybe more. No matter how much I want to." I add the last part in a murmur.

He glances at me as we merge onto I-4. "Why not?"

I've asked myself the same question for months, and he just put it out there. At first the answer was Paul, but it goes deeper than that.

"Because," I say. "Because that's not how I am. Because it's so far. Because I'd be alone and I'm never alone. Because . . . everything about it scares me."

"Being scared is normal, though," he says. "It means you're breaking out of your comfort zone."

I shake my head, my long hair waving. "Nope. No. Being scared means I *don't* do the thing that scares me. I like things that are comfortable and predictable. I love my comfort zone. Good comfort zone." I pet the dashboard.

One side of his lips rises. "I think you're not giving yourself enough credit. If you want to go, you should go."

My eyes widen because his mind reading is freaking me out. "I don't want to go."

"You said, 'No matter how much I want to.' So you've thought about it, want to do it, but talked yourself out of it because it's out of your comfort zone."

I startle. I've never been with someone who's listened to me this closely. And yes, there's a part of me that still dreams, despite everything. That imagines a life where I can just take off to Paris and become a world-renowned chef. And I never had to deal with that part of me because Paul liked safe, solid, and predictable too. But being around people like Aaron and Eugene and even Justin, who pursue what they want, makes me think . . .

No. The comfort zone is good. Bad things happen when you step out of the zone. I learned that lesson the hard way. Twice.

"You don't know me," I say.

He shrugs. "Maybe not. But I'm learning. And I like what I do know."

My face feels like it's on fire as we pull into downtown. But I can't be too focused on my hellish blush because in the distance, on Lantern Street, is Lantern & Jacks.

CHAPTER TWENTY-NINE

DAVEY'S PRICKLY FAMILY GROUP TEXT
MAY 29

Cousin Wesley
So when do you all pay up?

Cousin Crystal
Um, south of Never, because Eugene is totally going to win.
They're perfect together

Cousin Joe
Isn't she going to Aaron's baseball game on Saturday? Bring
vapors, she's going to swoon

Cousin Madison
Oh, because women are so fragile? LOL

Cousin Wylan
Here we go again. Thanks, pal

Cousin Madison

Oh, whatever, Wylan. It was a bad joke

Aunt Kim

I heard she and Justin Michael looked really close at the tea bar. It's still a shame you guys didn't want to include Simon. He likes her!

Aunt Rosey

Is everyone coming to Mabel's party on Sunday?

Aunt Minnie

Of course

Are the boys going to be there?

Uncle Carlos

I mean . . . it's not a horrible idea

Cari

It's a horrible idea

Uncle Carlos

Why's that?

Cari

Because she'd be bound to figure it out. She's already asking her friends questions because things feel off. Let's just

stick with the plan, guys. Don't go rogue. Teagan and Joe
could've really messed it up by showing up at her froyo place
last night

Cousin Teagan
Sorry! We just . . . wanted to see

Cousin Joe
She didn't figure it out

Cari
I can't go over this again. She could've asked one of you for
the ride home and then what? Then she'd have to 'accidentally' run into Aaron again? It's going well. Let's not mess up
now

CHAPTER THIRTY

Eugene fobs into the parking garage and pulls into a spot reserved for Lantern & Jacks employees.

I hop out of the truck and he waits for me by the tailgate. He stares at me as I walk, and it feels like I'm the only person in the world. I want to look away because his attention makes me nervous, but I can't help but look at him too.

He smiles as I stop in front of him. "Have you been to the restaurant before?" he asks.

"No, but I've really wanted to go," I say.

"I'll give you a quick tour before prep, then. Let's do this right."

We leave the garage, and Eugene puts his hand on my back to turn me around the corner.

"This way," he says.

His hand lingers, and I would go to the ends of the earth with him leading me like this. Instead he brings me to the main entrance of Lantern & Jacks.

Two beautiful lanterns flank the door, and there's an understated sign above them. Enormous windows run the length of the outside.

It's perfect.

"So here we are," Eugene says. "My dad's first restaurant of his own. The lettering on the sign is my mom's handwriting. Dad wanted to make sure she had her signature on here."

I love that.

I looked up more about his family (because I'm a creeper) and found out his dad's parents disowned him when he was addicted to drugs in his early twenties. His mom's parents disowned her for marrying someone they didn't choose.

Reading that made me so sad, but also grateful that my grandparents are open minded. They're Filipino immigrants on one side and Italian second generation on the other, but for all their differences, they have a weird amount in common. They go to the same church and have the same values. Plus, Grandpa Yap and Poppy are best buds and oddly competitive in bocce. But most important, they want their children to be happy. And now our family is everything from Laotian/ Dominican with Davey, to Aunt Regina's children who are Black/Filipino, to Uncle Richard's kids who call themselves "garden-variety white."

Eugene pulls open the restaurant door and I take it all in. The overall style is clean, comfortable, and a little understated. Everything is soft and sculptural, from the lights to the chairs. Small lanterns surround large fresh-flower arrangements that are scattered throughout the room. It's totally different from the way Ventura's Bistro used to look, but it fits the space so well.

The servers work quietly, setting the tables with rulers. They say hi to Eugene and stare at me as we pass.

"So this is the main dining room," he says. "Oliver Underwood did all the furniture. Dad tried to stick with local designers and manufacturers, and it turned out exactly how he'd imagined it."

I thought the style looked familiar.

"Mr. Underwood is my friend Emily's father. You met her at the party, I think."

"I did," he says. "They were actually here the other night for dinner. I came out and said hi."

I tilt my head. It's strange, really strange, that Emily didn't mention seeing him. But I can't dwell on my unsettled feeling, because Eugene continues with his tour.

"Our wine cellar," he says. He points to a glass room that's sealed to the high ceiling. "It's temperature controlled. The whites on the bottom, the reds on top, where it's naturally warmer."

"How do they get the bottles down?" I ask.

"There's a hydraulic arm. It's a great design by Al Ventura."

My mouth falls open. "Uncle Al."

Eugene's brow furrows. "Al Ventura is your uncle?"

I nod. "He's my mom's brother. I never knew he worked on this."

Weird that in all my research I'd never heard this, but I guess people don't shout out their architect.

Eugene's dimple shows. "Is there anyone in Central Florida you don't know or you're not related to?"

"No, I don't think so."

"That's pretty nice." He smiles.

That's a different reaction than I'm used to. Paul would complain it was impossible to keep my eighty-two cousins straight. I don't have eighty-two cousins. Well . . . not first cousins.

"The private dining area is over here," Eugene says. "If we don't have a large party, it becomes a communal table for the tasting menu. My dad believes food should be a shared experience, and I agree."

The tasting menu is $400, before any additions, like a gluttonous amount of truffles. I've read the reviews that were skeptical of paying that much without having their own table, but everyone enjoyed being able to discuss their courses.

"My dad's office is upstairs, along with some storage," Eugene says. "Between you and me, they're thinking about adding dining space up there, but my dad has concerns about the maximum quality he can put out at once. If I were to join him permanently, we could . . ."

He trails off and swallows the words I wanted to hear. If he joined his dad permanently, then what? Then he'd be a professional chef living in Orlando instead of a student in New York, and I know which I'd prefer.

Eugene frowns. "Anyhow, it's not interesting up there." He clears his face and smiles. "Ready to see the kitchen?"

The change in expression ended my chance to ask about his thoughts. Instead, I say, "Absolutely."

He swings open the door, and I was not, in fact, ready.

The kitchen is a dream.

I expected chaos like I remember in Jay's bistro, but instead it's the most peaceful space I've ever been in. Everyone is in a clean white jacket or a black apron. No one is talking other than to say "hot" or "behind" as they carry pans.

Soft classical music emanates from somewhere, and the kitchen is bathed in light from a picture window. Behind the restaurant is a small garden. I read in *Food & Wine* magazine that Lantern & Jacks grows many of their own ingredients, thanks to Eugene's mom.

The chefs look up from their prep and nod or smile at Eugene, but their eyes stop on me. There are a dozen people in the kitchen, but I'd recognize Chef Matthews anywhere. He strolls up to us with his white jacket on. Tattoos peek out from the cuffs of his jacket. He's probably six feet tall and barrel chested, but he has the same gentle smile as Eugene.

"How'd the deliveries go?" Chef asks.

"Got them all done," Eugene says.

"And one pickup." His dad smiles.

"Dad, this is Jasmine. Al Ventura's niece."

He places his hand on my back for the second time today, and his touch is so warm. I'm almost sad when he drops his hand away.

"Get out of here. Really?" Chef looks at me. I'm adopted, so the connection is never clear. Even with my dad's side, people don't think I'm Filipina, so there's always a pause.

"Nice to meet you," he says. "Eugene's told me a lot about you."

"Really?" I look from his dad to Eugene. I raise my eyebrows. "A lot?"

Eugene sighs. "He doesn't know what he's saying. Brain

damage from his molecular gastronomy phase. Ignore him."

"Ha!" his dad says, sounding just like Eugene. "Well, welcome to the kitchen, Jasmine. Eugene, who's told me nothing about you, says you cook as well."

I startle. "I . . . um, I mean, not professionally. I . . . just at home. I just make dinners at home. Sometimes."

Chef nods. "Everyone starts at home. But you're also Jay Ventura's niece, then?"

"Yes."

His lip protrudes as he nods. "She's one talented lady."

This is like Serena Williams saying someone is a good tennis player. I feel pride grow in my chest, because yes, Jay is talented. And even though my feelings changed on my aunt, I never stopped being proud of her.

"Are you hungry?" he asks. "We're doing staff meal in twenty."

Wait . . . Chef Matthews is going to cook for me? No. Way. I've died. I've definitely died and I'm in heaven and I'm good with that as long as my spirit can eat.

"I'd love to join you," I say. I look to Eugene for guidance, but he's disappeared. "If that's okay. If it's not, it's no problem. I don't want to impose. I can . . . well, I can just stand in the corner. I guess."

Chef Matthews laughs and turns to Eugene, who's rejoined our conversation. He claps his son on the shoulder. "Show her the garden, and then we'll need you to finish prep."

He checks his watch, and it's the same one that Eugene wears, although it looks newer, which is weird.

"Yes, Chef," Eugene says.

While we were talking, he put on his chef's jacket, and he looks disturbingly good. He carries himself differently with his coat on. More confident, more adult.

"Come on out back," Eugene says.

He opens the glass door to the walled-in garden. It's hot, herbaceous, and earthy back here. The smell of scallions, rosemary, lavender, and mint fills the air.

We walk along the paths that snake around the garden. The space isn't large, but it's well organized and labeled in his mom's distinctive handwriting.

Eugene picks off the few dead leaves as we go. "My dad comes out here to sit and think up a new menu or to clear his head. It also reminds him of my mom, and that's calming."

"Is she . . . not here?"

The Matthews family is well known enough that divorce or, God forbid, death would make the tabloid sites. But there could be other reasons for her to be gone.

He shakes his head. "She left a week ago to go to California to study horticulture, which she's always wanted to do. She should be back before I leave for Spain. If not, they'll visit me in Europe."

"Oh."

Spain again. I'm beginning to resent an entire location.

"She gave her all to this restaurant, and it's her turn to do what she's wanted. But it's really not the same without her."

I love the way he speaks about his mom, how clearly he adores her. I adore mine too and don't want to risk disappoint-

ing her. And so maybe I'll never try to have a dream restaurant like this, but that's okay. Pursuing a hopeless dream isn't
worth losing a family like mine.

Eugene sits on a stone bench and gestures for me to sit.
Once I'm next to him, he tips his face toward the sun.

"You look happy back here," I say.

He turns and looks me in the eye. "I love it. But I still
don't know if I love it for them or for me. And with my mom
gone, my dad has leaned on me more to make a decision."

I don't know what to say. What's the difference? And why
doesn't he care about making his parents proud? He's been
given everything, everything they've struggled to give him,
but doesn't know if he wants to have it all?

For the first time I wonder why I'm so drawn to someone
so opposite from me.

"Okay," Eugene says. "I have to get on the line. But stay
out here if you want. Otherwise, you can wait in the private
dining room—that's where we do staff meal."

"Is there anything I can do to help?" I ask.

"No. We have it all under control. I'll see you in a bit."

He brushes my arm with his hand and his touch wipes
away the questions in my mind. I inhale the clean scent of
orange blossoms and herbs and spices. I exhale all my doubts
and for a moment allow myself to dream of having this.

When my phone dings, I turn off the ringer without
looking at it. There's nothing I want more than to be in this
moment.

CHAPTER THIRTY-ONE

JASMINE'S IPHONE
MAY 29

♥ Paul ♥

Can I stop by tonight or tomorrow?
I really want to talk to you

I aced AP English, but I don't have words to describe staff meal. It was roast chicken—just a simple chicken and it was the best meal I've had in my life. The meat was perfectly seasoned and the sauce was so good, I wanted to lick it off my plate. Only decorum stopped me.

Barely.

The chicken was complimented by unbelievably rich mashed potatoes and a salad bursting with flavor.

I thought I knew how to cook. I very much don't know how to cook. And like my aunt said that one terrible night: I don't have what it takes to do this.

Eugene finished with his prep a little after five o'clock, and now we're slowly walking back to his truck. Waddling is more like it, as I had seconds of everything.

"So what did you think of L&Js?" Eugene asks.

"It was amazing," I say. "Please thank your dad again for me."

"He liked you," he says.

He unlocks his truck and opens my door. The little things he does, like come around to my side first, set him apart from

Paul. And it makes me wonder why I never expected Paul to treat me this way.

"He doesn't normally let outsiders in," Eugene continues. "But whatever you two talked about earned his approval."

"I have no idea what I said, but I'm glad. I liked him too. Really, it was an honor."

Eugene grins and shuts my door before getting in on his side. He starts the engine and air blasts out of the vents.

"He also liked that you helped clear dishes and chatted with Luke," he says.

"Why wouldn't I have talked to Luke?" I ask.

He was the dishwasher/garbage boy and the only employee around our age.

Eugene shrugs. "Some people only care about my dad or Collins, because they have the most power. But my dad values all the staff equally. I've done just about every job in his restaurants because he wanted me to see how each role is necessary to making the place run. I . . . suck as a waiter and I made a below-average host. I was yanked quickly from those positions."

I laugh. I'm 100 percent certain I'd be a terrible waitress as I've barely mastered handing tea across the bar at B&OA.

"It shows that he values them—they all love him," I say.

"It's a found family. Half of them came over from his old restaurant, so he's known them for a decade. Some even more than that."

"Which means they knew you when you were . . . nine?" I say.

He nods. "Braces and all."

I tilt my head, looking at him. "You had braces? You would've been cute with braces."

He makes a face. "I definitely wasn't. No braces for you, huh?"

"No."

"Just born perfect, then, I guess," he says. He puts the truck into reverse.

I blink a few times. I can't remember the last time a boy called me perfect. I'm not sure it's ever happened. Shawn used to go on and on about Emily's perfection when we'd all hang out (assuming they weren't screaming at each other). My beautiful queen this, my gorgeous girl that, while Paul and I sat silently. Even Justin Michael, who thought I was great when we were kids, never said I was perfect.

My family thinks I'm pretty good, but they're legally obligated to say that. And June and Emily aren't objective at all. Not like they're going to say: Hey, you're a troll. By the way, can I sleep over?

"I'm not perfect," I say. "Far from it."

He looks at me for an uncomfortable amount of time, and I feel the need to say something else.

"Cari is beautiful and perfect," I say.

"That means you can't be those things?" he says.

"Well, yeah, kinda," I say. "She's tall and graceful and popular everywhere she goes—even when people can't see her. She was class president *and* homecoming queen. I've accepted that I was born to play the sidekick. I'm Skipper to her Asian Barbie." I do a jazz hands motion, then put my hands back on my jeans because he's still staring at me.

"I get it now," he says.

"Get what?"

He reaches out and strokes my hair behind my ear. I'm so focused on the shivers he's sending through me that I almost miss what he says.

"You don't know how special you are."

He returns his hand to the gearshift, and I'm stuck in neutral, spinning on his words and his touch.

CHAPTER THIRTY-THREE

THE LITTLE BACHELORETTE PODCAST EXCERPT
S1, EP 1—JUNE 1

Anonyma: Hey, and welcome to the first-ever episode of *The Little Bachelorette* podcast. I'm your host, Anonyma.

To catch you all up, you're joining us exactly one week into a six-week competition. Three very different suitors have been selected to try to win the heart of my beautiful little sister—let's call her Ariel for the sake of this podcast. All three boys had unique meet-cutes with Ariel at a party last Saturday. All three had planned or accidental run-ins with her afterward, and this week she has spent time with all three.

We don't know who'll win the competition and become the Prince Eric to her Ariel. With five weeks remaining, it's anyone's game. Think of it like a teenage *Bachelorette* except for one thing: there's no rose ceremony. There'll be no confessionals with Ariel. And no real names because, here comes the shocking twist: she doesn't know about any of this.

I know what you must be thinking: What the hell, Anonyma? That seems . . . wrong.

But let me back up a bit. Ariel is eighteen and has only had one boyfriend: her high school sweetheart, a Resident Scumbag Player—we'll call him RSP for short. Despite him never being good enough for her, despite him not treating her well, and despite our family disapproving of RSP for those reasons, Ariel was getting ready to spend her life with him. That is, until we caught him cheating on her.

Messed up, right?

Well, it gets worse. He convinced her that he wasn't actually cheating, but that they should see other people this summer before they move in together. And my sister was willing to let him explore his options while she sat home.

The reason Ariel put up with him for so long and the reason we designed this contest are one and the same: Ariel, who has the biggest heart in the world, has never known her true worth. Our family tries. So do her friends. We tell her how great she is, but I guess we don't feel objective. And boy attention is just a different type of validation. We wanted her to see how many options there are out there. So we tried to come up with something to help show her how she should be treated and valued. And that's why we created *The Little Bachelorette* contest. We hope that through the contest she'll not only find someone to love but, more important, find herself.

The reason the competition is a secret though is because somewhere between her low self-esteem and her dislike of reality shows, she never would've agreed to something like this. No matter how much it would help her grow. So under the cloak of secrecy, our family found applicants, hand selected the top three bachelors, and intervened (and endlessly bickered among ourselves) to keep the boys in her path. We all have our personal favorites. We're all invested. But ultimately, it's her choice. She can walk away from this with a new boyfriend or just on her own. All we want is for her to realize how she should be treated. What she deserves.

Lately, however, there's been a wrinkle we weren't prepared for: RSP, who started this whole thing by wanting to see other people, now seems to be changing his mind. He's contacting her more and more. And none of us can get a handle on how much she's affected by it.

He showed up at our door (the nerve) the other night looking for her, and luckily, she was on a date with Bachelor Number Three. I told him she didn't want to speak to him and to leave. But we may, reluctantly, have four bachelors now.

Yes, that was a long-suffering sigh.

But let me get into the three chosen bachelors, what they bring to the table, and why each one might win her heart. . . .

CHAPTER THIRTY-FOUR

DAVEY'S OUTRAGED FAMILY GROUP TEXT
JUNE 2

Scumbag Paul was looking for Jaz AGAIN tonight

Aunt Jay
No way

Cousin Crystal
Ugh. Go away

Aunt Regina
Boy, bye

Cousin Wylan
What, and I can't stress this enough, the . . .

Aunt Regina
Language

Cousin Wylan
Heck

Cari
I guess he's been messaging her. He said he was worried bc she hasn't responded. It was a good thing she was at June's tonight

Cousin Mai
He needs to take a hint

The parents lost it on him. It was epic

Uncle Vin
Oh, this boy messed with the wrong librarian

Aunt Minnie
What did you do, Ferdy??

Dad
I told him he was no longer welcome at our home. Then I restrained Dee

Mom
You didn't restrain me

He totally did

Cari
Yes, he did

Mom
He shouldn't have shown up when I was cooking

Cari
Knives stay in the kitchen, Ma

Nonna
Good for you, honey

Cousin Mabel
Is she actually thinking about taking him back before the summer is over? Or at all?

Cari
I don't know. We decided not to tell her about him stopping by

Cousin Amberlynn
Why not?

Cari
She may see it as a 'grand gesture'

Cousin Amberlynn
But if she talks to him, won't she find out?

Mom

Hopefully she won't. But we can say we forgot—like when Davey 'forgets' to take out the trash bins

ONE TIME!

Dad

Let's hope she does the smart thing and continues to ignore him

Aunt Minnie

I'm sure she will—our girl is nothing but smart

CHAPTER THIRTY-FIVE

I'm meeting Paul for lunch, and I'm running a little behind.

He messaged every day for nearly a week, and I finally agreed to meet him. I picked Chuy's, but I'm late because Justin Michael sent a funny *Jeopardy!* video while I was getting ready and we wound up texting.

I'm still not sure if our movie night was a "date." We had fun, though, and that's what matters. We housed a pack of strawberry laces and fought over the half-popped kernels (clearly the best, rarest popcorn pieces). It was like old times, but also different. There was more . . . tension between us. What I felt in the bookstore returned tenfold. Rather than lying all over each other like we would've as kids, we kept a respectable distance. I kept wondering if he'd put his arm around me or get closer, but he didn't. I was both a little bummed and also wondering if I should make a move myself.

Spoiler: I didn't.

The only times we touched were when our hands brushed while reaching for snacks. It happened too many times to have been accidental, but can it be a date when it ends in a hug and at least one of your family members has been walking through the room or "looking for something" the entire time? Asking for a friend with a super-nosy family.

I also don't know if going to Aaron's baseball game qualifies as a date. Probably not, but it was really cool to see him pitch. I cheered for every strike, swept up in the excitement. Right after the game, he looked up at me and waved me down to the field. Everyone in the stands turned to stare, probably wondering how I knew their star pitcher. And I felt so special being singled out. Like I was a VIP. He took me on a full tour of the clubhouse and introduced me to the coaches and players. It would've been intimate, but both my siblings tagged along for every step. Can it be a date if you have two annoying chaperones? I don't think so.

He and I are going to the batting cages (alone) this week, and it's all my fault. When Aaron was talking about off-speed pitches messing with a hitter, I mentioned I've never swung a baseball bat. He swore he could teach me how to hit in one session. Because I haven't embarrassed myself enough lately and I said "bet," like a fool. So, it's on. He'll buy me ice cream if I don't get a hit on Thursday—the next day he's back in town. If I successfully connect with a baseball, I'll owe him a cone. I'll win and drown my shame in rocky road, so it's all upside.

My phone dings, stirring me from my thoughts. I shut the car off and check it. Okay, maybe I'm hoping it's Eugene finally texting. But even after he brought me to his restaurant, he hasn't messaged at all.

I frown. It's not Eugene. It's Paul asking if I'm still meeting him.

I take a deep breath and get out of my car. June and Emily said it's a really bad idea to see Paul again, but I know I can handle it. I truly haven't thought as much about him lately, but I do want to see what he has to say. And as he said—it's just lunch. It's not getting back together. I can do this.

I pull open the door to Chuy's, and the hostess greets me.

"Hey, there," she says. "Table for one?"

"Hi. Actually, I'm meeting someone," I say, looking around. The place is mostly empty since it's a Monday, but there are more people here than I'd expected.

"Oh, I think he's over this way," she says. "He's about this tall and pretty cute?" She smiles.

Lady, you're not helping.

But I nod, follow her, and find Paul sitting in a blue vinyl booth. Still handsome. Still so familiar. Old emotions flood my veins as he smiles and stands.

"Hey, Jaz," he says.

I stop close enough to smell him. His cologne sets off so many memories. Each one is tinged with good and bad.

He leans down to kiss me.

I stare at his lips. I want him to kiss me.

No. No. Bad idea. We aren't together. The last thing I need is the confusion of kissing him. What happened to the resolutions I just made in the car? Come on, Jasmine. Make it a full minute.

I turn my head at the last second, and his lips mash against my cheek.

It's as awkward as it sounds.

He clears his throat, looking thrown for a moment before composing himself again.

"Thanks for coming," he says.

I utter an mm-hmm and slide into the booth across from him. He only has water. I guess this time he waited to order, despite my twelve-minute lateness. I open my menu right as the waiter arrives.

"Hey, can I get you guys something to drink?" the waiter asks.

"Ginger ale," Paul says, not waiting for me to order. He never used to wait, but this is the first time it's occurred to me to mind.

"I'll have a Coke, please," I say.

"Not diet?" Paul says.

I stare at him. "I'm not on a diet."

"I'll be right back with that," the waiter says, clearly eager to get away from us.

"I didn't mean you were on a diet, but I thought you liked Diet Coke better," Paul says.

"I hate it, actually."

"But you used to get it all the time," he says. He's genuinely confused—he used to wear the same expression when trying to do his trig homework. As his girlfriend, I tutored him for free. He was my worst student.

"I made a lot of choices I wouldn't make again." I give him a pointed stare and return to the menu.

Everything looks good, but it's hard to focus because I actually landed a shot at Paul and that's never happened before.

The silence drags on and I glance up. Paul is staring at me. He tilts his head. I swallow hard and brace myself for his reaction.

"You've changed," he says.

"In a good or bad way?" I ask.

"Good," he says. "You seem . . . more confident. You look great, by the way. Did you do something different to your hair?"

Now he compliments me? I wish I could say it doesn't matter, but it does. The part of me that was starving for his approval drinks it in and revels in the fact that Paul Reyes thinks I look great.

The Coke and ginger ale arrive and the waiter scurries away.

"No, my hair's the same, but thank you," I say. I can't resist adjusting the silk headband holding back my hair.

I took a page from my sister's book and dressed to impress. Turns out, when I dress up, I feel more confident. It's a self-esteem cycle.

"What are you going to get?" I ask.

He frowns at the menu. "I don't know. I'm in the mood for a burrito, but I'm not sure if I'll like theirs and they come with cheese."

"They're really good and also enormous. You'll like them. You can ask for no cheese."

"Big As Your Face Burrito, huh?" he says. "Would that be bigger or smaller than my ego?" He raises his eyebrows.

"Definitely smaller," I say. "They don't have that kind of room here."

Note: the place is massive, with high ceilings.

I look away. I can't believe I just said that to him. I never would've made fun of him a few weeks ago, but everything feels different now. There isn't the pressure of trying to make him happy or walking on eggshells to avoid a fight, because we're not really together. And I've never felt that before. I used to care so much about his feelings that if he had a bad day, I'd absorb it and have a bad one too. It's refreshing to not feel that weight. A small voice in my head wonders if this is how we could be going forward, if we've both changed for the better, but it's too soon to tell. Right?

Paul laughs, actually laughs. It's confusing because Paul has no sense of humor. But the waiter comes back and we order. He gets a cheeseless burrito and I order the appetizer sampler. The sampler has queso, but that's okay—it's just for me.

He rests his arms on the table after the menus are cleared. I keep my hands by my legs, my foot shaking.

"How have you been? I was worried about you," he says.

"Why's that?"

"Well, it took you a while to respond to my messages," he says.

"I've been busy," I say, playing with my straw wrapper. "I'm sorry."

Honestly, I'm not that sorry, but it's easier to appease him.

He clears his throat. "I know you're still mad at me," he says. "And you have every right to be."

"Actually, I'm not." I say, then I think about it and it's

true. I'm not mad. I was hurt and I wanted things back the way they were before, but I was never angry.

I take a sip of Coke—it's so much better than diet. As the bubbles fizz on my tongue, the question dances in my head: Could I keep this newfound me if I got back together with Paul? Or would we revert to the way we were last year?

"I, uh, I stopped talking to her, by the way," he says.

I blink a couple of times, my train of thought derailed. Is he really going to tell me about his relationship status with the Instagram girl? Okay, now I'm annoyed.

"I just . . . I miss you, Jaz," he says. "I didn't say it when you texted, and I probably should've because it's true, but I needed more time to think about things. This . . . us . . . it's a lot. Before this summer we'd only ever dated each other, really. And I got a little freaked out about going to college a virgin, and moving in together, and all that. But I miss you. And I miss us. I drive by Tijuana's and I miss going there. That was our place—not here."

It was everything I wanted two weeks ago. All the words I would've paid to hear. Paul doesn't do emotional declarations like this, and it means a lot. He's really trying. But for some reason my heart doesn't leap for him the way it did in the past. And it's not the Instagram girl. Not really. It's more feeling like I deserve more now. That this isn't enough.

My phone dings and breaks up the silence.

I glance at the screen, secretly grateful for whoever interrupted the conversation, but it's Eugene. Happiness bursts in my chest like a firework. I try not to smile because Paul will think it's about him. And it's not. Maybe it's the possibility of Eugene, of something better, that holds my heart back.

Paul still waits for me to respond, obviously expecting me to make some sort of declaration in return.

"It's . . ." I pause and put my phone away. "Why did you ask to meet?"

His brow wrinkles. "Well . . . we miss each other. I thought we'd stop this summer apart thing. It was a mistake."

"Oh. No," I say.

It's as hard and definite as those two words—oh and no. But I sit with my mouth open because it's impossible that I said them out loud.

"No?" Paul repeats.

He looks confused and I am too. For four years I was willing to do anything to keep us together. So why wouldn't I jump back into this? I feel the pull of him, of our history. How could I not? But a bigger part of me feels that I owe it to myself to see this through.

I shake my head. "I . . . I need more time, I think."

"Why? It's not like you're gonna find someone better," he says.

I stare at him. It's so . . . mean. And manipulative. Not to mention that it's untrue. There is better. Or at least there are guys who'll treat me better. I don't feel the same ease with Paul that I do with Justin Michael, or the same rush of stardom like with Aaron, or whatever it even is with Eugene.

The words "It's over" should come out of my mouth. Now. Like right now. But for some reason I can't say it. I'm still holding on. I can't let go of the plans we made for the future. And yes, even though I don't want to leap back in, I'm still hoping he'll change. And there is a worry deep inside me that the weird attention from boys will fade as quickly as it arrived. That I'll play myself for a fool like I did years ago. That in the end, Paul is right—I won't find better than him.

He reaches across the table and his hand lands on my arm. "I . . . that didn't come out right."

At that moment the waiter arrives with our lunch. Paul retracts his arm as the waiter puts my sampler in front of me and Paul's huge burrito in front of him. Paul immediately digs in with a fork and knife.

He takes a hesitant bite, chews, and swallows. "This is . . . really good," he declares. Like he still doubted me.

I stare at him, not touching my food until he puts down his fork.

He gives me a look like he doesn't know why I'm not eating. I raise my eyebrows to remind him that I'm still waiting.

"What I meant to say is that you and I belong together, Jaz," he says.

"You weren't so sure last time we spoke," I say.

He frowns. "She was . . . something I needed to get out of my system before going forward with you."

I don't even know what to say to that, and it appears Paul is done, so I eat my flautas and dip them in queso. We don't talk much as we eat our lunch. Instead, I roller-coaster through the emotional high of him saying that we belong together and the new low of him saying I'd never find better. The memo-

ries and familiarity push me back, and the brand-new thought
that we don't fit together anymore pulls me away.

Once we're done eating, we argue over the bill, but in the
end Paul pays and we walk out together. After Burrito Fridays
we'd usually get into his car and go park and make out somewhere, but I take my keys out of my purse. I'm leaving alone.

We stop outside in the muggy heat. His BMW is to one
side of the parking lot and the Rolla is on the other.

"Well, thank you for lunch," I say.

"I want you back, Jaz," he says. He looks sincere—more
than he did even a few minutes ago. "She didn't mean anything."

I barely suppress a laugh at how he's trying to downplay
this. "Well, she meant a lot to me."

We stand in silence as I stare at him, squinting in the sun.
Normally, I would've looked away, but not now. Not on this.

I take a half step away.

"You once said you couldn't live without me," he says.
"Didn't you mean that?"

My breath catches. That day feels like it was yesterday,
even though it was a year and a half ago. My mother called to
tell me Paul had been in a car accident with his dad. I didn't
know how serious it was at the time, and I rushed to the hospital to find him with his head bandaged. I'd later find out it
was a concussion and a few stitches, but I sat by his side and
told him I couldn't live without him.

I hadn't thought he'd heard me. And he'd never mentioned it since.

"I don't know what to say, Paul." I shake my head as the rest of my words leave me. "I just need more time to think."

I turn to go to my car. I know in my bones that if I stay out here, I'll give in. And I don't think that's a good idea.

"Wait, Jaz. I wanted to give you this," he says.

He reaches into his pocket and pulls out a key chain. I recognize it immediately. I bought it for him in sophomore year. He had to go on a long cruise with his family and didn't want to leave. So I bought him a Florida-shaped key chain that said "Jasmine" so he could take a piece of Florida with him. It was twelve dollars plus tax, and that amount of money was a lot to me. Like Davey now, I was on a small allowance to cover food at school and some random things if I saved up.

Paul, who's never had a job, had taken the key chain and said thank you, but I hadn't seen it since. I assumed he'd lost it.

"I thought maybe you'd want to have this back," he says.

He hands it to me and the faux gold plating is worn, which is weird. He never had it on his BMW or house keys—I'd looked.

I knit my eyebrows, turning it over in my palm.

"I used to . . . I used to keep it in my pocket for good luck," he says, looking at the sidewalk.

I had no idea. I didn't think he cared about anything I gave him. I could never afford flashy presents the way he could. My Fendi purse, noise-canceling headphones, and sapphire earrings I find too fancy to wear were all from him. I gave him things I made or that meant something to me.

I hoped they would mean something to him, too, though I always doubted it.

But he has everything and valued a cheap key chain? What does it mean that he would be sentimental? And never once told me? The same way I didn't know he'd heard me in the hospital. How many secrets can fit inside one relationship? How many things can go unsaid?

I think for a second that he's lying, but the key chain is worn and not scratched. The only way it would look like this would be from someone gripping it in their palm over and over again.

"You really kept it for luck?" I ask.

"Yeah. I don't think it worked today, though," Paul adds with a sad smile.

My foolish heart reaches for him, wants to call off this whole time apart. I manage to stop myself, though.

"You . . . never told me," I say.

He puts his hands in his pockets and shrugs. "It would've sounded . . . I dunno. But that cruise with my parents wound up being one of our only good trips, and the key chain was a reminder of it and you. Then once I was back, I don't know, having it made tests easier—I'd remember your tips and something about rubbing it for luck seemed to work."

He's always been superstitious. Especially when it involved football. But all sports players seem superstitious. June, Justin Michael, and Aaron all have set, unbreakable game routines.

"You should keep it," I say. "I gave it to you."

I extend my hand. He reaches out and closes his fingers around mine.

"I know," he says. "But you should have it. I don't need more reminders of what I'm missing."

He sounds so sorry. He definitely wasn't on Burrito Friday, and even at lunch he wasn't truly apologetic, but now he is and it breaks my heart in a new way. I want to say, "Let's just be together," but once again the words refuse to leave my lips.

"We . . . um . . . we can still talk," I say.

He nods. "I'd like that. So you'll answer me if I text you?"

"Yes. But I have to go."

Truth is, I can't stand here another minute with so many questions and emotions swirling in my mind. It feels like I'll drown in them.

"Okay, Jaz. I'll see you soon." He kisses me on the cheek, and this time it isn't awkward. This time old feelings reconnect.

I walk to my car and haven't even started the engine when I grab my phone. I ignore the text from Eugene. Instead, I message Emily and June that I need to talk to them stat.

CHAPTER THIRTY-SIX

Emily responds immediately. She helps out at Macrebelle's, a clothing boutique owned by her mom's friend, where socks cost, like, $45, but she was finishing up when I texted.

I meet her in the store parking lot and hop into her white Mercedes. She's already behind the wheel with the AC and music blasting.

"So The Paul is back, huh?" she says, lowering the volume of the rock station.

Emily started calling him "The Paul" in junior year. I was upset one night because he went to a party without me, and she said, "He thinks he's the shit when he's really just . . . The Paul." And she and I laughed until we cried. It stuck.

I buckle my seat belt. "I . . . no . . . I don't know. I met him for lunch and I was fine, I swear, right up until he gave me this. Do you remember when I got this for him?"

I show her the key chain.

"Yes," she says. She lowers her old-school aviators to look me in the eyes. "Loser."

I scrunch my nose at her.

"So he wanted to end this grand experiment?" she says.

"Yeah."

"Hmmph," Emily says, before throwing the car into reverse.

All the swirling emotions of lunch made me forget about Emily's driving. Let's put it this way: if I could wear a crash helmet, I would.

I grip the armrest as she peels out of the parking lot and cuts off oncoming traffic. We're meeting June at the Winter Park Club, where she teaches tennis. Emily's a club member and has a parking decal. That's the *only* reason she's driving right now.

I do a little sign of the cross as we blaze through a solidly yellow and possibly red-tinged light. I wish I had my Saint Christopher's medallion, but it's in the Rolla.

"So, tell me what happened . . . or do you want to wait until we have the angels together?" she says.

Yeah, she means Charlie's Angels because we're *such* losers.

"Let's wait until we have Junie," I say.

"Okay, text her and let her know we'll be at the clubhouse in ten."

I pull my phone out and unlock it. There's a red notification, and I remember that I never read Eugene's text.

CM

Captain Eugene Crunch

So I finally have a day off tomorrow. It was supposed to be today but there's a staff event. Are you free Tuesday or will you still be waiting around for your cereal to marinate? 😫

I laugh and it draws Emily's eye. I point to the windshield for her to focus on the road and fire off a quick text to June.

"Uh-oh. I know that smile. Who's texting you? Is it The Paul? I really hope it's not The Paul. Because, Jaz . . . what he did wasn't right." She frowns.

"I know," I say. "It's not Paul."

"Oooooh. Then whoooo?" she says. "I can't wait to hear which one of the bachelors is making you smile like *that*."

She's taken to calling my newfound boy attention "the bachelors." It's obnoxious, but I know what she means. It's almost like that show Cari is obsessed with—where a bunch of dudes try to date the same girl.

But I'm not dating anyone. Not really.

Emily does a gossip shimmy as we pull up to the sprawling grounds of WPC. WPC is a standard, fancy country club, and most of Winter Park society belongs. Needless to say, my parents aren't members. Neither are June's, but Emily's dad got her a job here.

June has a lot of downtime between lessons on these hot summer afternoons, and that's why she meets us a few minutes after we sit down in the lounge. A couple of old guys turn and stare. It's gross, but she takes it in stride and starts greeting them by name.

"Hello, Mr. Preston. Good afternoon, Mr. Johannsson," she says.

The gawking stops as they remember she knows them . . . and their wives . . . and their grandchildren.

June Bug crashes into an armchair across from us and crosses her long legs. Sometimes people think we're related because we're both East Asian, but really, we look nothing alike.

"So, The Paul is back, huh?" She wrinkles her nose like there's a bad smell in this beautiful room.

Now would be a good time to mention that my friends don't like Paul. Emily tolerates him. June tried in the beginning, but by senior year she'd find any excuse to disappear if he was going to be around. And by senior year, I understood.

It's not that their opinions didn't matter, but I always thought they didn't *know* him the way I did. And maybe that's true, but honestly, now I'm not sure.

"The Paul isn't back. . . . I don't know," I say. "I really was just going to hear him out, but then he gave me the key chain. He held on to it this entire time. And he remembers when I told him I couldn't live without him. I think maybe he's changed. Or maybe we just didn't share enough of our feelings."

June and Emily exchange looks.

"You know I'm in no place to judge you," Emily begins. "I took Shawn back too many times. But . . . why would you take Paul back after everything he put you through?"

"I . . . I said we'd talk. Nothing else."

June frowns. "You have much better options now. You shouldn't let Paul mess with your head."

"I don't have options," I say.

June sighs at me. "Justin Michael is back. Aaron is taking you to the batting cages this week—"

"They just want to be friends," I interrupt.

Emily rolls her eyes so hard, I'm surprised they don't fall out of her head.

June blinks like she's looking for strength behind her lids. "You had that amazing dinner with Eugene, and although he hasn't texted, I'm sure he will."

Eugene is the one I can't deny. There's just something with him. It's not friendship. And it confuses me because he seems to like me but then . . . doesn't. And I maybe like him too, but how could that be when there's Paul? Not to mention that Eugene and I are so different. But I can't deny how good it felt to hear from him.

"Um, actually, he texted earlier today," I say.

"I knew it!" Emily does a circular motion with her fists. "I *knew* it. She got this look on her face when she checked her phone, and I knew it was him."

"Who knows if he actually likes me," I say.

One of the clubhouse staff drops off lemon ice water for us. Emily and June both say hi. When he leaves, we fall into awkward silence.

Emily looks at June. "We still have to drag her along even with everything. It's like she's purposely ignoring what's in front of her face. I cannot."

"You know how Jaz is." June shrugs.

I tap my chest. "Hey, by the way, I can hear you. I didn't

disappear." I wave my arms around to make sure they can still see me.

Emily gestures with her hand out and June nods. It's like they rehearsed this.

"The bachelors want to date you," Emily says. "It's why they're in the . . . it's why they're hanging out with you."

I shake my head. Okay, I've thought that, but what are the chances of three boys wanting to date me in one summer? Paul liked to point out that he was the only one who ever asked me out. I was never sure if he meant no one else would want me or if we were meant to be. I never wanted to ask.

"You don't know that," I say. "Justin Michael is in town for an internship and we're old friends. Aaron just wants to get to know people in Orlando. And Eugene . . . well, he leaves for Europe soon, so what could that even be?"

Emily glances over at June again. June gives an almost imperceptible shake of her head.

"Okay, what? This is bugging me," I say. "What's with the looks?"

June folds her hands on her lap. "You know Justin asked you out years ago. Those feelings don't just disappear, and you've said Aaron makes you feel special and that there's something about Eugene."

"It doesn't mean that they like me though."

"Okay." Emily places her water glass on the table. "What's with this low self-esteem pity party?"

"Oh, so it's a tough-love day, huh?" I say. I try to joke, but her words sink their claws into me. "I . . . I don't have . . . I'm just realistic."

"You're not though," Emily says. "You think guys who obviously like you can't because Paul fed right into your self-doubt to keep you with him. Because you don't think you're as good as your sister. Because some asshole in middle school was a jerk to you. And I don't know . . . just how you naturally are. But it's some bullshit."

Emily sits back and June widens her eyes and looks at her. Emily closes her mouth and purses her lips like she didn't intend to say all or maybe any of that.

Emily doesn't understand. She didn't go to middle school with us. She wasn't there when one of the popular girls, Morgan Weller, told me that the most popular boy, Kyle McGovern, had a crush on me. She wasn't there for the whispers by the lockers and how all of a sudden I was inter-esting to everyone. She wasn't there for my shy waves at Kyle and for his winks and smiles at me. And for the thrill that ran through me from someone noticing me. And how I tried out Jasmine McGovern because . . . well, I was in eighth grade.

Emily wasn't in our school when I finally worked up the nerve to talk to Kyle at lunch. How he was sitting at the table with Morgan and all the coolest kids in our year. How they moved aside so I could be next to him. How amazing it felt to be welcome by people who really had never paid attention to me.

Neither Emily nor June were there when they invited me to hang out with them at a bonfire that night. They weren't there as I watched Kyle smiling and talking as I sat next to him. They didn't pass around a bottle of stolen rum and watch me work up the liquid courage to try to kiss him. They didn't see him back away in disgust. They didn't hear the giggles from the group. They didn't hear him say "ew." They didn't see my confusion as I looked to Morgan, who stared blankly at me. They didn't see Kyle's face when I said, "I thought you liked me." They didn't feel his sneer as he said, "Not you. Never you." They didn't hear his laugh when he said, "Morgan, when I said I liked Yap, I meant Carissa, not her ugly little sister."

They didn't see the tears in my eyes as I ran away. Or how I hid for a while to cry. Or how I walked all the way home alone, trying to shake off the shame of what would've been my first kiss.

But then Paul came along and saw me and loved me. For me.

"We're way off topic," June says. "What are you going to do about The Paul?"

"I said we could talk, but that we won't make any decisions before August first, like we agreed to," I say.

Emily stares at me without blinking, and June sighs.

"You're going to ruin the whole—" Emily begins. June's head whips toward her. Emily exhales loudly. "You're going to ruin your chance to find someone, something, better."

"You guys don't think it meant something that he kept the key chain? Like he felt a lot more than he could say? You know his parents aren't loving to him and it's hard for him to love."

Both June and Emily look at me like: Do you even hear yourself right now? And, yes, I hear myself, but he surprised me.

"Throw it out," Emily says.

"What? No." I clutch it closer to my chest.

"He gave it back to you so you'd think about him," she says. "So he'd ruin how you felt about seeing other people, even if you're 'just talking.'"

Emily uses some hostile-ass air bunnies.

"No, I can't throw it away," I say. "It has . . . memories."

Emily gestures over to June and says, "Welp."

"Maybe I should hold on to that," June says.

"Why?" I ask.

"Because . . ." June draws a long breath. "Because you'll start thinking he wasn't that bad because he kept one thing you gave him, and, Jaz . . . he was that bad. Especially this past year. You want to think the best of people. You always do, but in this case, it's just a key chain. And Emily's right—it'll ruin how you feel about anyone other than him. It's manipulative."

She gracefully extends her arm and waits with her palm open.

I clasp it tighter, but that reaction tells me she's right. He knows me and what will hit deepest, and I've never been able to see when he's being manipulative. I always think of people as being sincere.

I'm pretty sure I've been good cop/bad copped, but I drop the key chain in June's hand. She puts it into the pocket of her tennis dress, then stands.

"I didn't think this would turn into a full-on intervention," I mutter, crossing my arms.

"We intervene out of love," June says. She kisses my forehead. "You can sulk if you want, but I need to get back to the courts."

"You should text your favorite suitor instead of sulking," Emily says.

"Whoever that happens to be." June winks.

As she leaves, I know two things: My friends are the absolute worst, and I don't know where I'd be without them. And one day very soon I'm going to lose both of them, and then what will I have if it's not Paul?

CHAPTER THIRTY-SEVEN

"I thought maybe I'd gone too far with the puke-face
emoji," Eugene says as I get out of my car. He smiles and
that one dimple shows. As I step closer, I realize I missed his
dimple. I missed him.

I texted him postintervention and he immediately
responded. We decided to meet on Tuesday after my day
shift at Berry Plum.

When I was done with work, he texted me an address.
That was all I got—just an address. I asked where we were
going, what we were doing, and what I should wear, and he
didn't reply. So I did what any normal girl with a crush would
do: I threw on a sundress, got in my car, and drove more than
half an hour to meet a boy I barely know.

If this were a *Dateline* special, I'd already be dead.

"You're entitled to your wrong cereal opinion," I say.

He smiles and shakes his head. He's leaning against his
truck, and I have the now familiar urge to press myself against
him and sniff his neck.

Yeah, I don't know what's wrong with me either.

Safe to say, I remain where I'm standing, playing with my
car keys. "So what are we doing here?" I ask.

We're in the parking lot of Speedway, a huge whitewashed building off the Florida Turnpike.

"Well, you won't get on my bike, so I thought go-karting might be the next best thing," he says.

"I've never been," I say.

He smiles. "You're in for a treat, but I'll warn you, it's addictive. Come on. Let's get your headsock."

"My what?"

He doesn't answer, but I follow him. He holds open the door for me, and as soon as the tracks come into view, I know this is a terrible idea. I don't like going fast. Speeding and taking chances are Emily's thing, not mine. These Formula One–looking race-carts will not be my cup of tea. Speaking of . . .

"Maybe we should get tea somewhere instead," I say.

"Nervous?" he asks.

"Well . . ." I gesture to the general track area.

We walk to a computer and he swipes a card before touching the screen.

"There's a little kids' track too," he says. "We may want to do that since I'm not sure if you're tall enough for adult races, anyhow."

He puts his hand on top of my head, fake measuring.

I skew my face. "Can your big head fit into one of the helmets?"

"Ha!" Eugene laughs.

He pulls up the waiver of liability form, and I take a look. It's all about death and injury and maiming. "Maiming"— they actually use that word.

He scrolls down to the signature portion and waits for me to sign with my finger. I glance at the form, at him, and back again. Like . . . nope. There's no way.

"There's a really nice tea shop not far from here," I say. I look up with what I hope are pleading eyes.

"I swear it's safe. You wear a helmet and you're strapped in. It's just fun."

We obviously have different definitions of fun.

He purses his lips. "I tell you what, because I can't resist good tea: Do two races with me and we'll go afterward."

"Two races? One."

"Two. I already paid."

Dammit.

I hesitate. There's nothing in me that wants to hop aboard a maiming machine. But he smiles when he's excited and his teal eyes go a little wide, and well, it's only serious, permanent injury.

"It's once around the track?" I ask.

He laughs. "That would take, like, a minute. It's sixteen times around, fastest time wins. You try to beat your best time every lap."

"Sixteen times? Like, one, two, three, four . . . sixteen? No, thank you." I shake my head vigorously.

He smiles like I'm cute instead of stubborn and leans closer to me. "Bubble & Co. is nearby and has Thai milk tea."

My resolve waivers. When he's this close, his scent floods my senses. "Yes" sits on the tip of my tongue.

"And . . . bubble waffles," he whispers in my ear.

Every hair on my arms rises, reaching to be nearer to him.

"What are bubble waffles?" I say, nearly breathless. We're talking about a midafternoon dessert, but it doesn't feel that way.

"You'll have to race me to see. Winner buys." He stands straight again.

I turn my head toward him. "Wait . . . what? It should be loser buys."

"If you think I'm not Asian enough to fight for the bill, you have another thing coming," he says.

I laugh.

Paul never understood the war-over-the-check Asian cultural dynamic. Weirdly enough, my mom's side, which is not Asian aside from Aunt Kim's family, is just as bad as my dad's. So all fifty people may go in for the bill. It's a blood sport.

A girl in a tight Speedway T-shirt comes up to us. She's around our age. She winks at Eugene and types a bunch of things rapidly into the screen. The next thing I know, I have a cotton thing in my hand, a membership card, and jealousy flowing through me.

But Eugene doesn't seem to notice anyone but me as he leads me to the racks of helmets. He slips a cover over his head and looks like a knight's squire.

"What the hell is that?" I say.

"It's a headsock. You have one too." He smiles.

So that's the cotton thing. I will look very, very fetching in this.

He grabs a helmet and holds it in his hand.

"Come on, Miss Safety. Put on the headsock and let's find a helmet that fits you."

I raise an eyebrow, but he laughs.

After I have both a headsock and helmet on, we wait to be loaded into the concussion-carts.

I can't believe my life has come to this.

The best part is, I'm not just racing against Eugene. I have to do sixteen laps against a bunch of people I don't even know.

"I swear it's not hard," Eugene says, like he's reading my mind. "That kid can't be older than thirteen—if he can do it, I'm sure you can too."

He points to a father and son ahead of us, and the kid is definitely middle school age. He reminds me of Kyle McGovern's popular crew. He's spent the entire time mocking the guy giving the safety protocol, because of course he has to act above safety.

"But I don't know what I'm doing," I say. It comes out as a semiwhine. There's little sexier than whining, I'm sure.

"You'll figure it out," he says.

He rubs his hand over the center of my back, and suddenly it's hard to remember what we're doing here. It's hard to focus on anything other than him touching me.

Our time comes and because I'm a total sucker, I get in the go-kart. The steering isn't exactly a wheel. It's more like a video game controller, which Davey would be great at. I, on the other hand, will probably die, as I suck at *Mario Kart*.

But I stay in my harness. There's a countdown and the traffic light turns green. Eugene floors it and I'm waved forward. He rounds the bend and shakes his head as I putter along, trying to get a feel for the accelerator.

I'm about three-quarters of the way around when Eugene pulls up beside me. He's lapped me. He stares at me then zooms off again, and I know that look. That's catch me if you can.

I shake my head. What am I even doing here? Paul never would've made me do anything like this. He knows my limits, my comfort zone. Eugene pushes me right out of it.

I've just started my second lap when the middle school kid passes me. He mocks me before speeding off.

Yes, an acne-faced twelve-year-old just heckled me for driving carefully.

And something about that makes me snap. I'm just fed up—with being teased, with being a doormat, with constantly trying to settle for safe. I started being like this because of a kid like him in eighth grade and what has it gotten me other than a broken heart?

I check my harness again and then I floor it. The speed makes my stomach knot, but I'm a great defensive driver. I know it. I can predict what people are going to do before it happens.

That's how I knew the middle schooler would try to sideswipe me for fun. That's why I hit the brake, so when he swerved, he missed me and crashed into the tires. I pause for a millisecond to look at the wreckage, then accelerate past him. Now I want to pass Eugene, who is a "regular" according to the girl who was flirting with him right in front of me. Like I was invisible yet again.

My small feet push against the rests, my body tensing and begging me to think about the safety of this plastic wagon hurtling at thirty-five miles an hour. The scenery blurs by me, but I focus only on him.

He's a better driver than the kid. As soon as I gain ground, he puts distance between us. But he has to go around a slower cart, and I gain on him. He also has to slow into the turn. I accelerate, mentally calculating the widest arc where I won't have to decelerate but won't hurl myself off this track. Unlike Paul, I never cheated on my math homework. I've got this.

I pull up beside Eugene and he does a double take. I see it in my peripheral vision, and because he slowed down to look, I pass him.

Eugene fist pumps the air, cheering for me. I let out a laugh.

Fourteen laps later, the race ends and we return to the starting positions.

Eugene unbuckles and then helps me out of my harness. He takes off his helmet and headsock. His hair is cutely messed up.

"That was amazing!" he says. He points up to the board, where I'm listed as fifth. He came in second. "You sandbagged me!"

I laugh. "I promise I didn't. I'm not sure what came over me."

"You're a competitor at heart. I knew it."

I try to stand, but I'm wobbly getting out of my cart. Really wobbly. It's like my legs and the ground are Jell-O. My hands have a noticeable tremor.

"Whoa, I got you," he says. He puts an arm around my waist. I lean into him. It sounds romantic, but it's not because I'm kind of a rag doll at the moment.

"It's a lot of adrenaline," he says.

He walks me over to the rack and I take my helmet and headsock off. After he puts our helmets away, he wraps his arms around me again. I'm not sure if I need it, but I want it. I lean into him and feel his heart beat through his T-shirt. And this is worth the merry-go-round of maiming carts.

"You surprised me, Jasmine," he says.

I like the way my name sounds when he says it. Other people call me Jaz, but he uses my full name and it's adult, even sexy, spilling from his lips.

"I surprised myself."

He smiles. "We don't have to race again. That one was pretty epic," he says.

It's everything I wanted to hear.

I look up at him. "Are you sure? I thought you paid for two."

"I did, but you can come back anytime. Come on. Let's go. I think you earned your bubble waffle."

We leave Speedway and head over to Bubble & Co. A few minutes later I sit at a café table with my first-ever bubble waffle—which is a normal waffle but with air circles instead of pockets. Mine holds vanilla ice cream, chocolate chips, strawberries, and chocolate sauce. Eugene ordered chocolate ice cream, bananas, and a caramel drizzle.

I tried to pay because, technically, I did beat him once. He gently pointed out that he bested me the other fifteen times. I don't think those count, but he insisted, so here we are.

I'm staring at my bubble waffle, trying to figure out if I'm supposed to eat it like a gyro or with utensils, when Eugene comes back with two spoons and our Thai milk teas.

He sits across from me and we dig in at the same time.

"So, was go-karting your worst nightmare or actually a good time?" he asks.

I smile slowly. "Okay, I had fun."

On the ride over, I thought of ways I could've gone faster on the track. So he was right: it's addictive. Once I broke through my initial fear, it was a rush.

And Eugene helping me out of the cart was the real win.

"I may need to go back," I say.

Eugene smiles widely. "Yeah?"

"Maybe—if you join me," I say.

I try to cut the waffle with the spoon, but that's not happening, so I pick it up and bite into it. It's soft and perfect. Eugene stares at me with a look I can't place. Maybe I was supposed to eat the waffle with a spoon. Am I a cavewoman who can't eat properly?

We lock into a conversational pause, and he doesn't look anxious to break it. I, on the other hand, am unnerved.

"So . . . why are you looking at me?" I ask.

He laughs. "Where am I supposed to look?"

Okay, good point. But being face-to-face with him is . . . intimate. Paul tended to scroll his phone or we'd be surrounded by his friends. We were rarely face-to-face like this, except for Burrito Friday.

Eugene's stopped eating, so I put my spoon down. He sits back in his chair. He's handsome when he's mulling things over, and his teal eyes take on a faraway look.

Not that I'm staring.

Note: I'm totally staring.

"What?" I ask.

He leans forward and I mirror him. He bites down on his lip and I want to bite down on his lips too and I need to stop being *such* a creeper.

"I like you," he says.

I blink a few times. "You like me as . . . as a friend, right?" I say.

"Um, no," he says, an amused expression lighting his face. "I mean, yes, I do, but I also like you in the dating way."

It feels like someone set off a rocket in my chest. It's everything—joy and ecstasy—to hear him say that. But then I come back to earth because who even talks like that? Paul would say I love you back, but I can't remember him saying "I like you." Ever. My head fills with all the reasons Eugene shouldn't like me: I'm awkward. I'm short. I'm not that pretty, or talented, or special.

And all right, maybe Emily had a point about about my self-esteem.

"But I mean, this isn't a *date* date. Is it?" I say.

He laughs but his eyes focus on my mouth. "It isn't? I guess I have to try harder."

I barely have time to register his words before his lips meet mine. My eyes shoot open then drift closed. He tastes like chocolate and tea and miracles. It's a kiss so good, it takes my breath away. It's the kind of kiss I've only ever read about, but never in my life have I experienced anything close to this. Not in all the make-outs after Burrito Friday.

His tongue encircles mine, and I feel like I'm floating and maybe I am . . . until my arm feels damp. I break our kiss and look down. I knocked over my milk tea.

Typical.

Eugene and I scramble for napkins to sop it up. We catch each other's eyes, smile, and clean up the spill. Once the napkins are thrown out, we go back to our bubble waffles.

But even though I'm eating a delicious dessert, all I can think about is the taste of his kiss. And how I can't wait to kiss him again.

CHAPTER THIRTY-EIGHT

DAVEY'S WORRIED FAMILY GROUP TEXT
JUNE 4

Cari
So a few things are going on and almost none of them are good

Aunt Tammy
Is someone in jail?

Aunt Minnie
That cannot be your response every time

Aunt Tammy
I mean, it's a possibility

Uncle Vin
Is it though, love?

Cari
No one's in jail, but Jaz met Paul for lunch. He's still trying to get her back

Cousin Madison
Why would she meet him?

Aunt Kim
Well, they do have a lot of history

Cousin Joe
Come on. She has three guys after her

Cari
There's more

Dad
Well, it can't be worse than Paul

Cari
Her friend Emily almost told her about the competition and doesn't want to be involved anymore

Cousin Wesley
Surprise. It got worse. What? Why?

Cari
It took Emily a while to get onboard, but . . . she thinks we're underestimating Jaz and that this will hurt her in the long run

(Ten seconds of silence.)

Cousin Joe
Well, shit

Cari
And there's one more thing

Aunt Minnie
I think I'd prefer someone being in jail at this point

Cari
Um, it's a long story, but I made an anonymous podcast about all of this and . . . well, it's gone viral

Aunt Jay
That is *not* good

Aunt Tammy
Oh, Cari

Cousin Wylan
How many episodes are there? What's it called?

Cousin Joe
Are we all famous now?

Cousin Teagan
Focus on Jaz. The more hits, the more likely it is to reach her

Cousin Wylan

Gentle reminder that she has no tech skills

Uncle Carlos

But if it gets big enough, won't she eventually hear about it?

Mom

I can't believe you didn't ask us first

Cari

I know, Ma. But I didn't think it would go anywhere. But the downloads keep rising and someone asked me on Reddit if I was the host

Mom

You have to shut it down. Immediately

Cari

I didn't expect it to take off

Nonna

You need to shut down the podcast

Cari

I will

CHAPTER THIRTY-NINE

THE LITTLE BACHELORETTE PODCAST EXCERPT

S1, EP 3—JUNE 8

Anonyma: Hey, and welcome back to *The Little Bachelorette* podcast. I'm your host, Anonyma.

We are officially two weeks into *The Little Bachelorette* contest and things are heating up. Ariel has been on second dates with the three bachelors—The Boy Next Door, The Pro, and The Cook. And, I'm sorry to report that her week began with lunch with RSP. At this point we have to admit that we officially have a fourth bachelor.

But enough of that disappointment. Joining us to give some insight on Ariel and the four-bachelor situation is one of her closest friends. What should we call you?

Flounder: I guess Flounder if we're going with this *Little Mermaid* theme, but know I don't like it. *laughs*

Anonyma: We could go with a different nickname. Sebastian? Ursula? *laughs*

Flounder: Flounder is fine.

Anonyma: Well, welcome Flounder. Thanks for joining me on the show. I know you had reservations about this whole contest.

Flounder: I did. I didn't like keeping Ariel in the dark, and Em . . . Sebastian, her other close friend, brought up some really good reasons we shouldn't do this anymore. But after talking to your family yesterday, I think you guys are right. Without this contest, she would've sat home thinking about how great RSP is when he's not. She wouldn't have dated and she wouldn't have believed she deserves anyone better than him. And she definitely would've taken him back by now. She's changed so much just by meeting the bachelors and it's only been two weeks.

Anonyma: I totally agree. Okay, let's get right down to business. I've heard a rumor that Ariel kissed one of the bachelors this week.

Flouder: I can confirm that she kissed The Cook.

Anonyma: And she got cozy at the batting cages with The Pro on Thursday.

Flounder: She hit a baseball. There's a first time for everything . . . allegedly.

Anonyma: *laughs* I saw the video clip. It actually happened. But let's talk about The Boy Next Door, because their date was at a theme park. And you've known him for a while. . . .

Flounder: Since we were kids. We all used to play together. I think he's wonderful, and between you and me, he's the one I'm rooting for the most.

Anonyma: Your secret is safe with me.

CHAPTER FORTY

It's Sunday, which ends a totally confusing week or begins a new one, depending on how you look at it.

Aaron just texted. He wants to play disc golf when he's back in town as he continues to not accept my nonathleticism. It didn't help that he won our bet—I actually hit a baseball on Thursday.

After the thrill of go-kart racing, I got right into the batting cage and was no longer terrified of new things.

Just kidding. I was totally terrified.

Aaron rolled with it, though. He patiently adjusted me a million times. I could've sworn his hands lingered on me, especially when he moved my hips. But only for a second or two, nothing pervy.

It would've been so sexy, him standing behind me with his hands on me, except I smacked him with a bat.

Yeah.

He said something I couldn't hear, so I turned around. Unfortunately, I swung while turning.

In that instant, I saw his future Major League career going up in flames. But his reflexes are lightning quick. He shifted out of the way before I could do real damage. I hit his back though, and I'll continue to be horrified by that moment for the rest of my natural life. After that, my ghost will be embarrassed.

Even through the haze of my shame, it was amazing to watch him bat. The baseballs popped and sailed into the distance, farther than anyone else's. Everyone, and I mean everyone, turned to stare. And he was there with me.

After we were done, I bought him his winning ice-cream cone (and an ice pack). We sat in his Audi with the AC blasting, listening to country. We sang along and he is, in fact, terrible, but he said I have to visit Nashville. He offered to show me the town and the Country Music Hall of Fame. One day I'll have to find the nerve to take him up on it, because between the music and the hot chicken, it sounds like heaven.

It was all casual and fun until he mentioned that he hadn't always lived in Nashville, and I asked why he'd moved.

"Bullying in middle school," he said. He looked away.

I knit my eyebrows. "You . . . bullied someone?" I asked.

He smiled sadly. "No. I was the target."

And looking at the star, the playboy in front of me, I couldn't picture it. It must've been reflected in my face.

"I was smaller, scrawnier, and easy to pick on when I was twelve. My dad was deployed, and my mom had so much going on with my younger sisters and all. I just thought . . . I don't know, that I should be the man of the house. I didn't say anything. I just . . . dealt, you know?"

Tears pricked my eyes. I did understand. It's not the same, but I didn't tell June, Justin Michael, or Cari about what had happened with Kyle. It was just too shameful. Eventually, I gave June a vague summary, but I never mentioned it to Cari. She would've felt bad and sorry for me and that was beyond the point.

Aaron took a deep breath. "But after I was pushed down a flight of stairs and had to go to the hospital, I couldn't hide it anymore. Mom pulled me out of school and we moved to Nashville. It was a new start. I never had to see those kids again."

He smiled like he could just wave it off, but memories from middle school leave a mark, a brand. I remember that bonfire like it happened an hour ago, the night at Ventura's Bistro like it was a minute ago. And his was much worse.

"I'm . . . ," I began, but I could tell by the look on his face the last thing he wanted was pity. Anything but pity.

"I wish we'd been in the same school together," I said. "We could've had each other."

I put my hand over his. He glanced down at it and smiled genuinely. Then he turned his hand and squeezed mine.

For the first time I felt like I got to know the real him—not the star—and all I wanted was to know more.

I don't know what's happening to me. I kissed Eugene. And went on a date with Aaron and also went on a date with Justin.

Or at least I think it was a date.

Somehow, he scored free passes to Universal so I met him after he finished work on Wednesday.

It wound up being the perfect night exploring what we remembered and what had changed. Neither of us had gone to the theme parks since we were thirteen. We rode the (few) roller coasters I was brave enough to go on and wandered around taking in the shows and people. He made me laugh with his nerdy factoids about the park, and I made him laugh by being absolutely horrible at the water-cannon game.

As we watched the nighttime lights at Hogwarts, I leaned back against him and he wrapped his arms around me. It was just so comfortable—like old times, like merging with a younger version of us. We still fit together like a clue and a crossword answer.

When we hugged goodbye, I didn't want to let go. The thought that he'll leave my life again when he finishes his internship physically hurts. He'll be yet another person moving on while I stay put. But I began to wonder if not wanting him to go is because I like him so much as a friend or whether it's something else. Whether my feelings for him have morphed and grown with us.

Right before I got in my car, he stared into my eyes and I thought he'd kiss me. My heart sped up, but he pressed his lips to my forehead and then looked at me again before saying good night. My heart beat in my throat and my hands shook as I unlocked the Rolla.

It might've actually been more intimate than a kiss.

And I don't know what to make of any of this.

These are my thoughts as I browse the aisles of Sephora. Emily's parents gave her a gift card for no reason, and she's treating me and June to new makeup. That's why I'm lost in this jungle of expensive creams.

My phone dings and I fumble through my bag to check it. It's Paul again. He's messaged every day since the key chain lunch. Lately, he's been sending me his favorite pictures. Some I've seen before. Some were candid of me I never knew he took—studying, waiting in the stands at his game, talking to someone at a party, or just looking out the window. I still think he cared more than he knew how to say. I still don't know what to make of that. Is it enough? I don't know.

"Paul wants me to meet him again," I say when June, Emily, and I find ourselves in the same aisle.

June barely pauses applying lipstick to sigh.

"He's the one you shoulda hit with a baseball bat," Emily says.

I frown at the makeup mirror. "Ha ha, guys. Thanks. I will continue to relive the thunk of hitting Aaron for the rest of my days."

June snickers and Emily snorts.

"But back to The Paul . . . ," Emily says.

"Are you really thinking about meeting RSP again, Jaz?" June says.

I look over my shoulder at her. June's chosen a bold red shade, but she's frowning at it.

"Who, June?" I ask.

"Paul," she says.

I shake my head like I'm clearing water from my ears. "That's not what you said."

"You're losing it. She said Paul." Emily applies a sparkly powder to her eyebrows. "Too many boys on the brain, including Mr. Kiss the Chef."

I sigh. "I'm no longer telling you fools a thing. We've now entered the cone of silence." I draw a circle around myself with my fingers, then sit in one of the tall chairs and pout.

I'm not pouting about their teasing. It's . . . everything about Eugene. He's so confusing. He said he liked me. He kissed me. And yet, he still won't message. I waited until Friday, hoping to hear from him, and . . . nothing. With zero messages incoming, I worked up the nerve to text first.

CM

Captain Eugene Crunch

The shelter loves the idea of families getting gourmet treats and being entered to win the gift baskets. Thank you again

My pleasure

What are you doing today?

Trying to improve your lap time?

I wish. I'm doing prep, then dinner service

With those less than enthusiastic replies, I let the conversation drop. It's for the best. I like him, but I don't get him. He makes it seem like working at the best restaurant in the country is a burden and not a privilege. He wants this life where he can backpack across Europe, so what could this possibly be? Maybe in the end, after all of this, I wind up back with Paul. Maybe that's not a bad thing. Maybe we are meant for each other and all of this will just help us grow.

My phone dings and I check it, expecting another trip down memory lane from Paul. But it's not Paul.

Like he could hear we were talking about him, Eugene messages me.

Sorry, I've meant to text more, but I've been so busy. I'm finally off tomorrow, though

Oh, it's the face," Emily says, craning her neck as if she can see my screen from six feet away. "I bet I know who's texting her."

"Who is it, Jaz?" June asks.

"Is it a boy with soft lips and burning teal eyes?" Emily says. She bats her long lashes and puckers up.

"Nothing to tell, you awful clowns," I say. But inside I'm beaming. I can't even help how happy I am to hear from him. And all right, maybe there's a part of me that still loves to dream. And I can't help but want to be nearer to someone who makes his wishes reality.

I'm trying to decide what to message back when my phone dings again. Both June and Emily turn.

Collins's dog had to have emergency surgery, so I was sous-chef all weekend

OMG. Is his dog okay?

He somehow swallowed a chef's glove, but he's fine

Phew. I'm glad

I really wanted to see you, but I was constantly at work. How about a beach picnic tomorrow?

I should play hard to get. Or make him wait for a response, right? I should seem in demand

That sounds amazing

My fingers are traitors

I'll pick you up at 11?

See you then

I'm smiling so hard, my cheeks hurt. I try to clear my expression as I put my phone away, but it's no use. June and Emily have been staring at me this entire time.

"Cheeeeeeesing," Emily says.

"Fine," I sigh. "Eugene and I are going to the beach tomorrow."

They open their mouths.

I put up my hand. "Not a word."

June tilts her head. Emily widens her eyes.

Emily gestures at me with her manicured talons. "Who's this new boss bitch?"

"I don't know, but I like her," June says.

I try not to blush. I fail. So there goes the boss thing.

"Let's check out and grab coffee," Emily says. "I need some caffeine. Did you find anything you liked, Jaz?"

I shake my head.

"I'm getting you this palette then," Emily says. She already had it in her hand, fully expecting me to not know what to choose at this giant makeup store.

I wait by the entrance as Emily pays with her gift card. I don't want to know how much that palette costs. Probably as much as a full day of work for me.

June and I thank her, but she waves us off. We get into June's Mustang and drive over to Wired, one of the cool independent coffee shops in town.

I order a vanilla cold brew, June's standard iced latte, and Emily's cappuccino. We grab them and camp out in armchairs. June and Emily relax with their long legs out. I sit toward the edge of my seat so my feet touch the ground.

"It's a beach date tomorrow, huh?" June says.

"Um, I don't know that . . . I mean . . . yes," I say. And I can't keep a grin off my face. I'm scared but also so excited to see him again.

June and Emily exchange smiles.

"Let's talk bathing suits, because you cannot wear that old lady skort or child one-piece like you normally do," Emily says.

"What's wrong with my bathing suits?" I ask.

Emily shakes her head. "Did you hear a word I just said—granny or twelve-year-old. We need to swing by Cabana and get you a bikini."

"I can't afford one." I hate to admit it, but I definitely can't afford anything in Cabana. I usually shop end-of-the-season clearance at Old Navy or something.

"I'll get it," Emily says.

I shake my head. "No."

"Yes. So there," Emily says.

"No. I'm not going to be your charity case," I say.

My parents taught me to be gracious, but not to accept help I don't need. I work to afford the things I want. And honestly, Emily is exaggerating. My bathing suits are okay . . . I think.

"We'll call it a graduation present," Emily says with a wink. Her eyes literally sparkle from whatever she applied at Sephora.

"I really . . . I can't. And you already gave me a graduation present."

It was a very generous check I put in a savings account for college, along with the rest of my graduation money.

"Your graduation present was compliments of Oliver Underwood and his guilt from scarring his youngest child for life. Your suit is on me. And, like, seriously—charity? How many times did you and June take me in over the past two years? Was that charity or because we're friends?"

I have nothing to say to that.

"Come on. Let's go to Cabana. I've got a barbecue later."

With that, we all get up and toss our trash. They're out the door before me, and it hits me again that come August I'll be at this coffee shop alone. Refusing to think about it hasn't prevented it.

And suddenly staying put in Orlando feels more like being stranded than playing it safe.

CHAPTER FORTY-ONE

DAVEY'S SCHEMING FAMILY GROUP TEXT
JUNE 9

Cousin Crystal
What's going on with Eugene? I thought the boys were going to get equal time

Aunt Jay
He's had some issues with keeping her in the dark, but he said he's going to text her

Cari
They're going to the beach tomorrow

Cousin Joe
Yawn. Doesn't matter. Aaron wowed her at the batting cages

Cousin Amberlynn
But she didn't kiss him, did she?
Which beach??

Cari
No

Cousin Amberlynn
No, what?

Cari
No, you can't just 'happen' to show up at the same beach on a Monday. Don't think I didn't see some of you at Aaron's game. We're lucky Jaz didn't notice

Cousin Amberlynn
I wasn't going to . . .

Cousin Crystal
You totally would've

Cousin Amberlynn
Rude

Cari
And we're lucky she didn't pick up on the betting talk at Mabel's birthday party. You barely convinced her the money was on fantasy football, Wes. It's not even football season!

She didn't figure it out though

Anyone want to change their bets?

Cousin Teagan
Nope. Justin Michael is end game

Cousin Madison
She doesn't need a boy in the end. It's more important she finds herself

Cousin Joe
Yeah, finds herself in Aaron's arms

Cousin Madison
You all are pathetic. I'm going to work on my thesis

Cousin Amberlynn
So, like, Cocoa Beach? . . .

Cari
Goodnight, all

CHAPTER FORTY-TWO

I retie the strings of my bathing suit top to make abso-
lutely sure I don't flash a boob at Eugene. Nothing, I repeat,
nothing, could be more embarrassing. No wardrobe malfunc-
tions here.

I could leave my cover-up on all day, but it's already ninety
degrees. And underneath is my new, very expensive bikini.
It's a red, retro-style halter top with booty shorts—kinda like
a fifties pinup. It's the opposite of anything I would've picked
on my own.

When we were in Cabana, I gravitated toward a one-
piece that turned out to be maternity wear. If you think Emily
and June mocked me endlessly for that, you'd be right.

So . . . I went with their choice.

Eugene is in dark blue trunks and a T-shirt, and he looks
great. He has on old-school aviators as he drives.

I try not to read into the fact that he chose to spend his
only day off with me.

Spoiler: I'm totally reading into it.

We park next to an access point for New Smyrna, a
smaller beach near Daytona.

"Do you want to leave your phone? I'm going to put mine in here," he says.

I'm surprised he's so easy about leaving the world behind. There's no way I'd convince Emily or Cari to give up their phones for a whole day. Even Davey would push back because he needs to be in touch with his gaming buds and bookmaking business. He's already branching out into taking family bets on fantasy sports, I guess.

I try to think if there's anyone I want to reach, but I'm with the person I want to talk to. I slide my phone into the glove compartment with Eugene's. They look nearly identical next to each other. He takes off his watch, then locks everything up.

And that's it. We're off the grid. There's something freeing and unsettling about that—pretty much being with Eugene in a nutshell.

"I'm going to grab the stuff from the back," he says.

"I'll help," I say.

We grab the chairs, cooler, and beach totes, and tread across the sand. We agree on a spot near, but not too near, the water. Eugene gets to work, and we soon have everything set up except the food. I can't wait to see what he brought.

"I'm going to rent an umbrella," he says, glancing up at the sun.

"Oh, I can do it," I say.

"Nah, I got it."

He wanders off toward the rentals. There's always some

guy with either a truck or a van who loans out chairs and umbrellas for the day. My family never gets them, as my father would rather go to war than pay for rented beach gear, but I've always been jealous of people who had them.

I reach for my phone but realize I don't have it. Instead of scrolling, I listen to the waves crashing and the gulls cawing overhead while I apply my SPF 10,000 sunblock. It's weird to be this . . . present.

Once I'm done, I sit on my chair and open the latest rom-com by Sandhya Menon. I'm only through the first page when Eugene comes back. He brings a guy with a large umbrella, which he plants between the chairs. The shade immediately feels great.

"So, are you hungry?" Eugene asks.

"Starving," I say.

He smiles, that dimple winking at me. "Good. Let's start with samosas. I made them this morning."

He takes a warming bag out of his beach tote and passes me one. I take a bite.

"Oh my God," I say, talking with my mouth full.

"I also made tandoori chicken skewers," he says.

Or I think that's what he says. Hard to tell with the flavor explosion in my mouth. The pastry is perfect and the potatoes are spicy without being overpowering.

"Marry me," I say.

"I'm not done." Eugene grins, then flips open the cooler. "We have white-bean truffle dip with toasted pita chips."

"Will you judge me if I eat that with a spoon?" I ask.

"Not even a little."

He rifles through the containers. "Assorted cheeses with honey-poached quince paste—because I remember someone really likes cheese. There's also ridiculously good speck. A corn salad. A potato salad that's pretty good if I say so myself. And ham, brie, and apricot sandwiches. I grabbed some candies from the restaurant and some other snacks. To top it all off is the best lemonade on earth. I can't take credit because L&Js's bar makes it, but I did go through the hassle of stealing it. What do you think?"

Eugene stops and looks at me.

"This is officially the best date ever," I say.

It truly is. It's beyond what I could've imagined for myself a month ago. He put so much thought and effort into this— things I never would've expected from Paul. Even if every bite is inedible, he's tried for me in a way no one else has.

Eugene smiles and takes a bite of samosa. "I'm glad."

We dig into lunch, and my little foodie heart is in heaven. He pours me a cup of lemonade and it's perfect—both tart and sweet at the same time.

As I sip, I know there's nothing better than this moment, with this boy, and this lunch, on a sun-drenched beach.

"It's really good lemonade," I say. "Almost as good as the potato salad. Almost."

He smiles and sits back with his sandwich. I know that pleased expression. I'm the same way when someone appreciates the food I made. It's the contentment of bringing happiness and also being recognized for creating something special.

We finish eating at a relaxed pace and close up the cooler. He throws some crusts to the seagulls, who waited a good twenty minutes for this opportunity.

"Thank you isn't enough," I say. "But thank you so much for lunch."

"My pleasure. You can return the favor by cooking for me someday," he says.

"No. Nuh-uh. Not with all of this going on." I gesture to the cooler. I can't compete with a lifetime in the kitchen. Like, thanks for the five-star meal, Eugene—here's peanut butter and jelly.

"Hmm," he says. "Let's go for a walk."

He stands and offers me a hand. I take it to hoist myself out of my chair. I'm super full, but I'll still have seconds when I can shove more deliciousness into my face.

To my surprise, he keeps holding my hand as we walk through the sand. And this is classic boyfriend/girlfriend, right? This is what couples do—stroll the beach hand in hand? Paul didn't really like holding hands, but this is what I'd imagined.

Eugene and I walk along the tide and the cool water feels good on the soles of my feet. His hand in mine makes the dream a reality.

"So talk to me. Why are you so scared?" he says.

"It's a charming facet of my personality?" I say, hoping to switch topics. We should talk about other things, like the recipe for that white-bean dip. Or him marrying me and us having a dozen foodie babies.

"Do you think I'd judge your cooking like a restaurant critic?"

I shake my head. "It's not that . . . well, it's a little bit judgment. But more that I know I can't cook the way you can."

"Just like you couldn't pass me on the track?" he says.

I see the challenge in his face.

I shake my head. "That's different. You're not the son of a Daytona 500 winner."

"Cooking isn't genetic, but I know what you're saying. Yes, I've had my dad mentor me since I could walk, but you're related to Jay Ventura. My dad says she's one of the best chefs in Florida. She didn't teach you how to cook?"

"She did, but . . . ," I say, trailing off into my thoughts.

Suddenly, I'm not on the beach anymore. Mentally, I'm fourteen and reaching for the back door of Ventura's Bistro. Every Monday, instead of going home after school, I took the bus to my aunt's place.

It was our little secret, and the only one I'd ever kept from my family. Mom was too afraid of everything hot and sharp in the kitchen to let me help out at the bistro. But after the bonfire, when I dreaded going to school that Monday, I confided in my aunt. She was the only one I told the details of what had happened with Kyle. Jay said if I was brave and went in, she'd teach me how to make her special French onion soup after school.

From there it became a tradition that on Mondays, when the restaurant was closed, I'd stop by and help her prep for the next day. Every time, she'd teach me a new skill or a new recipe.

But that Monday was different. The back door was open as usual, but the kitchen was dark. There was no bass-pounding music, no lights, no amazing aromas coming off the stove. I got an awful sinking feeling and maybe everything would've been okay if I'd listened to my gut, but I didn't. I forged ahead, searching for my aunt.

At that time Josephina Ventura was a force to be reckoned with. She was frequently in the paper or tagged on social media, either because celebrities came in or it was just the buzz about her restaurant. She was everything and I was so proud of her.

But that late afternoon I found her in her office with her arm curled around an empty bottle of wine. It wasn't even dark out, but she was asleep on her desk. It was hard to take in the sight of my passed-out aunt, but other things caught my eye. I went a step closer and saw bill after bill marked past due in angry red stamps. Legal papers crumpled up. There was a tearstained envelope in her hand that just said, "Goodbye."

I couldn't decide whether to stay or go, but Jay raised her head.

"What are you doing here?" she asked. She rubbed her face then hastily swept the bills and the envelope to the side.

"I thought . . . well, I thought we'd prep or cook today," I said.

She breathed out a laugh. "What for?"

"Well, for tomorrow. It's Monday." I hoped to jog her memory. I could tell she was drunk.

She shook her head like she was sorry for me. "Go home, Jasmine."

And maybe I should've. So many times I wish I'd just left then. But I didn't.

"I just . . . I can help," I said.

Jay finally focused on me and narrowed her blue eyes. "You think you can help me? Like you're so special?"

The bite in her words was so unlike her that I was stunned for a second.

"No," I said. "But you are. You can do anything."

Her face softened a little.

I took a small step toward her and found the words to say what was in my heart. "I want to be just like you. I want to have my own restaurant one day."

Her expression changed, hardened. She closed her eyes like the thought was painful. "Jasmine, you don't have what it takes. No one does. Now get out."

She didn't need to say the last few words, because I was already backing out of the office.

I ran to the bus stop, and as I waited her words shredded my dreams. I cried waiting for the bus, on the bus, and then walked around for a bit after my stop until it looked like I wasn't crying at all. The tears faded, but the hurt never went away.

Within two months, Ventura's Bistro was closed. Jay bounced around for a while trying different jobs before opening her catering company. When my mom asked what I wanted to be, my dreams having died the night before, I said maybe a nurse. She was so happy, so proud that I wanted to be like her that I've never found a way out. And my aunt and I were never the same.

"I can't . . . ," Eugene says. "I can't figure it out."

His voice brings me back to the present. To the beach. To four years later. I shudder off the memory and look up at him.

"Figure what out?" I ask.

"Why you have all this strength, but you won't use it. I can't understand why you don't go after what you want."

Something about the way he says it gets under my skin. Maybe it burrows because I was just reliving the moment when I lost my dreams. Maybe because I've been through things he couldn't possibly understand. He doesn't have any fears. And he's never had to struggle. He's had the keys to the kingdom handed to him, and the worst part is, he doesn't even know if he wants them.

"What are you so afraid of?" he says.

"Everything!" I yell. I drop his hand and my palms slap against my thighs in frustration. With the memory, with him.

Eugene stops walking and faces me.

I continue on. "I'm afraid of hurting my family. Of failing. Of not being good enough. Jay was so talented and her restaurant closed. Tens of thousands of my parents' money, just gone, and our house put in danger because they gambled on her skill. My parents have struggled to pay two mortgages because they weren't afraid and should've been. And if Jay couldn't make it as a chef, I have no shot."

He opens his mouth, but I'm not done. The frustration

I've felt since I met him bubbles over and the words fly out.

"Look, I don't view life as this adventure where I can take off to Spain by myself or step in as sous-chef at the best restaurant in the country on a moment's notice. I'm not you. I haven't been given everything yet stand here wondering if I actually want it. I know what it feels like to struggle to keep the shreds of what I have. You don't. You've never been told you're not enough."

Eugene is silent for almost a full thirty seconds. My heart pounds, and as the anger fades, regret floods in. What the hell did I just do? I yelled at him. I yelled things at him I don't share with anyone—even June and Emily. The debt my parents went into. The jealousy I feel at how he can choose, that it occurs to him to walk away from the dream I can't have. That the deepest fear I have is that I'm just not good enough.

As the moments drag on, I realize he couldn't have known about the restaurant debt or how I wanted to cook professionally. For all he knew, I was vaguely interested in cooking as a hobby. I don't know why he kept hammering me on it— like he suspected I wanted to be a chef. Maybe I haven't kept it as secret as I thought. But either way, I'm positive that he's about to say we should leave. Paul would've and I wouldn't even blame him. Who acts like this? Who raises their voice to someone they like?

Eugene quietly gives me that appraising look.

"Restaurants can fail for any number of reasons," he says. "Jay's restaurant closing doesn't mean yours would too. Unfortunately, the business isn't always skill. The right venue, the right kind of cuisine can take off while others that were better fail. And I understand how I must come off to you—poor heir to an empire. Poor prince who doesn't know if he wants the throne. Believe me, I know. I see it. But at least I know what I want and I'm honest about it."

"What do you want?" I ask. I lean forward toward his certainty.

He stares at the horizon beyond me. "I want time. I want to know that when I walk down a path, it's because I chose to put my foot on it. But my dad wants me to decide now, because he wants to convert the upstairs into a communal dining space and strike while the iron is hot. Because restaurants are about timing and I do understand that. But I'm not ready. Not yet. Yet if I hesitate, time could decide for me. I've thought about it since my freshman year ended. It was what I was thinking about when we ran into each other in Publix."

He refocuses on me. "But what do you want? Really want?"

"I just want . . ." I trail off.

What do I want? I want the restaurant still. Even after everything that happened, even after getting my heart broken, even after seeing my parents struggle, I never stopped wanting it. I pushed it down and away, but it never disappeared. Not fully. I still cooked. I still watched YouTube tutorials, still experimented in the kitchen, still consumed endless documentaries and articles about the chefs who did make it. But I also haven't tried to pursue it. Because my mom would be so disappointed. Because it would be a slap in the face to everything they worked so hard to avoid. Because although I'm not enthused with going to Valencia and becoming a nurse, it's real and it's stable.

"I want things to be safe," I say.

"That's all?" he says. "That's what makes you feel alive?" He doesn't look like he believes me for a second. Like he knows there's more I'm not saying. And I wonder if I really am that transparent.

"There's nothing wrong with that. I want to stay where I am and that's okay. I want to stay on dry land. I don't even swim!"

Eugene's teal eyes drift from corner to corner. "You don't know how to swim?"

That . . . that's what we're going to talk about? He raises his eyebrows and lowers the tension between us.

"I know how to swim," I sigh. "But I don't go into the ocean. There's current and it's just . . . it's too unpredictable."

I close my eyes for a long blink. I really am eighteen going on eighty. This was one of the things Paul would mention—that I wasn't fun anymore. I'm not sure I was ever fun to begin with, not by the time he met me. I'd resolved to be a different person in high school, to not take the risks that would get me hurt like I did with Kyle or Jay.

Eugene purses his lips. "So between cooking for me and getting in the water right now, you would choose . . ."

"How are those my choices?" I say.

He stares at me.

"Swimming, I guess."

I can't believe this is what we're debating.

"Well, I happen to have lifeguard certification and it's pretty warm out," he says.

I knit my eyebrows, trying to figure out his meaning. Before I can say a word though, he takes off and dives, yes, dives, into the ocean. I'm left standing midgesture as his feet disappear under.

WTF.

I stare at the surface where he went in. One second goes by. Two. My breath catches. What the hell? Where is he? Did he hit his head? Is he unconscious? Has he been caught by a riptide? It's not hurricane season really, but it's possible. How do I unlock his truck and call 911? Do I have the strength to haul him into shore? I've seen people under stress pull trucks and things with their teeth, but maybe those video clips were fake? I don't know.

Eugene breaks the surface, and relief courses through me. He laughs—because of course he does.

"You're killing me," I say.

"Seems like you're fine. You're still standing there looking cute," he says.

I smile, despite myself. Despite the fact that I was trying to figure out how to save him a moment ago, and that I kind of want to strangle him for a few different reasons. I don't know how he's managed to take my mind off everything, but suddenly all that matters is the two of us calling to each other over the tide.

"The water feels great," he says. "What would it take to get you in with me?"

"A miracle!"

He laughs. "I don't think I have any of those. How about bribery? You join me for a swim and I take you to dinner this weekend?"

Oh. Oh no. Bribery is so very effective on me. I worry my bottom lip considering it. To get in the water, I'd have to leave my comfort zone, and that keeps me in place.

"I know you're thinking about it," Eugene says. "Saturday night. It's not inventive, but we could do L&Js. You said you've never been, and chicken for staff meal doesn't count. We could do the tasting menu and Collins will hook us up. He owes me."

Whoa, wait. The tasting menu at Lantern & Jacks? How badly does he want me to get into the ocean? And why?

My muscles itch to comply. The comfort zone claws at me and asks if I'm really willing to risk it all for fine dining. But yes, yes I am.

And I'm also so very tired of being . . . me. Of this obsession with staying safe. Of pushing away what I want.

I step in ankle deep. "How far in do I have to go?"

"Farther than that," he yells. "Far enough to show me you can swim, because I'm starting to doubt it."

He's treading water some yards out. I don't like to be where my feet can't touch the bottom, which means I don't go in far at all. But I also don't go to fine-dining places, either. It's one thing to read about and see the food. It's another entirely to taste and smell it.

I take off my cover-up and he whistles.

"Did you just whistle at me?" I ask, tossing my cover-up onto dry sand.

"Me? No. I don't know how to whistle. But when I find the guy who did . . ."

I laugh my weird deep chuckle. I've always felt self-conscious about my body, and Paul fed into it with his skinny burrito suggestions. But Eugene looking at me feels so different. Like he's admiring me instead of criticizing.

With my confidence temporarily boosted, I get into the water. I walk in until I'm about to my waist. He likes me. Really likes me, and that draws me in.

I go to where the water is at my top. He makes me feel like I can do things. As if dreams are possible. Like even if I go in over my head, I'll be okay.

The comfort zone crumbles around me, and I say screw it and start swimming.

I'm not great. Let's not kid ourselves. I'm serviceable and maybe won't drown.

By the time I reach him, I'm a little winded. He's all smiles though.

"So you *can* swim," he says. "Or whatever that was."

My mouth opens in the shape of an outraged doughnut. I take my hand and hit the surface, splashing him.

I'm still in shock. I haven't behaved this way since . . . probably seventh grade. Before the bonfire and bistro. Before I found it easier to hide in Paul's shadow than to risk being me.

Eugene runs a hand down his face, wiping water droplets off his nose. "Oh, really," he says.

I yelp because he comes at me. I try to swim toward shore, but I think it's pretty obvious I don't make it. He swims after me and tackles me in the water. A wave crests and we're under for a second before breaking the surface.

We wind up close enough to the shore that he can stand in the water. And I'm wrapped around him and breathing hard. His chest is rising and falling rapidly too, but he barely exerted himself.

"Are you okay?" he asks.

My hair is plastered to my face, but I nod.

He strokes it back. "You're so much more than you think you are," he says. "You can do whatever you want—whatever you truly want. I know it."

And right now, here in the ocean with this boy whose smell makes my stomach flip, on the best date of my life, wrapped around him because he dared me to swim, I feel it.

I lean forward, and this time, I'm the one who kisses him.

CHAPTER FORTY-THREE

CARISSA'S PODCAST NOTES
JUNE 10

I know, I KNOW, I said I would shut down the podcast but . . . I didn't say when. Yes, that's a loophole, but they do know I'm prelaw, so . . .

It would've been easy to delete the podcast if it weren't a hit. The Little Bachelorette is so organically popular. I haven't even promoted it—not really. I accepted a couple of spotlights, but it's mostly been word of mouth. Episode one already has 35,000 downloads and is trending toward 40,000. Better yet, there's not much of a drop to episode two. In fact, the third episode numbers are an uptick from the second. Bringing June on was key. If I brought the boys in, I'm sure I could pass 50,000 downloads.

But the family is right: every hit only increases the possibility of Jaz finding out. Every time the numbers creep up, I'm both thrilled and fearful. But only the one Reddit user linked me to the podcast, and I ignored the comment. Hopefully no one else will notice.

The family has agreed to never tell Jaz about any of this.

The full competition is only six weeks long. It's a blip—a summer of love when she should've been seeing other guys anyhow. Who cares how she wound up meeting them. And it's not like the guys will suddenly, suspiciously disappear when this is over. Justin Michael has said he'll remain friends with her regardless of whom she chooses. And Aaron said he'll keep in touch. The only wild card is Eugene, and he's been that way from the start. Unfortunately, it looks like he's the one she truly likes. I worry about him, and to some extent Emily, going rogue and telling her about the competition. And there are times, when they express doubt, that I wonder if we've done the right thing, but she's so happy that it's hard to say this was wrong.

And, okay, yeah, there's something in it for me, too. I've wanted a new challenge, and Jaz is changing for the better. So I don't know—is that okay? Do the ends justify the means?

I swear I will shut this down soon, but before I do, I think I'll invite Aaron onto the podcast. People are clamoring to hear from the boys. And I'm the closest with him. Plus, he's the most entertaining. He's also a big fan of my other podcast, and we message a lot about it. He'll know the style and flow I'm looking for and he tells the best stories. The listeners will fall for him just like Jaz should've.

CHAPTER FORTY-FOUR

When Eugene starts the truck, I'm shocked to see it's already five thirty p.m. The day flew by in a blur of swimming, amazing food, and even better kisses.

He unlocks the glove compartment while I wipe sand off my feet. When I climb into the passenger seat, I smile at Eugene, but he's wearing a troubled expression. The whole day since we swam has been smiles and laughter, so this is an icy shift I feel across my back. He's upset with me. He doesn't have to say a word. It's the same way I can tell someone's tone is off via text. Even the weather seems to have changed, with clouds rolling in.

"You, um, have some messages," Eugene says. He hands me my phone. "I didn't mean to look. I thought I'd grabbed my own phone."

Immediately, I think it's Emily and feel awful that I locked my phone in the truck. She probably needs to talk. Her family therapy session was today and she was going to tell her parents *everything* she's feeling.

I swipe my screen and I have six notification previews. But, they're not from Emily—they're all from Paul. Five are "remember this" pictures, as he continues to send me a virtual scrapbook. The last one is him saying he can pick me up from work tomorrow, which we never discussed. And he's still saved in my phone as ♥ Paul ♥ because I am the slowest donkey in Donkeyville.

"He's . . . Paul is . . . it's complicated," I say.

Eugene nods and begins to drive. "You're dating him?"

I turn my phone over and over again in my hands, trying to figure out what to say. The truth is probably the right answer. One I should've told him a while ago, maybe after our first kiss. Probably before.

"No," I say. "He . . . well, I was. But he wanted to take a break this summer and see other people. We were together for all of high school and he was the only boy I'd ever dated. And up until very recently, he was the only guy I'd kissed. We were supposed be apart before deciding whether to move in together before college and . . . I don't know."

Eugene is silent for a while and it's awful. The day is slipping away from me and all I want to do is claw it back. And it's all because of the limbo with Paul. The one I accepted, leaving August 1 hanging over us because I was too scared to lose him. Too scared to lose what little I had. Maybe I'm the one who needed the safety net.

"I should've told you. I'm really sorry," I say.

"So, you're thinking about going back to him once the summer ends?" Eugene asks. He said it casually, but his jaw is locked.

I shake my head. "That's what he had in mind—a break until August where he could do whatever, and I guess whomever, he wanted. And I was ready to go along with it even though my friends and family told me I should move on. I just . . . I guess I didn't think I deserved better. And then I met you. . . ."

I take a deep breath. It's been so long since I've put myself out there, but at this point what do I have to lose? If I don't take the chance, he'll be gone. I can tell. So I say what's in my heart.

"I've never felt this way," I say.

A small smile crosses Eugene's lips.

I exhale, relief coursing through me.

As we pull onto I-4, the tension in the cab clears. He rests his hand on mine and it feels like a lifeline.

"I've never felt this way either," he finally says. "I get why it would be hard for you to just end things with him, even if it wasn't great. I've never dated someone for that long, but my parents say a partner becomes a part of you after a while."

I nod, eagerly. "It's exactly that. It's hard having years tangled up with someone, and honestly, the most difficult thing has been letting go of the future, of all the plans we made. He's a part of me, but I'm not sure he fits anymore. It's like my eyes have been opened to the spots that warped over time."

The truth of my own words hits hard. I felt it at lunch with Paul. I've thought it since I had a better time at my graduation party without him—that he doesn't really fit together with me anymore. But it was too difficult to admit it.

"I understand," Eugene says. "Really."

"I'm sorry I lied to you."

His brow wrinkles. "You didn't lie."

I shake my head. "I did. I should've been upfront about the situation with Paul. I didn't tell you the whole truth and that's the same as lying. Maybe worse because I knew I was keeping you in the dark."

Eugene looks to the side even though we're going straight. Something about it is off. But I don't know what.

The atmosphere in the cabin shifts, and his hand returns to the wheel. My lifeline is gone and my stomach drops. I wait for him to talk again, to say something, but nothing comes. And I don't know how to fix this, because I don't know what I said.

He doesn't say a word, but somehow as we drive away, I know we'll never have another day at the beach again.

CHAPTER FORTY-FIVE

Well, it's official: I'm a web stalker. I've looked up Eugene's socials so many times that he's the first suggestion when I click the search bar. I should have my mail forwarded to his Instagram, since I live there now.

I messaged him Tuesday morning thanking him for the beach day, and although I stared at my phone, I got nothing back. Then I playfully texted after minigolfing with Aaron on Wednesday (I'd suggested mini-golf certain I'd be better at it than disc golf and he still kicked my ass), and nothing. I keep checking my phone, trying to will him to message me, but it hasn't worked. I've started hearing phantom dings when there isn't a sound.

I guess he can't get past me being dishonest. At some point I'll have to accept that. But it feels like I opened up again only to have the response be: Not you, Jasmine. Never you.

In truth, I'm really not in the mood to go to the Orlando Museum of Art right now, but I pull into the parking lot anyhow. I promised Justin Michael I'd meet him and I won't stand him up during a couple's painting night. Plus, it'll be nice to spend time with him. Maybe it'll make me forget about Eugene.

I smooth my black dress as I get out of the Rolla. Justin's waiting by the entrance because he's punctual like me. His long legs are out in front of him as he leans against the wall. When our eyes meet, he stands up straight and smiles. And seeing him does make me feel better. I was so wrapped up in Eugene that I forgot about the instant comfort of being with Justin. How I can be myself, not some girl who has to break out of her comfort zone every thirty seconds. I'm good enough as is with my old friend.

"Candy," he says. "Right on time."

I smile and he picks me up in a hug. I sigh contentedly. I've gotten used to his new smell of aftershave and mint, although I miss the newsprint.

"You look great," he says.

I comb my fingers through my hair. I let Cari use the diffuser thing on me today.

"You're looking good too," I say.

Justin raises his chin and adjusts the collar of his button-down like a model. I laugh.

"Ready to do this?" he asks.

"Ready to watch you paint? Yes, I am," I say.

Justin was always more of an artist than me. He and June would doodle elaborately. I liked to draw, but I have no style of my own. I'm a good copier, so I might be okay at paint-by-number or whatever this is tonight.

We walk into the entryway of the museum and follow the signs to the art night. We find the right classroom and pause in the doorway. We are the youngest people here by about four decades. I can't help it, I start laughing. Justin tries to maintain a straight face but ends up laughing with me. It's like we walked into a nursing home. But we're used to having a world of two, so we make our way through the elderly.

The instructor is a smooth sixty and gives us a look. She clearly has no idea why we're here. Neither do I, but we put on our smocks and take our seats.

"Welcome to art night at the museum," she says. "This is a paint and sip, but I think we have a couple of painters here who are a bit too young for the sip part."

The elderly stare at us and break into chuckles. Heat hits my face as I blush and shrink in my seat.

Justin leans into me and whispers, "Do I know how to show a girl a good time or what?"

I laugh and the instructor gives us another side-eye. I clear my throat and give her my most innocent face.

"Well, then, tonight we'll be continuing our cubism series with a look at Jacob Lawrence's work. Are any of you familiar with Lawrence?"

The room is silent until Justin raises a finger. Of course he knows.

"He was a Harlem Renaissance painter. Famous for his migration series," Justin says.

I glance over at him. He's *such* a nerd.

The instructor lights up, visibly impressed. "Very good! Jacob Lawrence is arguably the most famous Black American painter of the nineteen hundreds."

She moves to the center of the room and unveils a painting. As she drones on about the art and the life of the artist, I watch Justin listening with rapt attention. He always loved to learn. No one teased him in middle school, though, because he's a boy, good at basketball, and so likable. As his popularity grew, people wondered why he hung out with me. *I* wondered why he still hung out with me.

"So tonight," the instructor says, "let's create portraits with the abstracted treatment Lawrence shows here. But instead of self-portraits, I want you to paint a likeness of your partner."

You're kidding, lady. Where's the *Starry Night* paint-by-number?

I look around and maybe two other people seem skeptical. I glance at Justin, who smiles like he's completely into this.

"Let's do this," he says. He angles his chair across from me.

"You know I don't have any . . . what's the word," I say. I tap my chin. "Ah, yes, 'talent.' Fresh out of talent."

He raises his eyebrows. "That's not true. I've seen you draw."

"I can copy," I say.

"That's a talent. This is just adding paint after drawing," he says.

I shake my head.

"All right, then you can model for me instead." He squints and frames me with his fingers, and yeah, okay, this is worse.

I make a face at him.

"There's my muse," he says.

I full-body sigh, but my shoulders shake as I silently laugh. "Fine."

I grab a pencil to sketch and he smiles.

"You don't have to pose or paint," he says. "I was only kidding. If you don't want to do a portrait, you can just keep me company. I'm going to paint what I remember, anyhow."

"I'm just glad it wasn't nude night," I mutter.

Justin laughs so hard, he spills his water. "Now *that* would've been a date."

I laugh too as I start my sketch. It's not going to be good, but at least it's supposed to be abstract.

"I mean, if you want to disrobe, I won't stop you. . . ." Justin peers around his canvas and waggles his eyebrows at me. I flick some water at him.

"Stop interrupting the genius at work," I say. I sit importantly behind my canvas as he laughs again.

After a while, the instructor walks around, probably just to make people feel self-conscious. She, of course, takes time to admire whatever Justin is working on.

Teacher's pet.

He won't let me see his painting until he's done. I've asked, like, a dozen times.

The instructor comes behind me and is less than impressed by my offering. I get some kind of "hmm" sound and that's it before she moves on.

Still, as I paint over my sketch, it's not bad. It's not going to be acquired by this museum, but I followed the guidelines well enough. I might've done a lot better if I were allowed to have the wine the adults are guzzling instead of a bottled water. Plus, I keep wondering what Justin is working so hard on. It's not like him to keep things from me.

After another hour, time is up and we put our paint-brushes down and clean our hands. We return to our seats and untie our aprons. I peer over at Justin, who is being unusually cagey.

"I still can't see the masterpiece?" I say.

"You can," he says. "But let's turn them on the count of three. One . . . two . . . three."

"Ta-da," I say.

I turn my canvas so he can see my mediocre attempt, including the triangle for his nose, but I'm struck by his. It's me. It's abstract but it's me when I was fourteen. I'm standing by the weeping willow tree in his backyard. The tree looks sad, its branches limp like it's actually weeping. Blood drips from the "C + S" carved in it. And I know the exact feeling of his art because it tore me apart too, when he had to move.

Justin is watching me, but when my eyes meet his, he looks away.

"I remember that day," I say.

He nods. "That's why I didn't need you to pose. I'll never forget that."

Emotions flood through me. It's sad, of course, but also filled with warm memories. And he's just so talented.

I smile. "I love it."

He smiles too, relieved, I think. "I'm glad. You can have it."

"Really?" I say.

"Of course."

"You're such a good friend," I say.

He stares at me for a second. But what I said is true. I missed him as a friend. I don't feel the kind of way about him as I do with Eugene, but I'm so happy and content to be near him again.

"I'm glad I found a way back into your life, Candy," he says.

"Me too," I say. I lean against his arm. "Come on, Stardust. I know a place we can actually be served drinks."

"Boba?" he says.

"Exactly. On me."

We leave our "art" to dry overnight and walk out of the museum. It was fun—a lot more than I thought it would be—and it was good to spend time with Justin. But I still check my phone once I'm in my car.

No new messages.

I sigh and start the Rolla.

CHAPTER FORTY-SIX

THE LITTLE BACHELORETTE PODCAST EXCERPT
S1, EP 4—JUNE 15

Anonyma: Hey, and welcome back to *The Little Bachelorette* podcast. I'm your host, Anonyma.

We are now officially at the midpoint of *The Little Bachelorette* contest!

For those just joining us, it's hard to believe this all started a few weeks ago with my family's idea of finding three boys to compete for my little sister's heart.

So much has changed. Ariel has been on some great dates and truly is coming into her own. Through getting to know the bachelors, she seems to be understanding how she should be treated and what she wants. She may even be falling for one or more of the boys.

As the competition is now halfway over, I have a special treat for you all. For the first time ever, we're going to hear from one of the contestants himself! Stay tuned to find out which bachelor will be joining us.

First, let me recap this important week of the competition. Ariel has now been on third dates with each of the boys. This week she went to an art museum night with The Boy Next Door, minigolfing in the evening with The Pro, and she had a day at the beach with The Cook.

RSP, our uninvited fourth bachelor, showed up at her work with takeout, but she turned down his offer to spend time together. Instead, she went home with me—something she never would've done before the competition.

I asked if she's still thinking about going back to him in August, since it's only a month and a half away, and she denied it. She was uncharacteristically quiet, though.

I have to say the downside to this competition has been having less time as a family. She hasn't confided in me much since between the boys, her work, and her friends, she's been so busy.

But, here with much more knowledge about Ariel's whereabouts these days is none other than The Pro. Welcome, Bachelor Number Two.

CHAPTER FORTY-SEVEN

It's Father's Day, and I'm trying to keep a smile on my face. As we do every Father's Day, Mom and I made Dad's favorite breakfast: sunny-side-up eggs and tocino—it's a Filipino sweet bacon. We served it with Cuban coffee, which was a habit Paul's family introduced. My dad used to prefer Grandma Yap's traditional tsokolate.

We had breakfast together and I forced down some food, but really, I haven't been hungry. I didn't even care when Davey stole half my tocino.

I've had a lot on my mind—Eugene, mostly. I messaged him one more time and now it's undeniable: he's ghosting me.

I kept trying to rationalize his silence—that he works full-time in a demanding kitchen, that we communicate differently, etc. But after the paint and sip, I knew in my heart something was wrong. And I know I'm going to sound like a megastalker, but on Friday I was so worried, I drove by the parking garage near Lantern & Jacks to check if his truck was there—i.e., if he was still alive. I saw it and drove off.

For everything people say about Paul, he never did anything like this to me. Never just dropped off the face of the earth without another word. He never left me worrying and wondering without an explanation. I know it was wrong to keep Paul a secret, but Eugene could've just told me he didn't want to talk to me anymore. This is just . . . heartless.

Needless to say, I didn't have dinner with him at Lantern & Jacks last night. I tried to not let it get me down. But it really hurt. Maybe he took another girl instead. Maybe that girl who was flirting with him at Speedway.

But my week wasn't all bad. Paul showed up at my work on Tuesday with my favorite soup. It's from a Vietnamese restaurant located all the way across Orlando. And just the smell of the broth lifted my spirits.

"Thank you," I said, walking out of Berry Plum. He brought it in at closing and waited around for me to be done.

"Anytime," Paul said. "Can you maybe hang out for a little while?"

I shook my head. "I can't."

"Oh," he said. "I thought maybe we'd eat together."

"You don't like Vietnamese," I said.

He hated the soup and used to complain that it stunk up the car if I brought home leftovers.

"I know," he said. "But I could get something else and we could have dinner at my house. My parents took Gloria on their friend's yacht. I'm all alone."

My heart wrenched because I knew how he hated being alone in that huge house. "I . . . I can't. Cari is on her way to get me. She'll be here any minute. . . ."

"It's okay," he said. He stood with his hands in his pockets.

"Thank you again for the soup, though," I said. "It was a really nice surprise."

"It's nothing," he said.

"It's not nothing," I put my hand on his shoulder.

He glanced at it and then into my eyes. "I guess I've been trying to remind you of our good times—that we had them at least. And we could again. It'd be different, Jaz. I know what it's like to lose you now."

He reached out and stroked my cheek. My eyes drifted closed like they used to.

"I hope you think about it," he murmured. "Fifty-one days left."

He looked past me as Cari pulled up in the Rolla, then he kissed me on the forehead and got into his car. I crashed into the passenger seat, thoroughly conflicted, and Cari took me home.

I know everything that happened between us was bad, but I can't shake that Paul is really trying now. And the soup was amazing. It warmed and comforted me in a way that only good food can.

We still have forty-seven days left until August 1, but maybe I should end this experiment and just be with Paul. Maybe we do belong together, like he says. I've changed, but he has too, and maybe we'll fit together again.

Only, why does the thought make me sad?

I managed to smile through Dad opening his present from us. It was a group gift. Mom, Cari, Davey, and I chipped in and bought him a tablet specifically designed for editing photos. It'll keep him busy for the rest of the day, maybe the year.

After that I mindlessly helped clean up after breakfast, then retreated to my room. Someone has to stare at my phone. Might as well be me.

"Hey, Jaz," Cari says, knocking on my half-open door.

I shake off my thoughts and force myself to smile as I lie on my bed. "Hey, Cari."

"You look . . ." That worry line appears by her eyebrows. "Mom wants me to run over to Qi Dragon. I guess some family is coming over in a few."

"Oh," I say. I don't want to have to fake being okay in front of more people, but I don't have much of a choice. It's Sunday—family day, and Father's Day.

"I feel like I haven't seen you all summer," she says. "Would you come and keep me company?"

I bounce off my mattress with as much speed as I've shown all week, eager to spend some time alone with Cari as well as avoid my other relatives for a while.

"Sure," I say.

We get in the car and we're barely out of the neighborhood before she lowers the music. I should've known something was up when she put on country. My siblings hate country.

"So, tell me what's going on. You're not yourself," she says. "You haven't been in a few days."

"Boy drama," I say. I'm as weary as I sound.

I wish it were something meta or more globally important than waiting by the phone, but it's as complicated and as simple as a broken heart.

"Paul?" she asks without looking at me.

"No. It's . . ." I sigh. I guess admitting to being ghosted is a new layer of humiliation in my life. "Eugene cut off contact."

"What? Why? I thought you guys had a great date. You were beaming when you got back from the beach. You even watched some of *Bachelor in Paradise* with me."

She's right. I did. I got bitten so hard by the romance bug that I was willing to watch a fake show to absorb more of that feeling.

I shake my head. "I wasn't honest with him and now he hates me."

"I really doubt that. . . ."

"I didn't tell him about the Paul situation and I should've. I lied, maybe not by saying anything false, but definitely through not telling him the whole truth. And that's just as bad."

The worry line hasn't left her brow, and Cari is frowning. She almost never frowns.

I sigh. "So it's all my fault and I can't do anything to change it."

"Have you messaged him?" she asks. I give her a look of disdain and she startles. "Okay, that wasn't a good question. So he just cut off contact? Oh, Jaz, why didn't you say anything earlier this week?"

I shrug. "I don't know. By the time I'd figured out he was ghosting me, it was after art night. Then Friday I worked all day. Saturday you were prepping for your show or whatever, and I was at the shelter most of the day anyhow. It wouldn't have mattered, though. There's nothing you could've done. He probably met someone else."

Cari is a good driver so she normally keeps her eyes on the road, but her head swivels in my direction. She purses her lips and nods.

We're headed across town. Qi Dragon isn't far from the Vietnamese restaurant where Paul picked up my soup. It's a good twenty minutes away.

We're silent for a while as Cari turns the music back to normal volume. Eventually, I make it lower.

"The reason I can't let this go is because he doesn't seem like the kind of person who'd ghost. When I explained everything on the way home on Monday, he seemed okay. It feels like I'm missing something and it's killing me. Maybe he just never really liked me."

Cari shakes her head. "No, that's not it. He likes you—really likes you. Maybe he just needs time to think about everything. He's probably confused and gathering his thoughts."

She's trying hard to cheer me up. She wants to believe everything is a love story like on *The Bachelor*. But not everyone has a happily ever after.

I sigh. "I didn't think I could get rejected twice in a summer, but ha ha. Joke's on me"

"Jaz, I . . . I'm really, really sorry," she says. "I never wanted anything like this to happen."

I shake my head. "You don't have anything to be sorry about. I'm the jerk who wasn't honest."

She pulls the car over, but we're not to Qi Dragon yet.

"What's going on? Why did we stop?" I say.

She looks at me, but her eyes are behind black sunglasses so I can't read her. She parts her lips a couple of times and I wait, but no words come out. Cari looks away then back at me.

"You have a good heart—" she says.

"You're the same," I interrupt.

She shakes her head.

"We have the same heart," I say. I take her hand in mine.

"I didn't want to . . . if he can't see how great you are, then it's his loss," she says.

And it means a lot. Although she's chosen to be single, my sister has had an endless number of suitors, yet she sees value in me. Even when I can't see it myself.

"Want to go to that playground for a while?" she says.

I glance through my window and there's a kiddie park. It's tempting. It's somehow not a million degrees, and playing around seems worlds better than being asked about my love life by my well-meaning but overbearing family. The three boys I've been hanging out with are endlessly fascinating to my cousins. I have no idea why.

"Don't we have to go to the bakery?" I say.

Cari shrugs. "We'll tell them there was a long line. And you know people will bring pastries over anyhow."

Unlike me, Cari can lie and think on her feet. It's impressive.

"When was the last time you were on a swing?" she asks.

"I don't know. When I was thirteen maybe. Probably Justin Michael's tire swing—so fourteen."

"I think it's time, then." She shuts the car off. "You can't be sad on a swing. It's science."

I arch an eyebrow at her sincerity. "So glad you're prelaw not premed."

We get out of the car and make our way to the swings. I sit on the rubber seat and Carissa jumps onto the one next to me. Because of course she just dives in.

Old memories come rushing back as the chains rattle. Mom used to bring us to playgrounds all the time. Davey would be in her arms, but Cari and I would play for hours. Before I met June, before I really got to know Justin Michael, Cari was my first best friend.

I reach over and take her hand. I'm so glad I have my sister. We are different, that's for sure, but I love her.

We start swinging low together. Then we drop hands and swing on our own. Oddly enough, she's right. The more I swing, the farther away everything feels—the ground of course, but also everything weighing down my mind.

I look at Cari, her long curls waving behind her, a carefree smile on her face. She's always wanted the best for me. But I somehow fell into believing I deserve less than her. Yes, she's good at nearly everything, but that doesn't mean I'm good at nothing.

I push higher. If she can do this, I can try.

With a few more leg pumps, I'm at the end of my comfort zone. As much as I broke through it with Eugene, his ghosting me made me retreat, hard. I even started looking at apartments for August. Because I put myself out there and got burned yet again.

We swing a little higher and my stomach swoops. I put my legs out to slow down, to stop. But Cari isn't stopping. In fact, she's leaning back more. And just as I'm ready to accept that I can't be like her, I try.

I pump my legs and grip the chains through the spike of fear, and something happens: nothing. Nothing happens. I don't fall. I don't get hurt. I may not be as carefree as Cari, but I can do things too.

I keep swinging, holding on tight, until it feels like we're flying together.

CHAPTER FORTY-EIGHT

NEWS CHANNEL 2
JUNE 18

"Good afternoon, this is Felicia Strong with your news at noon. Our top story this hour: The governor has declared a state of emergency for all twenty-six of Florida's Atlantic coast counties projected to be in the impending path of Hurricane Beverly.

"Your News Channel 2 weather team has been monitoring the storm since it formed days ago. As we reported this morning, Beverly was upgraded to a Category 4 hurricane by NOAA, making it the first major storm of this early season.

"The massive hurricane is on track to make landfall in the Caribbean within the next twenty-four hours, bringing with it damaging winds and torrential rains. Current projections have Beverly maintaining strength and striking Florida by Saturday morning.

"While the storm may change paths at any time, meteorologists predict Beverly will directly impact the Central Florida region, bringing high winds and a dangerous storm surge to the Daytona area. Florida coastal residents are urged to make evacuation plans and to heed mandatory zones. The Orlando area has been placed under a hurricane watch, and residents are encouraged to take storm precautions.

"Stay tuned as News Channel 2 will continue to update you with the very latest."

CHAPTER FORTY-NINE

A hurricane watch for Central Florida meant two things for me: 1) a total shift in focus to the storm, and 2) manual labor. So much manual labor as my entire family helped one another prepare for Hurricane Beverly.

In the Ventura/Yap households, the regular storm protocol of checking hurricane shutters, assembling supplies, gassing up chain saws and cars, and storing patio furniture somehow gets paired with a midsummer clean out. I don't know why, but it's a tradition. And lately the cousin generation is put to work while the aunts and uncles supervise from a dining room table or claim to be too weak to lend a hand.

Yeah, it's some BS.

But Aaron helped out on Tuesday at my grandparents' houses, and that was both fun and super embarrassing, as my family could not help themselves. Between Nonna commenting on how I'd "blossomed" (kill me) and my cousins inviting him to my neighborhood hurricane party even though they don't live on my block, I was not looking forward to Justin Michael lending a hand the next day.

But the family is more used to Justin and less starstruck,

so he and I replaced and painted a windowsill at the bookish Venturas' house in peace. Mostly. My cousins still stared over at us every 0.2 seconds and Aunt Kim offered us lemonade no fewer than six times.

As I finally took a glass of lemonade, I immediately thought of the beach with Eugene. In the time since they announced the hurricane watch, I've thought about him a lot—whether he'll be okay, what will happen to L&Js, and whether his mom will come home. But he obviously hasn't thought of me.

It's Friday now, and I've stopped expecting to hear from him. And that has made life a little more bearable. We finished family hurricane prep yesterday and the storm was downgraded to a Category 3 overnight. Orlando, however, was upgraded from a hurricane watch to a hurricane warning. Central Florida will be hit starting tomorrow morning with Daytona taking the brunt of the storm. The hurricane should weaken as it comes this far inland, but it'll still cause a mess.

Most of the stores in Winter Park were cleaned out of canned goods, chips, and bottled water earlier this week. My family has been partially responsible. We now have a swimming pool's worth of bottled water stacked around the house.

As I walk into the kitchen, my home is peaceful even with everyone here. Cari sits at the table having tea. Davey is on his fifth meal of the day, and Dad is reading in the living room. Only my mom looks harried.

"Okay, guys, you know I'll be at the hospital," Mom says.

Ever busy, she's wiping down the counters and putting things away. Technically, she doesn't have to work until tomorrow morning, but she wants to be at the hospital because, in her words, "babies don't care if there's a storm—when it's time to be born, it's time," and women who are nearly due will go to the hospital early, so they'll need extra staff tonight. She said I'll see when I'm a nurse. I tried to ignore the churning in my stomach that the thought provoked.

"I'll try to get home as soon as the storm is over," she says. "But I'm not sure when that'll be. I hope early Sunday. I love you all. Be good for your father and text me if you need anything."

She picks up an overnight bag and kisses all of us before heading out the door. Yes, she actually told us to be good like we're eight years old.

Granted, "good" is relative since the hurricane party is tonight. It's basically a boozy potluck/block party, but a little more apocalyptic. There's an end of the world, invincible feeling to them.

It's a Florida thing.

June and Emily are coming to my street because it's more fun than where they live, and Justin Michael and Aaron will be here too, so it should be a good time.

I'm not really in the mood to cook—I haven't been since Eugene ghosted me, but I need to make dishes to bring to the party. I open the fridge and stare, trying to think of what I can make. Sausage and peppers is the easy answer. We also have a million eggs, so I'll do an asparagus and ham frittata. Plus, we have enough ingredients to make chicken fried rice. I haul out the huge rice cooker and get to work.

While I'm prepping, everyone avoids the kitchen area. I rinse, chop, sauté at my own pace, while listening to music on my phone. And a familiar contentment returns—even if I was reluctant to do it. Loving to cook was never about a boy, although Eugene made it better. But he also made me dive into possibilities I'd shut in my mind, and now I'm just left . . . unmoored.

I remind myself that I can still cook, still make dinners when I become a nurse. And sometimes I can almost convince myself it's enough, but it's not. It feels like settling. The same way it does when I look at the apartment links Paul sends me. He's all for putting down a deposit right away. And now I'm the one dragging my feet. In everything. I haven't even officially accepted the scholarship to Valencia. I've never felt this unwilling to move forward, and there's never been a better time for a hurricane party.

As I finish the three dishes, the vultures descend.

"Go away," I say as I smack a fork out of Davey's hand. He was headed right for the rice as I was moving it from the enormous cast-iron skillet to a catering pan.

"It smells so good though and I'm so hungry," Davey whines.

I put the lid on. "It's not for you. We're bringing this over to the party. Dad, don't even think of cutting into that frittata. I see you."

Dad puts the butter knife aside. "They wouldn't have missed one piece."

Cari stole some sausage and peppers while I was busy with Dad. She stands there with her cheeks full like a very tall, thieving squirrel.

"You guys are helping me clean up," I say, throwing my hands up.

"We'll do all the cleanup . . . for a small plate each," Dad says.

"Gluttons. We're going to be surrounded by food in an hour," I say.

"All the reason they won't miss three small plates," Cari says. She's finally chewed and swallowed.

Note: I hate doing dishes. I'm holding out to give them a hard time.

"Small plates. Emphasis on *small*," I say.

I make them each a plate and myself one too. Everything came out well, but the chicken fried rice is the best.

We finish our food and I look at the oven clock. It's almost time to go outside.

"Can I actually trust you with the food while I change?" I ask.

"I mean, I wouldn't," Davey says. He's trying to peek into the rice again.

"Cari . . . ," I say.

"I got this. Go change." She folds her arms and raises the warning eyebrow at Davey.

"This is an estrogen conspiracy," our brother cries.

"Talk like Cousin Wylan again and we'll tell Mom," Cari says.

Davey shuts his mouth so fast, his teeth click.

I laugh and go to my room. I reach for jeans and a nondescript tank. The same thing I used to always pick. But I put them away. I can wear those tomorrow when we'll be cooped up inside until the storm ends. Tonight is a party.

Before I can think myself out of it, I put on a strapless sundress, leave my hair down, and slip on a matching headband. I dab some lip gloss on my mouth and apply blush and eye shadow from the palette Emily bought me.

"Oh my God, who even is this?" Cari asks from my doorway. I turn for her approval and she smiles. "You look great," she says.

"I'm going to dress better until I feel better," I say. "Fake it until I make it."

I try to smile, but tears prick my eyes. Cari steps forward to offer sympathy, but I wave her away. No use crying over a boy who doesn't like me.

"You're lucky you're a giant; otherwise I'd be raiding your closet," I say.

"You know I'd share. Speaking of sharing . . ." She hands me a mango spiked seltzer she'd hidden behind her back.

"Goddess," I say. I crack it open. "Cheers."

"To us," she says.

"To us," I repeat.

We clink cans and I take a long, fizzy pull.

"Love you," I say.

"Love you too, Jaz," she says.

We drink the seltzers down and hide the cans before we leave the house. Each of the Yap kids carries a tray of food, and for the first time in a while it feels like it's going to be a really good night.

CHAPTER FIFTY

JASMINE'S IPHONE
JUNE 21

PR

Paul

I need to talk to you. Call me as soon as you get this

CHAPTER FIFTY-ONE

By dusk the block party is in full swing. Cars block off both ends of the street, long folding tables laden with food line the sidewalks, and tailgating chairs are strewn around lawns. Kids play two-hand-touch in the street.

Justin arrived early and helped get the potluck set up. He knows so many of our neighbors still that he's been sucked into conversation for most of the night.

I'm grabbing a water from one of the coolers when Aaron arrives with a cake he bought at Publix. I'm still not sure how he makes a T-shirt and shorts look this good, but here we are. He even has muscle indents above his knees. I don't know what to call them let alone how to get them.

"Hey, darlin'," he says.

He leans down and kisses my cheek. There's a part of me that's flattered just to be around him and have him pay attention to me. It would be nice, though, if I could feel the same way about him as I did with Eugene. But my lousy heart won't cooperate. Only Paul comes close and lately . . . it's not that close.

"Where should I put this?" Aaron asks.

"Oh, I think the desserts are over there," I say. "By Cari."

"Okay. Thanks again for the invite," he says.

"It was like half my family who invited you," I laugh.

He grins. "Well, I'll assume you desperately wanted me here but were too shy to ask."

He winks and a smile spreads across my face. He's been friendlier, less guarded since the day at the batting cages. And I just like him. Even if he's a total sore winner at minigolf.

"Let me go put this down," he says. "I'll find ya later."

He takes off in Cari's direction, and once he's by the desserts, they start talking. She's laughing and a gentle smile lights his face.

They're such a beautiful couple.

As soon as the thought enters my mind, I can't shake it. They're so right for each other. They both have the easy confidence of being gorgeous. They're the eldest siblings in their families who take the responsibility seriously. They're ambitious and see their way to success. For him it was baseball, for her it was her "brand," law school, her podcast—anything she puts her mind to, really. Nothing stands in their way. They're both so likable and kind and . . . tall. The way he stares at her, the shy way she smiles back . . . it could be the spiked seltzer but suddenly everything is clear: they belong together. More than he and I ever did.

Thinking back to our "dates," it never seemed like they were really dates. He never even tried to kiss me. At the time I thought he was being a gentleman, but maybe it was a lack of interest. Maybe he only likes me as a friend.

But, he's always asked about Cari. Even when we toured

his stadium, he talked to her and escorted her around. I'd thought he was being polite, but now I realize he was into her.

Maybe he was cozying up to me to get to her this whole time.

I search myself for a reaction. This is the Kyle situation again—where I think a boy likes me but instead he's after Cari—except it feels totally different. There's a prick of jealousy, but it's pointless to be jealous of Cari. And I also have no claim on Aaron. I like and I enjoy his attention, but . . . there's only one boy I want. And ever since the beach, I can't deny that. The same way I can't deny that I really want to be a chef.

I check my phone a last (desperate) time. I have a message! But it's not from Eugene. It's from Paul. My chin drops to my collarbone and I stare at the pavement as Emily's shoes come into focus.

"What's up?" she asks.

"Nada," I say.

I try to shake off the sadness, but I know she caught it. June, Emily, and I have talked at length about Eugene, as I continue to be unable to let it go. Like Cari, they both think he really liked me, but 1) I don't know why they believe that, and 2) it doesn't help.

"How are things at the Underwood residence?" I ask.

She takes a long breath and sighs. "He's going to move back in. He pretty much has, but they're going to ride out the storm together and make it official. They 'heard' me at therapy, though."

"How . . . how do you feel about it?" I ask.

She shrugs. "It's their lives. They're going to do what they want, but they swore they'd continue with therapy. And, I'm out in August, either way." She drinks from her sweet tea. "But . . . I hope they make it work."

"Really?" I ask, raising my eyebrows. This is the calmest I've seen Emily about her parents in years and, frankly, it's freaking me out.

"Yeah, we all deserve to be happy, you know?" She looks me in the eye. "You should text him."

She doesn't have to say who. Lately his name feels like taking a bullet, so she avoids saying "Eugene" aloud.

I want to talk to him more than anything, but I cannot bring myself to send him a fourth text. Quadruple texting friends is fine. Quadruple texting a guy who's made it clear he doesn't want to talk to you is a restraining order.

"I did text him, remember?" I say.

"I know, but maybe he's thinking it's been too long and he can't text you now."

"That's nonsense, but I love you." I throw my arm around her.

"I love you too," Emily says. "Where is Cari hiding the White Claw? June drove me over and I could use a good white girl drink."

I laugh. Spiked seltzer is the unofficial sorority beverage, but it's so tasty. I take her to Cari's stash in one of the coolers. While we're by the tables, I check our catering pans. The chicken fried rice has been a huge hit and it's already gone. The frittata and sausage and peppers are also low; meanwhile, every other dish looks mostly full. I can't help but take some pride in that.

I'm wondering whether I should make more when a familiar boy comes strolling down the street.

And I swear my heart stops.

Like it or not, whatever I think about texting, however brave I am behind a keyboard, he still has an effect on me.

"What is he doing here?" Cari asks. She nearly hisses. Aaron looks confused.

"I don't know," I say.

My pulse pounds as Paul gets closer, probably from the alcohol. But also, I'm kind of happy to see him. He's tried so hard lately—all the messages and attention. He's been consistent when Eugene hasn't been, and maybe I should give things another chance. Really, what am I waiting for?

But I get a bad feeling as Paul approaches. Something's off in the way he's walking. There's a negative aura in the set of his shoulders. It's like the time he got into a fight after a field goal was blocked, and I could tell it was coming. That same energy radiates off him—the way you can feel electric charge in the air before a storm.

"Hey, Jasmine," Paul says.

He eyes Cari and Emily. June and Justin Michael are at the other end of the table. My dad and Davey, who I haven't seen all night, suddenly appear.

"Oh, hey," I say.

"Hello, Yap Family. Well, part of it," he says. His tone is so hostile that I want to step between him and my loved ones.

"You're not welcome here," my dad says. His hands ball in fists at his sides.

"And why's that?" Paul asks. "Because I think I have an idea."

I glance from my family to Paul then back again. Everyone is so tense.

"You know damn well why you're not welcome here," Dad says. "We've always been kind to you, but not anymore. Not after the way you treated my daughter."

In all my life I've never seen my father so . . . aggressive. He's a peace-loving librarian and right now it's hard to recognize him. Davey stands to his left, like he's ready to back up Dad in case this becomes a fistfight. Which is all ridiculous.

"Wait, what's going on?" I say. I put my hands up. "Dad, Paul and I are okay now. If he wants to be here, he can be. There's no reason for all of this."

"You're so sweet," Paul says. "So sweet and naïve, Princess Jasmine. Or I should say, Princess Ariel." He stares at Cari, and I could not possibly be more confused.

"What?" I say. "Are you drunk?"

"No. Sober up, Jaz. Your family and friends have been playing you."

"You're the only player here," June says.

He whips his head toward her. "Hey, Flounder," he snarls.

June closes her mouth.

I must be so much drunker than I thought, because did he just call her Flounder? I giggle, but I'm the only one laughing. It's quiet all around me.

A crowd of neighbors has gathered around the highly unusual sight of my dad willing to physically fight someone.

Paul's hazel eyes are glued to me. I try to figure out what is going on. Flounder. Princess Ariel. What?

"Why are you talking about *The Little Mermaid*?" I ask.

"I'm not. I'm talking about *The Little Bachelorette*," he says. "You."

"Huh? Little . . . what are you talking about?"

"Oh, Jaz, of course you still don't know." He pauses and shakes his head like he's very sorry for me. "How could you know?"

"Know what?" I say.

"Your family set you up. They found three guys to fake date you this summer—a boy next door, who I assume is your old friend Justin Michael over there." He waves his hand in disgust. "A pro sports player. And a cook. They left you in the dark and made a game show out of it. Your cousins, your whole family set you up and they're betting on who you'll choose, with your brother playing bookie. You are supposed to choose one, by the way, to bring to your grandparents' party, and that boy will be the winner. In case you're wondering, I'm known as the Resident Scumbag Player—RSP for short. Isn't that right, Cari? I mean, Anonyma?"

He turns and points to her, the drama probably for the audience.

"She did a whole podcast series about it," Paul says. "You should look it up. It's a big hit. You're famous now, babe."

My brain has trouble absorbing his words and I hate

being called babe, but the one thing that sticks is "RSP." I've heard those initials before, but where? Then I remember. When we were shopping for makeup, June asked me about RSP. I thought I was hearing things. Emily played it off like I was. But June had slipped and used the podcast term for Paul—Cari's nickname for him in her podcast. About fake dating. About *me* fake dating.

A boy next door.

A pro player.

A cook.

Justin Michael. Aaron. Eugene. It was . . . all fake and . . . broadcast for people's entertainment?

The horizon slants and the world spins as I look from guilty family member to friend to apparent contestant. I want them to deny it. I want someone to deny it. But I can read in all their faces it's . . . true. My entire family teamed up to lie to me. To make a fool out of me as if I don't do that well enough on my own.

Paul looks at me and smiles—the one happy face in this crowd.

"All the 'chance' meetups you had this summer, all the dates. They were all set up. All lies," he says. "The boys were playing you to win. Every member of your family lied to you. Even your two friends got in on the action—although I guess Emily had a brief moment of conscience. But . . . it's not like she told you what was really going on. I'm the only truth. I'm the only one who actually cares about you, Jaz. Who's cared for you since we were fourteen. What you and I have is real.

The rest of this . . ." He looks at my family and friends with disgust. "Is a *reality* show."

I lock eyes with Cari. Deny it. Please. Deny it all and I'll believe you.

I wait. Her eyes are glassy, her lips parted.

Words fail to leave my mouth and it's almost like another voice says, "Is it true?" But it was me. I just asked my sister if she set up an entire dating charade.

She looks away. And I know: Everything I experienced this summer was a lie. And everyone I know and love was in on it.

So, I do what any intelligent, grown woman would do: I turn and run away before I start crying in front of everyone.

CHAPTER FIFTY-TWO

DAVEY'S SORRY FAMILY GROUP TEXT
JUNE 21

Cari
Jaz knows about the contest

Uncle Steve
Oh noooo

Cousin Joe
What? How?

Cousin Wylan
Oh shit. Who told her?

Aunt Regina
Language. But, oh shit

Mom
Wait, I thought you all were at the block party. What happened?

Scumbag Paul showed up and told her about
Cari's podcast

Uncle Steve
Oh NO

Aunt Minnie
That boy. You should have gone old country on him, Nonna
Ventura

Nonna
I'm saying. My sweet Jasmine, though

Cousin Teagan
Poor Jaz. How is she?

Dad
She ran off. We've really messed up, fam. I couldn't even
argue with what that boy spewed because it was true. We
crossed the line, we bet on the boys, we all lied to her

(One full minute of total silence.)

Aunt Regina
We got carried away

Uncle Carlos
We lost sight of what was best for her

Cari

It's my fault, guys. I . . . I pushed the idea. I wanted the podcast more than I wanted her to be happy. I didn't shut it down. I should've and I didn't. I loved having the success

Mom

Oh, Cari

Aunt Jay

No. It isn't just your fault. It's all of us. We wanted to do this for Jaz. And, yes, we went overboard, but it came from a good place. And for a while she was happy. That has to count

Cousin Madison

It does, but we still took away her ability to choose this. We thought we knew better

Cousin Wylan

Damn, sis. You're actually right

Aunt Tammy

I feel so bad, y'all. She must feel . . . betrayed

Mom

Has anyone tried to talk to her? I wish I could be there, but I can't leave until the storm passes. I've texted her, but she hasn't replied

Aunt Kim

We can all come by after the storm is over

Cari

I don't know how to say this, but she doesn't want to talk to any of us. We've all tried and she won't answer. Aunt Jay, can you have Eugene text her? He may be the only person she'll talk to. I just don't want her to be alone rn

Aunt Jay

I'll try

CHAPTER FIFTY-THREE

I thought I knew heartbreak earlier this summer when Paul wanted to see other people, but apparently that was just a dress rehearsal, because this, this is the deepest I've ever been hurt. It's hard to breathe. And I have no one to turn to because every single person in my life betrayed me. The thing that I feared the most in the world just happened: I'm truly alone.

And, God, does it suck.

I clutch my pillow as my tears rain onto my blue floral pillowcase. The party is still going outside. There's music, kids playing, and laughter while I'm in my bedroom crying, and somehow that makes everything worse. The earth stopped for me, but not anyone else.

Someone knocks on my door again.

After I ran in here, I locked my door for the first time since I can remember. There have been various knocks with my supposed friends and loved ones trying to talk to me. I don't bother answering. It doesn't matter who it is.

They knock again softer and I ignore that too. Then footsteps move away from my door.

My phone dings yet again and I don't check it. It's someone

trying to explain and there's no point. Paul explained everything. They all lied to me. They thought I was so pathetic that
they set up a whole fake dating contest to . . . what? To get
rid of Paul? So that I wouldn't be such a saddo? Because they
didn't think I could meet boys on my own? Thanks, I guess.

All the things that didn't make sense this summer come
flooding back. The aunties at my party talking about a contest. Crystal and Amberlynn saying "winning" at Publix when
I was with Eugene. Joe and Teagan happening to stop in for
frozen yogurt before Aaron showed up. The family talking
about bets and then seeming odd when they said it was fantasy football. Emily and June insisting I change shirts before
volunteering at the shelter. Justin just happening to come to
the bookstore. Eugene running into me at Publix.

These were orchestrated. They were all playing a game.

My phone chimes one more time and I don't know why,
but I'm compelled to check it. I want to hurl it across the
room. I want to throw it into the sea. But I'm too logical. I've
always been so logical and grounded and yet I was able to be
duped for weeks.

I've downloaded all four episodes of Cari's podcast, but
I haven't hit play yet. I have a whole day tomorrow where I
can relive every moment of this humiliation. I just can't do it
right now.

I have new messages from Mom again, Paul, Emily,
nearly all my family, but there's a text I didn't expect: it's from
Eugene.

And even in my worst moment, I wipe my face like he can

see me and sit up. On my screen are the three unanswered messages I sent and the one from him.

CM

Captain Eugene Crunch

Thank you so much again for the amazing beach day

So I definitely need the recipe for that white bean dip. What's a girl gotta do to get it? Sky diving? Ax juggling? Bull running?

Hey. What are you up to?

I've really wanted to respond to these, but I didn't want to lie to you anymore. You deserve better

I stare at his response and the first feeling is anger. Overwhelming, surging anger. Of course I deserve better. My fingers pound against the glass screen of my phone as I peck out a reply.

I guess lying to me the rest of the time was okay

Gray bubbles appear as he types and types. Every time he pauses and the bubbles disappear, my heart stops like he's not going to reply. Finally, a message comes through. I expect a novel, but I don't get one.

No. It was never okay. But I didn't expect to fall for you

My breath leaves my lungs. I stare at the words—he fell for me. He fell for me the same way I fell for him. Our time together, our words, those feelings, those kisses, all meant something. It wasn't just in my head.

A relieved thrill courses through me. I almost smile, but . . . I shouldn't feel anything because how can I trust his words? They feel real, but everything felt real and none of it was.

The truth is, I can't trust him or my feelings. He's a contestant in a game show. For all I know this is another twist. I doubt it's a coincidence he's messaging me tonight after being MIA this whole time. He knows I learned the truth, which means people are still working behind the scenes.

This is just another cruel ploy.

I close my messages and toss my phone to the other end of the bed. The little spot of hope made everything that much bleaker.

I put my face back in my pillow and cry myself to sleep.

CHAPTER FIFTY-FOUR

When I wake up, rain lashes the house with winds so loud, it's like there's a vacuum cleaner running in my room. It's a maddening, constant whirring sound that never shuts off.

The same thing is going on in my brain.

Beverly is here, but not as a Category 3 hurricane. It was downgraded to a tropical storm as it moved inland. But it's no gentle rain. With winds gusting over fifty miles per hour, we still have to stay inside.

Before last night I would've liked to spend the day with Cari, Davey, and Dad. In past years, with cable and internet out during storms, we've played board games, told ghost stories, and cooked strange meals to pass the time. This year I'm hunkering down in my room alone.

"Jaz?" Cari says from the other side of the door. "Jaz, the bathroom is free if you want to shower."

I do want to shower. I didn't even brush my teeth before I fell asleep last night and I'm gross. I need coffee and some food, too, but I don't want to see or talk to any of them.

I keep replaying last night. How glowing Paul looked when he told me. How guilty my family, friends, and . . .

contestants seemed. How all the neighbors saw. How many people must know me because of the podcast. I've never been so embarrassed in my life. And every time I relive it, it poisons me a little more.

My phone chimes every few minutes. I have messages from just about everyone I know. Texts and voice messages from my family and supposed friends fill my inbox, but I don't answer. Eugene is the only person who hasn't messaged again.

I don't bother to respond to anyone because what is there to say? My family had no faith in me. The boys lied to me and used me. After everything we've been through from elementary school to high school, June didn't have the decency to be honest. And although I guess Emily didn't like the contest, she never told me about it. Everyone was in it for celebrity, or to win, or whatever. My entire fifty-person family went behind my back to orchestrate this whole charade. And the worst offender was Cari. I thought I'd always have my sister in my corner. I was wrong.

I grit my teeth thinking of how she sat in the Rolla listening to me wonder about Eugene on Sunday. She had a chance to tell me about the contest right then as I searched for answers. She didn't. She was probably just gathering more fodder for her podcast. Like when she did my hair and was asking questions about Aaron.

With nothing else to do, and fired up with anger again, I settle in and listen to her show. Paul explained in his texts last night that he overheard two girls talking about how they loved *The Little Bachelorette* podcast. They thought the host was the local girl with the teen *Bachelor* show. He tracked it down and listened to it on Friday.

I put in earbuds although I don't know why. I'm sure my whole family has already heard this. Cari must've been eating up the fame with a spoon—her ambition paying off yet again. I'm sure some of my cousins must be enjoying the limelight too.

My sister's voice plays in my ears and my hands tighten into fists. But I'm surprised she introduces herself as Anonyma instead of Cari. Still, I'm close to shutting it off in disgust as she eagerly explains the contest when she says:

Ariel, who has the biggest heart in the world, has never known her true worth. Our family tries. So do her friends. We tell her how great she is, but I guess we don't feel objective. And boy attention is just a different type of validation. We wanted her to see how many options there are out there. So we tried to come up with something to help show her how she should be treated and valued. And that's why we created *The Little Bachelorette* contest. We hope hope that through the contest she'll not only find someone to love but, more importantly, find herself.

I pause the podcast and stop in front of my mirror. This was all done . . . for me? To help me find myself?

The girl in the mirror's hair is a bird's nest, her eyes are puffy from crying last night, and her lips are chapped. Makeup is smudged all over her face, and it's just wrong.

I shake my head. I couldn't be further away from finding myself.

But is that true? I look a little harder. Not at my hazard-ous reflection, but at myself.

I've changed since Burrito Friday. I can't deny that. Even when I went to lunch with Paul, I could feel how different it was to be around him, and the difference wasn't him—it was me. I was more confident, more sure of myself. And I'd changed in no small part because of Justin Michael, Aaron, and . . . Eugene.

I wince at the name, but getting to know him changed me. He challenged me and he seemed to believe in me—believe I was stronger than I've ever thought. Even if it was all an act, that opened my eyes to a lot of things. When I was with him or Justin or Aaron, I couldn't avoid seeing how much I'd put up with over the years. How I'd shrunk myself instead of grown, and how I've settled for stable in all aspects of my life. How I've believed I was not good enough for the things I really want.

But I hate that it was all a lie—an elaborate one from the people who are supposed to love me the most.

If this was all for me, as my sister claimed, why didn't they tell me? Even if I can accept that they were trying to help, I can't get over how they didn't ask me. How they let me believe it was real. What could justify that? If they wanted me to be on a game show, why not tell me?

I pause and think about the timing. If the contest started with my graduation party, they had to have put it together days or weeks beforehand. That would've been while I was home, cyberstalking Paul, or when they knew about the

Instagram girl but I was in the dark. When they couldn't figure out how to tell me. When all I wanted was to be with him.

If they'd told me their plan then, would I have agreed to do it?

No.

If I'm honest, I can't think of a time where I would've agreed to participate in a dating game.

I want to be angry. I know I deserve to be angry, but yes, if this was their only idea, I can admit they had to keep me out of the loop. But *how* was this their only idea? Whatever happened to boundaries?

With more confusion than hostility, I unlock my door and go into the bathroom to shower. I still don't want to talk to them, but I can't keep wallowing in here.

CHAPTER FIFTY-FIVE

**DAVEY'S JAZ WATCH FAMILY GROUP TEXT
JUNE 22**

Mom
How is everyone holding up in the storm?

Aunt Kim
We're good here. Reading some books. Charlotte is painting. How's Jaz?

Cari
She finally came out to shower

> She went right back into her room after. We're
> thinking about cooking something for lunch.
> Maybe she'll help

Mom
Do not set fire to anything while I'm gone

Aunt Tammy
We're all good here. Did Jaz say anything? I haven't gotten a
text back yet

Aunt Minnie
None of us has. We're fine here

Nonna
Keep us posted on our girl. Poppy and I are riding out the
storm

Dad
Everything is fine here. We're on Jaz Watch and going to
make some lunch

Mom
I mean it. No fires

CHAPTER FIFTY-SIX

I'm pretty sure my family has set fire to something in the kitchen. I guess burning down the house is one way to get me out of my room.

The distinct smell of smoked oil wafts under my door. Gross. They must've also burned toast, which is impressive since . . . it's toast. But I don't take the bait—they can make their own inedible lunch. I stay in my room listening to Cari's full podcast series. Then I listen to it again from the beginning.

I have to hand it to her: she's a great podcaster. I never listened to the ones she did for *The Bachelor*, but I'm sure they're just as good. There's a reason she's number one. She is, in fact, good at everything.

My sister has a great voice and a way of speaking where you want to keep listening to see what she'll say next. She has funny asides and a good way of breaking things down. But it's her interview with Aaron where she really shines. They have instant chemistry and he's almost as charming as she is. It would all be super entertaining if it wasn't about my life.

After listening to the four episodes twice, I'm struck by two things:

1. Just how deeply my family meddled in my life.

2. How much work they put in to do it.

But I still have questions, and it's because of those questions that I finally leave my room. I'm done with accepting things, especially secrets.

I find Cari, my dad, and Davey in the kitchen, waving around dish towels, trying to clear smoke out of the house without opening a window. Our hurricane shutters are down, but the wind can still crack the glass if they unlock any panes. There's a light haze in the air that makes everything fuzzy around the edges. I'm surprised the smoke detectors haven't gone off, but then I see they've removed the batteries.

I sigh, go into the kitchen, and turn on the overhead vent. I get the can I use for grease out of the freezer, pour the smoked olive oil in, and put it back.

"Thanks, Jazzy," Dad says.

It's hard for me to look at any of them. My dad, even my dad, who's always kind, who's always loved me, joyfully deceived me.

"I need to talk to you," I say in Cari's general direction.

"Oh, um, sure, yeah," she says.

She walks with me back to my room. My bedroom is a mess of tissues and dirty laundry, but I don't care. I sit at the desk and leave Cari standing by the door.

"How are—" she begins.

"I don't want to chitchat. I just want answers," I say.

She nods. "Okay."

"When did you come up with the reality show?"

"After Paul told you he wanted to see other people. We just wanted—"

I hold up my hand, cutting her off again. "Where did you find Aaron and Eugene?"

I figure Justin Michael was easy to include, if he actually has an internship with Disney. It would be an elaborate hoax if he didn't since I've seen his employee card, but I wouldn't put it past my family. He keeps apologizing via text and voice messages, but I don't want to hear it now.

"Aaron and I had a Facebook mutual," Cari says. "Justin Michael just wanted a way back into your life. And Aunt Jay found Eugene—I'm not sure how, I think because she knows his dad."

"Why did he ghost me? I'm sure you know."

She looks away. My stomach drops as rage bubbles through my chest. She knew. She let me spin out and obsess and she knew all along why he didn't text me.

"He . . . something you said at the beach had an effect on him—something about lying by omission. Since he couldn't tell you the truth without destroying the whole competition, he decided he couldn't talk to you anymore. He was never a fan of the setup, but he liked that we were trying to help you."

I bark out a dark laugh. Cari frowns.

"He had a lot of reservations after meeting you at the graduation party," she continues. "He wasn't going to be a contestant, but then you really accidentally ran into each other at Publix and he waited for you to text him, but you didn't."

"How nice that something was real," I say.

"Everything you felt when you were with him was real, Jaz. You should give him another chance. He really likes you. You really—"

"I'm good without relationship advice from you," I snap. "You have your shows, but you don't know anything about love, do you?"

She winces. Guilt pricks at me. I never talk to my sister like this, but she deserved that barb. She deserves a lot worse.

"I think he's a good guy," she says quietly.

"I thought you were all good people. Look where it's gotten me."

She opens her mouth but sighs. "I never wanted to hurt you, Jaz. I just . . . I just . . . we just wanted you to be happy."

"Thanks," I say flatly. "Close the door, please."

She does and I spend the rest of the day alone in my room.

CHAPTER FIFTY-SEVEN

The storm passes as all storms do, but I'm left sorting through the wreckage of my family and friends. I'm not as furious as I was yesterday. I'm just . . . empty. And that may be worse.

Most of Orlando lost power, a mobile home park was seriously damaged, and there's severe flooding in some areas, but aside from debris and dangerous heat, Winter Park got off easy.

My mom came back in the morning, so there was another person I had to avoid in my not large house. She's usually a force to be reckoned with, but somehow she left me alone. The rain ending, though, meant family continuing to visit one another—inspecting damage, helping to remove trees, things like that.

I lucked out though. Instead of people coming over, Mom, Dad, and Davey left to check on our grandparents. They said goodbye as I watched a documentary on Chef José Andrés I'd downloaded earlier from Netflix.

Cari and I are now home by ourselves and the doorbell rings. I know she'll answer it, so I stay in my room. A few seconds later, though, there's a knock on my bedroom door.

"Jaz, it's me," Aunt Jay says.

I'm surprised she's here, but I give her my standard answer. "I don't want to talk," I say.

"It's not about that," she says.

And I can't help it—I'm intrigued. I get up from my bed and unlock my door.

"What's it about then?" I ask.

Jay is dressed for the kitchen in chef pants and a tank top. The sleeve of tattoos that my mom absolutely hates—knives and bread and mermaids, things like that—is on full display.

"I was hoping you could give me a hand," Jay says, her blue eyes serious.

I knit my eyebrows. "What?"

"I know you're upset and—" she begins.

I shoot her a look.

"Right," she continues, and clears her throat. "I don't know if you've heard, but they opened the Amway Center to people displaced by the storm. It's going to take a while to get the whole power grid up again and people need somewhere cool and safe to stay."

"Okay. . . ." I'm listening but trying to figure out what she wants. I know it's more than to give me an update on the state of Orlando. And this is probably the most we've talked, just the two of us, since the day at Ventura's Bistro.

"Almost all the restaurants won't open tonight, and trucks can't get through to restock the stores because of powerlines and debris, so some chefs and caterers are going to provide meals. I was hoping you'd want to cook with me."

What? Is she really asking me to cook professionally with her? We haven't cooked together in years.

"I could use another set of hands," she adds.

To say that I'm conflicted is an understatement. Memories war in my brain for supremacy. Laughing with Jay as she hip checked me away from looking in on the cake we made. Her teaching me the ways to pick the best produce at the farmers market. The walk around my neighborhood so it wouldn't look like I was crying. The family parties after the bistro closed where she tried to talk to me but I avoided her. And the day she stopped trying.

"I'd rather not . . . ," I say.

She doesn't react much beyond raising her eyebrows a little. "I have to get to my facility. Your mom wants you and Cari to help at Nonna's if you're not coming with me."

A deep groan rises in my throat and I suppress it. Barely. How did my life become this series of impossible choices? I guess secrets and lies will do that, but still . . . ugh.

I think about saying no to it all, but that would require turning down Jay and going toe to toe with my mother and I've never done that. I don't see it ending well. So it's either help at my grandparents' house with most of my family trying to talk to me or cook with Aunt Jay and Cari where there's so much unsaid.

I make my choice.

"Give me a couple of minutes to get ready," I say.

Jay nods. "I'll be in the car."

I put my hair into a braid, change into a tank and jeans,

and slip on kitchen clogs by the door. They're rubberized shoes that protect from knife drops. Jay gave them to me as a Christmas present one year. Mom couldn't figure out why my aunt bought me "ugly shoes."

Everything still feels so familiar from four years ago, but today will be different. For starters, Cari will be there. I bet she'll figure out a way to be great at cooking, too.

But when I get into the passenger side of Jay's red Jeep Wrangler, it's just the two of us.

"Where's Cari?" I say. "Isn't she coming?"

"Did she suddenly learn how to cook?" Jay says.

I almost laugh and it comes out as more of a snort. "They smoked olive oil yesterday."

Jay shakes her head as she reverses out of the driveway. We drive down the block and palm fronds are scattered across yards. Jay swerves around tree limbs in the street.

"It's not that I don't want her help," Jay says, "Well, I kind of don't. It's going to be hectic enough without having to worry about someone chopping off a finger."

"So why ask me?" I say.

Jay barely shrugs. "You're the only other person in this family who can cook."

I raise my eyebrows. My mom would resent that.

"If you tell Dee or Tammy I said that, I'll deny it," Jay says.

I almost smile again. The truth is, I missed my aunt and the way she just says things. How she never seems to be bothered by rebelling, by being the black sheep.

Jay makes the radio louder—she still listens to old-school hip-hop. I hang on to the handle as she weaves through Winter Park. She's a little reckless but not Emily-level dangerous.

Nearly all the traffic lights are out, and cops are parked in the busier intersections directing traffic. Some streets are closed for live wires or trees down. Everywhere there are crews trying to get power back up or clearing the mess. It's this way after every hurricane.

"I'm glad my facility still has power," Aunt Jay says. "Once everything is ready, we'll transport the food and supplies over. There's nonsense red tape about cooking and serving in Amway itself because of the concessions contracts."

"What?" I say. "It's not like there's a concert or a basketball game."

"I know. But, we're just going around it. The restaurants are setting up in the parking lot as a pop-up, benefit, or tailgate. Surprise, surprise, the chefs couldn't agree on what to call it or how to run it. So everyone is kind of doing their own thing or banding together in groups. Cari is handling the social for me."

"Are you charging?" I ask.

"It's pay what you will. Obviously, there's no charge for anyone in the Amway, and I'm donating all the ingredients. Any money we collect will go to the food bank. They'll need it in the coming days. The storm hits the people hardest who are least able to afford it, you know?"

I nod. Mom and Dad both talk about that. It's easy, living in a place as wealthy as Winter Park, to forget how privileged you are to not worry about where your next meal will come from. My family always wants us to remember.

"I should tell you that Jack Matthews will be cooking with us," Jay says.

I turn in my seat. "What!"

I don't even know how to feel. Am I really going to be cooking in the same kitchen as Chef Matthews? Never, even in my wildest dreams where I have my own successful restaurant, have I thought that was possible. But he's still Eugene's dad and I have a lot of feelings about that.

"Not his son," Jay says as if she can read my mind. "Just Chef. Eugene is setting up at the Amway. If he gets done early, he'll swing by to help us finish and load up."

"Drop me off, please," I say.

"Jaz." Aunt Jay looks over her shoulder at me, giving me a disappointed glance that's as cutting as any Mom has given me. "You're not this person."

Before I can stop myself, I explode.

"You all think you know what I should do, who I should date, what's best for me. What makes you so sure you even know who I am? This is the most you and I have spoken in four years."

"I know we haven't spoken," Jay says. "You wanted your space and I gave it to you. But I've always known you. From the moment you came here as a baby, when you became part of our family, I've known your heart. I know you care. And I know you're not going to go home when you can help dozens, maybe hundreds, of people today. You won't skip it just because a boy might be there. You're stronger than that—you didn't do that in eighth grade, you don't have a reason to do it now. And I'm sure you're still disappointed in me, but you're here. Put it aside. This is something you can do to comfort people who lost their homes, who lost everything. And it's something only you can do. You were the only one I taught because you were drawn to the kitchen and you wanted to learn. And now we need your skill. But . . . if you want me to drop you off, I will. You're not a hostage."

With that, we ride together in silence. There's so much and yet nothing to say.

CHAPTER FIFTY-EIGHT

We walk into my aunt's catering facility, and five people are already hard at work. Aromas of onions and spices and fresh bread fill the air—i.e., it smells amazing. The high-ceilinged building used to be an abandoned factory, but Aunt Jay revitalized the space with help from Uncle Al.

I recognize Chef Matthews immediately, and although I brace to see Eugene, he isn't here. Chef Collins is working with Chef Matthews, and there's a woman and two other dark-haired men in the space, but none is Eugene. I feel relief tinged with disappointment.

"Everyone, this is my niece, Jasmine," Aunt Jay says. "She volunteered to help us today."

All five people look in my direction.

"Nice to see you again, Jasmine," Chef Matthews says. He's butchering a slab of pork. "Do you remember Collins?"

"Yes, Chef," I say. "Nice to see you both."

"Thanks for helping out," Collins says from the stove.

"Come with me, Jaz," Aunt Jay says.

She hands me a chef's coat and I remember this coat. It's the one she got me when she owned Ventura's. She surprised me with it the second Monday I went to the bistro. I never knew what happened to the jacket after the day I ran out. I figured she threw it out, but she kept it this whole time.

I put it on and follow her. Jay stops next to the blond woman.

"This is Annie Holloway," Jay says. "She's the pastry chef at the Encore." Encore is an Orlando staple, famous for its elaborate desserts and after-dinner drinks.

"Hi, Jasmine," Chef Holloway says. She's running the industrial mixer with a huge amount of dough.

I follow Jay over to another stove.

"I think you've met Mario Gonzalez," Jay says. She gently touches him on the shoulder and it's an intimate graze that makes me look at her sideways.

He's braising beef, but he smiles. Like Jay, Mario has his own catering company. I met him at a food and wine festival when Jay used to have her restaurant and I was volunteered by my parents to help carry things.

"Hey, Jasmine," he says. "Glad you were able to come out."

He smiles then winks at my aunt. I give her a "what's going on there" glance that she pretends not to see. Instead, she leads me to another stainless-steel table where a chef is working on prep. He has a baseball cap on and his knife moves across vegetables at a dizzying speed.

"And this is Chris Wang. He's the executive chef at Cadence."

Cadence won best new restaurant in Orlando last year. They specialize in high-end Asian fusion. Like L&Js, I want to eat there. Like L&Js, I don't have the money to go.

He glances at us, nods, and gets back to work.

"So, the plan is simple," Jay says. "We're not doing fancy, haute cuisine today. We decided to go back to our roots and make comfort dishes, because what people need most right now is some comfort. Jack happened to have a hog at his disposal—don't ask. He and Collins are doing a riff on a boucherie—a nod to Collins's Louisiana roots. They're doing everything pork from salad to apps to the main, using the whole hog. Mario is making street tacos. Annie is baking bread and making éclairs and cookies because she's an overachiever."

Chef Holloway flips her off without turning around.

"Chris is making Szechuan chicken and vegetable bao. I'm going to do a four-cheese lasagna and meatballs. It's up to you what you want to make, but it would be nice to have a side dish option."

"Wait, I'm doing a cook?" I say. I point to my own chest like there's someone behind me.

Jay stares at me like I'm new.

"I thought I was helping out," I add.

"You are, but come up with your own dish too," she says. "I didn't bring you here just to be a prep bitch and fetch monkey. Cari could've done that."

"Oh," I say.

But why would she ask me to cook when she told me I don't have what it takes? Is this just guilt? Pity?

"Think about what you want to make while you give Chef Wang a hand," Jay says. "He's doing a million buns because he's also an overachiever."

Chef Wang stops for a second to raise his middle finger and goes back to chopping and stirring.

I wash my hands then walk over to Chef Wang's station. He's busy speeding through dumplings. He has a dozen on a tray already and he just started wrapping them.

"Thanks for helping out," he says. "You've made bao before?"

"A few times with my friend's family," I say.

"Great." He smiles. He's around Jay's age, maybe a couple of years younger. "Dive in."

Concern mounts in my chest. I can't pleat and move as quickly as he can. Those are hands like June's mom. There's muscle memory from having made thousands and thousands of bao in their lifetime. They could do it blindfolded and they'd all be perfect. My track record is not as good or long.

I hold the circle in my palm and spoon in the vegetable mixture. It's not even cooked and it smells amazing. Chef Wang must've made this dough earlier because it's super fresh. I wash the edges with egg wash and I try to get it to be any semblance of the ones on the tray. I finally finish sealing the bao and it's lopsided. I sigh—it's awful.

"You're trying too hard to be something you're not," Chef Wang says.

I look up. It's like he just read the story of my life.

"They don't have to look like mine," he says. "As long as they're closed, they're fine. Here, cup your hand and then pinch the folds quickly. Like this. The less you think about it, the easier it is."

I glance at him skeptically.

"Work," he says, pointing to my hands. Reluctantly, I try again.

"When I was growing up," he murmurs, "my mother and grandmother would tell stories while they made bao in our little kitchen. Everything about where I grew up was small—our apartment, my pullout sofa, my popo. Anyhow, ma and popo would tell me about the monkey king and fox spirits—probably so I'd sit still, but also to pass the time. No one was focused on getting it just right. See? Much better."

I look down and I've done one that's nearly perfect. I put it on the tray next to my abomination.

"Your family is Italian?" he asks.

I have to explain this a lot. "On my mom's side," I say. "My dad's side is Filipino, but I'm Korean."

"That's cool," he says.

I wait for the follow-up question about my heritage or being adopted or if I know my "real" parents, but it doesn't come. I keep working on bao.

"And you want to cook?" he says.

"Oh, no, I . . . I'm just helping Jay. I . . ." I sigh at myself. "I do, but I'm too scared."

He nods. "It's a life."

"It's not even the lifestyle," I say. "I'm not afraid of long nights or having no weekends or holidays off. I'm not afraid of the hot, cramped line, or the egos."

He stops stirring the chicken. "What's the hurdle then?"

"I . . . I don't know if I'm good enough. Actually, I do know. I'm not good enough."

He nods again. "Well, the world needs plenty of mediocre cooks."

I nearly drop my bao. "What?"

He shrugs. "Someone has to work in chain restaurants that have those two-for-twenty-dollars deals. Or diners. They always need short-order cooks. Not being good shouldn't stop you."

"I wouldn't be a cook at a diner," I say, shaking my head.

"Why not? You can't make eggs?"

"I can make eggs—"

"Eventually you'd learn. Scramble isn't hard, just whisk it a lot. And some people even use ketchup so they won't taste your bad eggs—"

"Because I'm better than that!" The words fly out and I stand there with my mouth open.

He stops what he's doing and stares at me. "Oh, so that whole not being good enough thing is kind of bullshit, isn't it?"

He smiles.

I didn't even realize he was baiting me. I am, however, flying through these bao.

"I have a sister who's like you," he says. "Two younger sisters. You can't fool me. Your problem isn't that you don't think you're good enough."

We're silent as he replaces the dough rounds with a new tray. He stacks the dumplings onto a catering cart.

"Then what's my problem?" I ask. I tip forward on my toes in anticipation. I haven't spoken this honestly since I last talked to Eugene.

"Complacency," Chef Wang says. "You want to play it safe. You don't want it enough, and in that case, you shouldn't be a chef, because you won't make it. It's a hard life and requires way more drive than you have and more work than you want to do."

I'm so insulted, I don't know what to do with myself. I make some kind of hassled sound and put down the last bao. I want to throw it at his face.

I walk over to an empty table and stand with my back to him because I'm both furious and thinking that he's right.

He's not right, though. I do have drive and I'm not afraid of work. And maybe I'm the only one who'll ever see that, but I know it.

I grab garlic and start smashing it. After everything that happened from the hurricane party to thirty seconds ago, it feels good to crush the bulbs. There's already cooked rice because Chef Wang was going to make congee. I grab it and an enormous sauté pan and start making garlic fried rice. Sinangag is one of my dad's favorite Filipino dishes. It's as simple as it is delicious.

Once it's done, I add shredded mozzarella. A lot of it. Next I clump the rice, roll it in egg wash, and coat it in sesame and gochugaru-spice-seasoned flour, then panko. Then I deep-fry it.

While it cooks, I chop scallions. Then I whisk soy, oil, eggs, sugar, lemon juice, and some of the fried garlic to make a sauce.

The timer goes off and I pull up the basket and put a dozen rice balls on a grate to cool. When I finish, the other chefs are standing around me. I hadn't even noticed them.

"That's clever," Aunt Jay says. "Nice to combine all the sides of you."

I glance at my aunt. She still gets me. Really gets me.

"Are those sinangag arancini?" Chef Matthews asks, peering over at the plate. "Can I try one?"

"Yes," I say.

I say a silent prayer to every deity that ever existed that they taste good.

We all take one, and I break mine open to cool it down. I take a bite a little too soon since it's still hot, but the flavors are all balanced. It's crispy, salty, savory, and a little spicy from the Korean pepper flakes. It's good. It's really good.

"Oh, there's sauce," I say. I push the bowl forward.

"It doesn't need any. I could eat a dozen of them right out of the fryer," Chef Matthews says. "Impressive."

Impossible. Chef Matthews couldn't have just complimented my cooking.

Chef Wang gives me a smug smile, tipping his baseball cap at me. Ugh. He was still baiting me when he said I had no drive.

With the compliments from the chefs, I feel like I'm invincible. I prep hundreds more like it's nothing.

And I know—there isn't anything in the world I want more than this. And I won't deny it anymore.

CHAPTER FIFTY-NINE

Once we finish prep and load Aunt Jay's van and Chef Gonzalez's truck, we drive over to the Amway. As Jay said, downtown is a mess with street closures and crews working. But it's not far away, and with a few detours, we make it to the enormous parking lot in about twice the time it should take in bad traffic.

I can't obsess over the fact that I'll be seeing Eugene, because I'm put to work unloading the van and getting our station set up under the tailgating tents. I am, in fact, a fetch monkey right now. I barely have a second to glance around, but I don't see him.

With no cooking facilities, everything had to be brought in from chafing dishes to portable wok burners. It's five o'clock when everything is in place.

"Do you know how to use this, kid?" Chef Wang asks me, pointing to the portable wok. It's like a barbeque grill, but with one open space for a single wok.

I shake my head no.

"Here, it's like this," he says.

He walks me through how to adjust the temperature. We're going to wok-fry my rice balls in batches because they don't hold up long in chafing dishes. It was my one misstep—making an item that will get soggy under a lid.

"Thanks," I say.

"You know I was just giving you a hard time before, right?" he says. "This business will kick your ass, and there'll be a ton of people who'll try to put you down. Especially you being you."

"What do you mean—me being me?"

"You're Asian, you're young, and you're female—those are three strikes against you in the kitchen. Take it from a guy who has two of those strikes. But you have talent and you're a quick study. You'll make it . . . if you want it. But you have to want it. Look at what this industry did to your aunt. Her partner stole all the profits and she lost her restaurant, but she picked herself up and now she has a catering business. You have to have a love for it."

I startle, but he walks away, and I stare with my mouth open. No one, not a soul, ever told me Jay's restaurant closed because someone stole money. I just assumed it went belly up because . . . restaurants do. Because she took a risk and she failed. But it wasn't talent, or the industry being hard, not really. It was . . . theft.

I think back to those bills littering her desk. How devastated she was. How I'd never seen her drink alone like that before or since. And the envelope saying "goodbye." I wonder if she'd just found out that day. Right before I came waltzing in, expecting her to teach me.

I don't have long to think about it, though, because the

lines of people are now massive around us and the other tents. There are a dozen news trucks covering the pop-up goodwill event.

Jay's dishes don't require any work, neither do Chef Holloway's or Chef Gonzalez's. They're all pros. Chef Matthews and Chef Collins are cooking things to order and fussing with plates and working with tweezers, because they can't help themselves. Chef Wang has steaming baskets that need to be rotated out. That's my job as well, but his Szechuan chicken is ready to go.

Chef Holloway is collecting money while Jay and Chef Gonzalez are serving. My job is to keep everything stocked and to fry my rice balls when they look low. We start service and I'm glad I'm here. The first people in line are a family who lost their home in the storm. They're from the Sunshine Pines mobile home park that was leveled in the high winds. Every chef greets them as they go down the line and choose what they'd like.

I can't imagine what it would've been like to lose everything in a day. Everything I'd ever had or loved gone except for my family. For me, the hurricane went the other way around.

But . . . that's not true. I didn't lose my family. In the face of people who actually lost everything, I can't say that. My family is still here. They're trying to talk to me. I'm just really hurt and upset with them.

We serve more and more people, most of whom lost power in the storm or lost everything. I've never felt more certain of where I should be. I belong here. This is what I want to do with my life—make good food that provides some comfort. A hot meal that lifts spirits. And I'm going to figure out how to do it, even if I have to take a risk. Even if I may not have the talent. Even if I have to tell my mother.

A reporter comes through and asks to interview us. For some reason, she focuses on me. Probably because I don't want her to at all, but I gather myself and smile for the camera. I am, after all, a reality star . . . of sorts.

"And here is one of the volunteers," Felicia Strong says. "Tell me, what sparked this idea?"

"Well, my aunt wanted to help the people affected by the storm," I say. "Josephina Ventura and the other chefs donated all the food and supplies to give back. The money raised tonight will go to the community's food bank."

"And what are you preparing right now?" Felicia asks.

"It's a Filipino rice ball," I say. I hand her one.

The camera guy zooms in on her plate as she breaks one apart and takes a bite. "Mmm! Amazing. What's the name of your aunt's restaurant?"

"It's a new catering company, actually—Ventura Catering," I say. "You can follow them on Instagram." I remember the plug Cari uses.

"And I will!" She smiles before turning to the camera. "World-class chefs are out here at the Amway serving more than just delicious dishes. They're serving the community."

I look over at my aunt and she mouths "thank you."

And it feels good. Really good.

At nine o'clock, we break down the area and begin to load the vehicles. The table in front of me is the last one to be cleaned up. Any remaining food sits out in case of stragglers.

I've just finished transferring the used wok oil for disposal when someone says, "Are there more rice balls like the ones I saw on TV?"

While putting the cap on, I point without looking. "Yeah, there are a couple in—"

I should've recognized the voice.

I look up and Eugene stands in front of me.

He locks eyes with me. He's wearing something similar to the first time I met him—a black T-shirt and jeans, but he just looks good.

"My dad said I had to try them," he says. "And so did the reporter." He puts two on a plate. The chefs are moving around us, putting things away, but it's hard to notice anyone but him.

"Thanks again for your help, Jasmine," Chef Holloway says. "We raised more than three thousand dollars for the food pantry."

That's an impressive amount considering half the people didn't pay.

"And thanks for the shout-out, Jaz," Jay says. "You didn't have to do that, but we added a bunch of followers tonight after the news segment."

I want to ask her why she never told me the reason her restaurant folded, but maybe she had tried when I was avoiding her. And now, in front of everyone, isn't the time to discuss it.

"No problem," I say.

"Will you take a walk with me?" Eugene asks.

"I—" I hesitate and notice the other chefs, including Jay, trying not to stare.

Note: they're definitely staring.

Yeah, better to take a walk because I have things to say to this boy.

I take off my chef coat and give back it to Jay.

"Thanks for keeping that," I say. I want her to know I remember the green jacket with the embroidered J and how much it meant to me—how much it still means to me.

I look up at her and hope to convey that I'm sorry about what happened to her. That I wish I'd known. She looks back at me a little surprised at first, but her face softens and there's so much love there. And for the first time in four years, it feels like I'm reconnected with my aunt.

Eugene waits for me and I walk with him. It's dark now and the breeze feels incredible. My body is buzzing from service, from working like that. There's an afterglow to surviving a dinner rush I hadn't expected to feel so acutely.

We pass the other pop-up tents breaking down for the night. I love how Orlando has this community. And maybe if I never leave, it'll be okay.

"These are fantastic," Eugene says. Somehow he's eating while we're walking. "I knew you'd cook for me eventually." He tosses out the paper plate in the nearest garbage can.

I stop and stare at him, but he keeps going.

"I want to apologize," he says.

"You should've started with that," I say.

"I know." He stops walking and faces me. "I should've figured out a way to respond to your messages after the beach. It was wrong to ghost you and I'm sorry."

I wait for more, but he's done talking. I blink rapidly. "That's what you're sorry for?"

"Yeah, and if it's any consolation—I missed you, a lot."

His words impact me and they shouldn't. They absolutely shouldn't matter. I'm done with this whole charade. But the corners of my mouth turn up a little—traitors.

"So all the faking and game playing was . . ." I wait for him to fill in the blank.

"What faking or game playing?" he says. "Everything between us was real."

I utter a strangled laugh.

"Yes, I knew your family was trying to set you up with dates, but I really brought desserts to the party. I really caught you when you tripped. I really ran into you at Publix. It was Cari's idea to stop by the shelter, but my family does do monthly donations to charities. We were going to stop because my mom left town, but my dad was on board to give to the shelter. And the rest was just us. Everything from bringing you to my restaurant to racing against you to the beach was all real. We both kept some pretty important details hidden from each other, but don't most people when they're first dating? If you want an apology, though, I'm sorry I knew you were going out with other guys, I guess."

It's . . . the worst apology. Ever. It's so bad, I'm speechless.

He's the one who actually seems annoyed.

"I meant every word I said to you, including Friday when I told you I fell for you," Eugene says. "I don't know how much more real it gets than that."

I stand there shaking my head as every rebuttal leaves me. I had points, I know I did. Good reasons I've been mad at him, Justin Michael, and Aaron for days. But Eugene looks sincere and I believe him when he says he fell for me. What's more is I felt it. That's why I was so devastated when all of a sudden he wouldn't talk to me, when I found out it was all a competition. And that's why I know I can't trust my own judgment.

"You just wanted to win," I say.

He sighs. "You didn't hear me at all, huh? I'm sorry then, Jasmine. I'm sorry for this whole thing."

We turn around and walk back. But my limbs feel leaden, like I want to stay right here with him. I shouldn't feel this. I said what I wanted to say and he apologized. I got what I wanted. There shouldn't be any sadness.

We return to where the pop-up was set up and it's empty. I look for the van or the truck, but I don't see them. Eugene continues through the space.

I pause.

"What's wrong?" Eugene says.

"I'm looking for my aunt. We were right here, weren't we?"

"Oh. She asked me to give you a ride home."

I slap my hands against my jeans, my body not knowing what else to do with this frustration. "You're kidding."

"No," he says. "She's going back to her kitchen then home. You live closer to me than her. And this way you won't have to help them clean up. Come on, I'm over here."

I hesitate. I really do hate washing dishes, but really? More interference? When I'd just started to rebuild good feelings with my aunt?

Still, I follow him to the end of the aisle, because part of me distinctly wants to go with him.

"Right here," Eugene says.

That isn't a truck.

He has his bike.

I'm going to kill my aunt.

"Oh, hell no," I say. I back up a step.

"It's easier to get around on the bike," he says.

I shake my head. "No. No, it is not."

"Your call." He shrugs. He takes two helmets out of the saddlebag and puts his on.

I don't have a lot of options —we both know that. In the aftermath of the storm, there won't be rideshares, and the bus, which disappears in perfect weather, isn't running at all. I'd either have to walk for hours at night or call Cari to come get me, and I'm not exactly on good terms with her. I'm also not speaking to Justin Michael or Aaron, who are not far from here. Or June. Or Emily. And I don't want to go there with Paul.

Wow, my options suck.

I sigh and put on the helmet. Sure. Why not hop aboard the SS *Death Trap*?

"Here, it's a little . . ." Eugene reaches out and adjusts the strap under my chin. "The only thing you need to do is to lean the way I lean when I turn. If you don't, the bike can get unbalanced."

"Oh, okay. I feel much safer now!"

He shakes his head, straddles the bike, and kicks it started. I hate every single thing about this.

"Get on on this side," he says over the roar of the engine.

I throw my leg over the seat and rest my feet behind his. I glue myself to his back and wrap my arms around his chest.

He repositions my arms to link around his stomach.

"I think you'll crack my ribs otherwise," he says.

With that we take off.

My hands are in fists so tight, I'm probably breaking what little nails I have, but his ribs will be fine. I squeeze my eyes shut as my stomach swoops like when I was swinging. However, while I was safe on that children's swing, I'm not safe at all right now. Anything and everything can go wrong.

After a few minutes I decide it's worse to be in the dark, so I open my eyes and the scenery blurs by. I look over his shoulder at the speedometer and Eugene is going the speed limit. A little under, actually. It just seems faster on the bike. I feel a lot more of everything, from the night air to the cars around us. The pavement is immediate, the stars, all of it.

A little more time passes and when we're not roadkill, I have to admit there's something thrilling about this. It's exciting in a way that defies everything reasonable.

Note: I will never admit this aloud.

He takes the turn off the highway for Winter Park, and I lean the way he does. And I'm certain we're going to fall and die anyhow. There's no reason to be at this angle. I take back what I said about it being thrilling, this is just death taunting. My heart is in my throat, but we finish the turn and we're upright again.

I will kiss the Corolla when I see it.

Once we're in Winter Park, we have to weave more than on the highway, and if possible, I hold him tighter. When we stop at a working light, he pats my arm and leaves his hand on me until the light changes. I think he says something. The vibrations of his voice echo through his back, but between his visor, my helmet, and the engine, I can't hear him.

We make it to my driveway, and he takes off his helmet and shuts off the bike.

"Make sure to get off on this side because the exhaust pipe is very hot," he says.

Great.

I slide off the bike, and once again I'm wobbly. He reaches out to steady me, and I put my hands up for him to stop. It may be silly since I've been pressed against him for a while, but it's different being face-to-face.

We lock into a wordless stalemate. There's so much I want to say, but none of it comes out.

"Thanks for the ride, I guess," I say.

He nods.

"Goodnight." I turn toward my door.

"Jasmine," he says.

I stop and look at him.

"You're not a competition or a game to me," he says. "You never were." He pauses and then says, "You're not like anyone. And you're perfect the way you are. I know you don't believe me, but I hope one day you will."

Eugene gets on his bike and kicks it started. He puts on his helmet and backs out of the driveway. I remain still and watch as his taillight disappears into the night.

CHAPTER SIXTY

By the end of the day Monday, some of Winter Park (the richest part) has power. By Tuesday night, the generator shuts off and my house has full electric again. By Wednesday, I'm back at Berry Plum.

I haven't heard from Eugene since he drove away. When I watched his bike disappear, I had a feeling I'd never see him again. I tell myself I'm okay with that. He lied to me like everyone else—even after I told him the truth about Paul. Bits and pieces of our conversation gnaw at me, but I can't process any of that right now because my life is in ruins.

I haven't forgiven my family, and it's become a constant weight around my chest. We've settled into a quiet truce where I ignore them and they cast looks in my direction every few seconds. It won't last forever, but for now they leave me alone.

I also haven't forgiven my friends.

With almost no one to talk to, I've spent a lot of time at the shelter and I picked up more shifts at work. Katia is in the middle of relationship drama with Lee, and she's talking about them nonstop. At least it's a distraction.

The only person I talk to lately is Paul, and although we're not officially back together, he filled out an apartment application and he's been accepted. He wants to put a $500 deposit down this week so we can move August 1—thirty-six days from now. I guess that's okay. It would, at least, get me away from my family. But I can't seem to say yes. I also haven't formally accepted the Valencia scholarship, despite their email threatening that I'll lose it if I don't respond soon. And I know this is what I've worked for, but right now it doesn't seem to matter.

I finish my shift at Berry Plum and walk out the door. June and Emily wait next to the Rolla.

"We didn't want to come in while you were working, but can we talk?" June says. She's still in her tennis whites.

"Maybe take a walk in town?" Emily says. "I'll treat to Peterson's Chocolates."

Dammit. Bribery. Peterson's Chocolates are wildly good, but wildly overpriced.

"Please," June says.

It's been five days since the hurricane party, which makes this the longest we've ever gone without talking. Emily and I have had longer breaks, but only when she's been out of touch on trips to places with no cell coverage.

They stare at me, waiting for a response. I sigh. I want to get in my car and drive away, but the truth is, I've missed them. And deep down I know I'm wasting what little time we have before they leave for college—before I'm left behind. I know that years and years of friendship mean they deserve to be heard. And in the end, they didn't organize the contest. Of course, they knew and didn't tell me, but all things considered, that seems like a lesser wrong.

"I'll follow you over there," I finally say.

A few minutes later I meet them in the small candy shop. I'm not joking when I say each chocolate-covered strawberry is five dollars, but they're enormous and my favorite.

"I'll have one," I say, pointing to the cloche.

"Just give us a dozen," Emily says. She hands over her credit card.

"That's way too many," I say.

"June and I will have them too. Whatever we don't finish just take home."

We stroll out of the store and toward the green space in the middle of town.

"So, we're shit friends and we're sorry," Emily says. She hands me the bag of strawberries.

I blow out a long breath.

"I'm especially shitty," June says. "We've been friends longer and I did the podcast. I should've told you, and I also held Emily back from telling you. I just . . ."

"You just what?" I say.

I bite into one of the strawberries, but it's going to be a mess to eat and walk, so I sit on a park bench. They both perch on the one next to mine. We sit in the sun-dappled shade of the large trees.

"I just wanted you to be happy," June says. "I didn't think about how you'd feel if you found out. Paul was so bad for you, and when he said he wanted to take a break, we thought you'd finally meet a better guy—but you said you wouldn't date. When your family told me about the dating contest idea, all I could think was it would be good for you. That other boys might help you see you the way we see you."

I shake my head. "I don't get it. Cari said something similar in the podcast. What does that mean—see myself the way you see me?"

June hesitates and makes a few false starts.

"You never acted like you were worth a damn," Emily says. June purses her lips but doesn't argue. "You kept settling and making excuses for The Paul's shittiness because you had this idea in your head that you needed to hang on to anything you had. That it was all you deserved. You were afraid to reach for anything new. But you changed this summer. I mean, I'm sorry as hell we had to lie to you, but you changed for real."

"You got into a batting cage, you raced go-karts, you swam in the ocean," June adds.

"I rode a motorcycle on Sunday," I say.

"Get the fu— . . . hell out of here," Emily says. She's been trying to curse less post-Shawn.

"What? How?" June says.

"More family intervening," I say. "I cooked for the pop-up dinner at Amway."

"Oh my God, yes! My family saw you on TV," June says.

"Well, Jay abandoned me afterward so Eugene would have to take me home."

June and Emily stare at each other and then at me.

"Wait, back up. You were with Eugene?" June says.

"You got on his motorcycle?" Emily says.

"I didn't want to, but there wasn't another way home," I say with a shrug.

"Oh, no. See, this is what we're talking about," Emily says. "Old Jaz would've either walked or waited around for a family member to come get her. How was it?"

"I lived."

"How was it seeing him again?" June says.

"I lived." I finish the strawberry and pitch the stem in the trash can. I actually make it. "He, um, he told me he really fell for me."

The two saps across from me nearly melt on their bench.

"Guys, no," I say. "He lied to me. He was a game-show contestant. How can I take anything he says seriously?"

Emily claps her hands together and dusts chocolate off them. "All right, I know we're supposed to be nice and super sorry and I am. What we did sucked, and I never thought it was the best, but do you even hear yourself right now?"

"Em . . . ," June says.

"No, seriously. She's going to be pissed at us for lying and I get it, but what about turning that around? You lie to yourself more than *anyone* lied to you."

"How do I lie?" I say. "I didn't tell him about Paul at first, but . . ."

Emily shakes her head. "What don't you lie about? You liked Eugene. He liked you. You don't want to be with The Paul, but you're too scared to end things. You don't want to be a nurse, but you're too scared to tell your mom. All that settling, 'I love the status quo' thing, was always such bullshit.

You want to cook in Paris, so go do that. Stop lying to yourself about what you want."

We're all silent for a while. I'm stunned, so is June, and even Emily seems taken aback by her own words.

The thing is: Everything she said is true. It's everything I've been thinking since my graduation party. Just said aloud. I do like Eugene. And I've been too scared to cut things off with Paul because what if I don't find better? What if I'm totally alone when everyone leaves next month? And it's been similar with my mom. How do I break her heart when I'm not sure if I can make it as a chef? But it's what I want to do. I want to be a chef. I want to learn to cook in Paris. But I'd have to leave everyone I love behind.

"I'm not you, though," I say. "I can't just say everything on my mind to my parents. And what if things don't work out? What if I can't make it as a chef?"

It feels so . . . naked, to have my worst fears out there. But June just tilts her head.

"They're your family, Jaz," June says. "They love you. This whole ridiculous thing happened because they love you and just want the best for you."

"Tell them what's up," Emily says. "Be that boss bitch we know you are and stop using your family as an excuse to not live your life. If things don't work out, then they don't. Then you go to Valencia. But that's better than never having tried."

As her words sink in, I realize how much I've been using my family as a reason to stay in place. There's nothing wrong with a family as a safety net—that's how things should be. But somehow things morphed in my mind and they went from being a safety net to a glue trap. I was scared I wouldn't be able to make it as a chef, and my family became the excuse why I couldn't. I let the comment Jay made when she was losing her dream stop me from pursuing mine.

And what is the worst case? In the worst case, I do fail. I'll be embarrassed. I'll be hurt. But I'll still have my family. And I can still go to community college here. Or even reapply to schools and go to a four-year college. But at least I can say that I tried.

I'm so struck by my thoughts that it's a while before I notice how quiet we've all been.

June glances around, worrying her fingers on a napkin. "Um, so, we really hope you'll find it in your heart to forgive us," she says. She shoots Emily a dirty look.

And I can't help it. I laugh. All three of us laugh.

"I missed you guys," I say.

"We missed you." Emily reaches across and I take her hand. June does the same.

"We love you, Jaz," June says.

"I love you both," I say.

And that's how, on a Wednesday afternoon, we sat crying on park benches in the middle of town.

We get ourselves together, and Emily adjusts her eye makeup with the tip of her finger.

"But seriously, what are you waiting for?" she says. "When are you going to actually live your life?"

"Right now," I say.

And I mean it.

CHAPTER SIXTY-ONE

"I'm really happy you asked to meet here," Paul says. He slides into a chair across from me at Tijuana Outpost. It's not Burrito Friday; it's Thursday lunch, but close enough.

He looks handsome in a soccer jersey and shorts. He used to love playing soccer as a freshman. It made him happy— until he realized football was way more popular at our school and more interesting to his dad. He was different back then. We were different back then.

"You didn't order anything, or are you waiting for your food?" he says.

"I never really liked the food here," I say. I sip my Coke.

"Oh." His eyebrows knit. "We could've gone somewhere else. Chuy's was good."

I smile. "It was good. But this place has more memories."

"Yeah, it does." He reaches across and puts his hand on mine.

I flip my hand over and take his. It's so familiar but different at the same time. I take a deep breath.

"Paul, most of those memories weren't good. Not for me," I say. "Not in the past year, maybe more."

"In the past year?" he says, his eyebrows knitting. "I know

we haven't had a good couple of months, but things were fine senior year. You're exaggerating."

I shake my head. "I'm not. Things were only fine because I put up with so much, and I won't do that anymore."

He withdraws his hand. "What do you mean?"

"I mean: I know we still have thirty-five days until August, but I've made up my mind," I say. "It's time for us to go our separate ways."

He shakes his head. "I thought . . . but we're back together. I got the apartment. We're moving in together."

"No," I say. "I wanted to meet to tell you in person that we can't move in together. I don't want to do this anymore."

He looks hurt, broken for a second, then his expression morphs into anger. Then calm, and that was always the worst.

Paul sits back and folds his arms. "You've chosen one of your contestants, huh?"

There's the snide I knew was coming.

"No. I want to be on my own."

Paul looks thoroughly confused. "I don't understand. I'm saying I want to be with you. Move in together. Start college together. What we've talked about for years. They all lied to you, Jaz. I'm the only truth."

He's right: they did lie, or at least didn't tell me the truth. I've thought about this for days.

"I know," I say. "But they lied to me to help me. I've wanted to get back together with you, I have. I've wanted to keep my life the same. But there's nothing to go back to."

"Nothing?"

I shake my head. "It's not your fault. I had this vision of us being together forever, and I wanted it so bad. I was so caught up in this safe zone where I wouldn't have to experience life that I was willing to do anything to stay. That's on me, not you. You never asked me to do that. And I don't think it was possible for you to respect me when I didn't respect myself. When I accepted any way you treated me. Instead of expecting you to expand your world to include me, I shrunk myself to fit into yours. And I can't fit back into that space. I won't again."

He's stunned silent, blinking at me.

"But I love you," he says.

And it hurts. It physically impacts my chest, and a soft sadness closes in around me.

"I love you, too," I say. "I think I always will. And if you want to be friends, we can be. I still care about you."

He shakes his head. "But if we love each other . . ."

"The thing is, just because there's love doesn't mean it works."

And just like Emily said, the second I stop trying to hold things together, I feel immediate release. I know for certain this was right.

I grab my purse. "I want you to know that I do remember the good times," I say.

"We could have more . . . ," he says. And his expression makes him look just like the boy I met. The one who didn't have his guard up all the time. The one who told me he loved my brownies. The one who still liked himself.

I reach out and cup his face with my hand. "We're moving in different directions and it's time. You knew it this summer before I did. We'd only hold each other back now. And I love you too much for that."

I get up from my chair and kiss him on his cheek. "You're going to be great, Paul."

With that, I walk out of Tijuana Outpost for the last time.

CHAPTER SIXTY-TWO

It's Thursday night and I'm making dinner. My entire family is home and they keep passing by the kitchen, looking at me. Their glances are everything from slight smiles to confusion to caution, like this may be a trap. But after I talked to Paul, and after I finished crying, I sat in my car thinking about what we'd said. When I pointed out that my family had lied to help me, it was true. I started the engine, then I went grocery shopping.

"Dinner's ready," I say.

They come out of hiding and take their places around the dining room table. I made pasta Bolognese, a simple salad where I tried to whisk together a dressing as tasty as the one at Lantern & Jacks, and the sinangag arancini I made at the pop-up dinner.

Mom and Dad sit at the heads of the table. Cari and Davey are across from me. I put my napkin on my lap and start passing the dishes around. My family looks confused, but they fill their plates.

"I . . . this looks great, Jazzy," Dad says.

"It really does, honey," Mom says. They exchange glances, and someone kicks Davey under the table.

"Yeah, smells good. When can we eat?" he says.

Cari full-body sighs at him. "Thanks for making dinner, Jaz."

But they're all waiting for me. Even Davey, who seriously doesn't want to.

"I know you all want to talk about what happened," I say. "So let me say this: You crossed every line as if personal boundaries don't exist. You lied to me and orchestrated a whole competition instead of just talking to me." I look at my sister. She stares down at her plate. "You treated me like I'm an extension of you and not my own person." I pause and glance at my mom and dad. "You bet on me like I was a pro sports game." I raise an eyebrow at Davey, who has the decency to look away. "And you did it all for me."

All four faces look up at me.

"Well, maybe not the betting, but you wanted me to understand what I'm worth. I'm not going to lie: there were better ways to do it than to set up an elaborate fake reality show. Couldn't you see it would make me think boys would only like me for the novelty of it? There were also better ways to get me away from Paul than to throw three guys into my world. But I get it. You were trying to help."

"We . . . we just wanted you to realize how great you are," Mom says. "I'm sorry. We're all sorry it got so out of hand."

"I shouldn't have taken bets," Davey says. "That was messed up."

"We should've had more respect for you and trusted in you more," Dad says.

I look at Cari. She has tears in her eyes.

"I'm sorry for all of it," she whispers. "The podcast, the reality show, everything."

"It was humiliating," I say. "You could've just talked to me. Especially you."

"I know," Cari says as her tears fall.

"But you put a ton of work into creating the competition, really searched to find guys who'd be the perfect fit for me. And you didn't do it for the fame. Because you already had that. You did it because you love me—and you got carried away, but it was out of love first."

Cari sniffles and nods.

"Can you forgive us?" Dad asks. "We love you, Jazzy. This thing was done out of very foolish love. The whole family loves you and just wanted to see you be happy."

"Are you going to start recognizing boundaries?" I ask, sticking a fork in my salad.

"We will," Mom says. "I swear it."

"Then yes," I say.

Everyone physically relaxes, lowering their shoulders. They pick up their utensils and start twirling their pasta or cutting into the rice balls.

"There's something else, though," I say.

Everyone freezes like we're playing red light green light.

"What's that, Jaz?" Cari asks.

"I've decided I'm not going to live with Paul," I say. "We ended things today."

My parents exchange glances of restrained glee.

"Oh, that's . . . good," Mom says.

"And I'm not going to go to Valencia," I say.

The look my parents exchange this time is less gleeful.

"Oh," Dad says.

"What?" Mom asks.

"Not this fall, anyhow," I say. "I've deferred admission a year. I sent the emails today."

"What . . . what do you want to do, then?" Mom asks.

I take a deep breath. It's now or never.

"This," I say, gesturing to the table. "I want to cook, professionally. I've always wanted to, but I've been afraid to try. I've been afraid because of what happened to Aunt Jay. Because of how our family lost money. Because of how your relationship changed with Jay. Because of how hard you and Dad had to work since you took out the loan to invest in her restaurant. Because I didn't know the whole story. Because I was afraid I didn't have what it takes. Because I've been afraid my whole life, of everything, really."

They are so silent, I can hear cicadas chirping outside. I might as well get the whole thing out there.

"Instead of going to college in the fall, I want to take a gap year. I want to go to Paris and work in a kitchen," I say. "I want to see if I can make it as a cook. And then if I can, I'll come back and go to culinary school."

And then it's out there. All of it. No more secrets or lies. Well, almost. I take another deep breath.

"When Jay had Ventura's Bistro, I used to go after school,"

I say. "I learned to prep and cook with her, and it was the happiest I've ever been."

"I—" Mom begins.

"I can see it," Davey says through a mouthful of food. "You're really good."

I shouldn't be relieved, because I've made up my mind, but it's nice to have someone's instant support.

"It's what I love to do," I say.

Mom blinks a couple of times. "You don't want to be a nurse anymore?" she says.

And it hurts. It stings to disappoint her, and I wonder if things will be as strained between us as they became with Jay. Still, I slowly shake my head. "No. I don't."

I hold my breath and wait for her to respond.

"Well, good," she says.

It's my turn to be surprised. I widen my eyes and stare at her. "'Good'?"

"You have problems with the sight of blood, Jaz," Mom says. "Remember a few years ago when Davey needed stitches after playing basketball? You went white as a sheet. I was never sure nursing would be right for you, but you seemed so determined."

I can't believe this. "You're not upset?" I ask.

"I'm a little upset that Jay was teaching you behind my back, but I'm hardly surprised." Mom sighs in the long-suffering way of an oldest child dealing with the youngest. Cari sighs at Davey in the exact same manner.

"I mean, that I don't want to be a nurse," I say.

Mom pauses and Dad talks instead.

"We want you to be happy," he says. "I'm shocked you want to go all the way to Paris. It is *far*. But if it's your dream, I support it. As you said: it's your life. All we've ever wanted is for the three of you to find yourselves and be happy."

Mom opens her mouth but just exhales and nods.

It's hard to believe these words are coming out of my parents. I thought they'd be so disappointed, so opposed. But it was just my own fear standing in my way this whole time.

"And these rice balls are amazing," Mom says, pointing with her fork.

Happiness bursts through me.

"Why didn't you ever tell me the story about Aunt Jay's restaurant?" I say.

"Ventura's?" Mom wipes her mouth and frowns. "It was really complicated, and you were only fourteen or so when everything fell apart. The money was one thing, but Jay was so hurt. She was humiliated by loving and trusting someone who betrayed her. Rick wasn't just her business partner—he was her boyfriend. She . . . we all thought they'd get married. But it was a ruse. He embezzled all that money, and now he lives in Venezuela with his wife."

"Argentina," Dad says.

"Somewhere that doesn't extradite. I forget. It was such a bad situation that it became something we didn't mention—we didn't want to hurt her more. But I had no idea it affected you. Or that you'd been working there." Mom stops and raises her eyebrow.

"Regardless, it's our job to worry about loans and payments—not yours," Dad says. "And if we had to do it all over again, we still would've supported your aunt. It's what family does."

"And, honey, Jay is okay," Mom says. "She got a lot of business from you appearing on the news. The local story was picked up nationally."

"It was?" I ask.

Cari nods. "She got a ton of Instagram follows and business inquiries from it—good job dropping the IG."

"That's great," I say. "But you're really okay with me going to France, with not being a nurse, Mom?"

Mom purses her lips. "It'll be hard—to have you that far away. But it'll only be for a year, and we can FaceTime. And when you'd said nursing, maybe I latched on to it too hard. But nursing is the last thing someone should do if they don't really want to."

"If it's your dream, Jazzy, go to Paris," Dad says.

Mom nods. And we're all silent for a second.

"We'll have to find you a place," Cari says. "One with an extra bed, because I'm definitely going to crash with you during winter break."

"We can all fly over for winter break," Dad says.

Mom smiles.

Their reaction is more than I ever could've hoped for—to not only have their support but to know I'll see them in a few months.

"But you don't have the money for that," I say.

"Oh, you control our finances all of a sudden?" Mom says. She raises her eyebrow—the scary one. "There's overtime. There's savings. And Jay has started to pay us back. I can't think of a better way to spend it."

She smiles gently, and I feel a glow radiating from my core.

We dig into our dinner and it's one of the best meals I've ever had, because I have my family with me.

After dinner, Davey goes back to whatever warfare game he's into now, and Mom and Dad retreat inside, probably to tell the rest of the family what's happened and figure out how they'll stay in constant contact with me while I'm in France. It still feels surreal, but there are two more things I need to do.

Cari is washing dishes at the sink. I pick up a dish towel and start drying.

"I can get those later," she says. "You cooked."

"I know, but I want to talk to you."

She glances over at me, her worry line appearing.

"I texted Justin Michael," I say. "He apologized again about the contest, and we're going to stay friends."

"That's good. That's really good, Jaz. I'm glad you decided to forgive him."

"Just wanted to give you an update for your next podcast," I say. I wipe a plate until it shines.

Her chin drops toward her chest. "Jaz, I . . ."

"I get it. You wanted something that was yours. And you love love."

"I did. I do," she says.

I put a plate to the side. "So, when are you actually going to experience it for yourself?" I say.

"What?" She turns and stares at me.

I lean against the counter. "You keep watching people fall in love. What about experiencing it for yourself?"

"I don't know, Jaz. It never . . . it wasn't a priority for me, I guess. I wanted to build my brands. I love my family and it . . . it's enough."

"It isn't, though, is it?" I say.

"I . . . It is." She frowns and picks up another plate to wash.

"Huh. Well, I texted Aaron back today too. He said he was sorry for lying to me, and I accepted his apology. He told me he really is into me and we're going to start dating for real now."

Cari drops the plate into the water. "What?"

I laugh. Okay, maybe it was a mean lie, but she's owed one and I got the reaction I was looking for.

"You should see your face right now," I say. "You like him and that's okay. We're not dating. We never were. But you two should."

She shakes her head. "I don't . . . no. It was for you . . . we . . . no."

"He did this whole thing to get to know you," I say.

She shakes her head. "No . . . he wouldn't . . . he . . ."

"Yeah, he did," I say. "We even talked about it earlier today while I was grocery shopping. He fell for you the minute you had coffee together, but you were so excited about the contest that he felt like he had to go along with it. He likes me—but as a little sister. Nothing more."

"He . . . did? He said that?" she asks.

"Yes. I don't think I'd lie about something that flattering. But you two are perfect together." I lean against the counter and fold my arms. "How about it? Both of us on our big adventures this year?"

"I . . . Jaz, I don't know."

I get her hesitation. We're more alike than it seems on the surface. She's confident and beautiful, but she has even less experience than I do when it comes to relationships. And taking any kind of chance is scary, but especially when your heart is at stake. It's easier to watch from the sidelines and never get in on the action. But that's not really living.

"You should think about it," I say. "It would be a great spin for your podcast. And a great thing for your life."

I open my arms and she opens hers and we hug in the kitchen.

"You are so very special," she says.

And the weird thing is: I know it. I'm not her little side-kick. I'm not her shadow. I'm her sister. And maybe the over-the-top bachelorette competition did help me see that I have my own value. It's different from hers, but not less.

"I love you," she says.

"I love you, too."

We go back to cleaning up. Just as we finish the dishes, the doorbell rings. She moves to answer it but I stop her.

"I'll get it," I say. "It's Aunt Jay."

Cari raises her eyebrows. She doesn't know what happened, but she knows that things changed with Jay years ago.

I open the door and let Jay in. I'd texted her at the end of dinner asking her to come by.

"Hey," she says. She hesitates in the doorway, but she's carrying a box. "I brought some brownies for dessert."

Jay was, of course, the person who taught me how to make them.

"Come in," I say.

Jay takes her shoes off and sets the box on the table. We stand on opposite sides of the dining room. Cari lingers by the entrance to the kitchen. We both look over at her.

"I was just . . . going. Yeah, I was going," Cari says.

With Cari's first less-than-graceful exit, my aunt and I are left alone. We stand in uncomfortable silence until Jay clears her throat.

"Thank you again for mentioning the catering company at the pop-up," Jay says.

"You're welcome again," I say. "Can I ask you something?"

Her eyes meet mine, and she moves a chair closer and sits down. "Shoot."

I pull out a chair and aim it across from her like it's an interview. "Why did you ask me to cook with you at the pop-up?"

She wrinkles her brow. "It's like I said: you know how."

"But you said I wasn't good enough," I say.

She shakes her head. "What are you talking about?"

"You said I wasn't good enough to become a chef," I say.

Jay shakes her head again. "I never said that. I would never say that."

"You did. When I was fourteen, we were in your office and you said I didn't have what it takes. It was the last time I was in your restaurant."

Jay's face falls. She puts her head in her hands, then rubs her nose and draws a long breath. "I don't remember saying that to you, Jaz. I swear. I love you. I've always loved you and I would never want to hurt you. Is that why you didn't talk to me after?"

I nod.

She gives me a rueful smile. "I'd always thought you avoided me because you were disappointed in me. Because I couldn't live up to your expectations. I barely remember seeing you in the office that day, but I do remember telling you to go home. But that day—the one where you came in—I'd found out that all the accounts I'd figured Rick was paying were left unpaid for months. He'd been stealing from the restaurant, from me, for such a long time. And he'd had his fill, I guess. He made his escape plan to go back to his wife in Argentina and left me so in debt, I couldn't run the restaurant anymore. He'd written me a goodbye letter and after I read it, I decided to drown my sorrows in a bottle of wine."

My aunt looks pained by the memory and winces.

"I only just found out about Rick today," I say. "I'm sorry."

"I should've told you. It's my fault, Jaz."

Her blue eyes are tear filled, and I hate that it took us so long to finally talk, but family secrets have a way of staying buried even when the hurt shows.

I reach out and take her hand. A small smile lights Jay's face.

"When Eugene told me you still wanted to be a chef, I knew you hadn't given up," she says. "That's the full reason I asked you to cook with me."

I frown at his name and how they'd been talking about me. But it makes sense why he thought I wanted to be a chef and why he kept pushing me on it.

"I'm going to try it," I say. "I talked to my parents tonight about going to Paris to become a chef."

Jay brightens and squeezes my hand. "Oh, Jaz! You'll do it! I know you will. And I'll help however I can."

She pulls me into a hug and I lean into my aunt. I duck my head and hear her heart beat. The same way I did in eighth grade after I told her what had happened with Kyle. And it's still so comforting.

"I'm sorry about what happened to you," I say.

Jay pulls back and strokes my cheek. "I know you are. Thank you, Jaz."

She gives me another hug, and we're still hugging when Mom walks in. I freeze, ready for them to go at it.

"Everything okay?" Mom asks.

Jay and I both nod.

"We're great, Mom," I say.

"Good, because I need to talk to you," Mom says.

She raises her eyebrow, the scary one, at Jay. Jay widens her eyes but laughs. Then Mom smiles. What the hell is this?

"Wait, what?" I say.

They both stare over at me, identical blue eyes unblinking.

"I thought . . . I thought things between you were . . . I don't know," I say. "After the restaurant closed, it seemed like things changed."

They look at each other and shrug.

"I guess things have been a little more contentious, but it seems no different to me," Jay says.

Mom nods. "I don't always approve of her choices—like for example letting a thirteen-year-old cook in a kitchen." Mom shoots Jay a look, and Jay purses her lips. "But I love her all the same."

"And Dee is an intolerable know-it-all, but I love her too," Jay says. "That never changes with family."

They laugh and I laugh too. Mom and Jay go into the kitchen to talk, and I know she's about to let Jay have it for things that happened four years ago. But she'll do it with love.

And as I bite into one of the brownies, I know that even though people claim romantic love matters the most, sometimes all you really need is the love of your ridiculous family.

EPILOGUE

AUGUST 15

The rest of the summer passed in a blur of paperwork and video chats. There was a mountain of little things that needed to be done before spending a year abroad. But with my mom and dad's help, I got my passport, residency card, and other documentation in order.

My sister was also busy in the late summer. With my permission, and my interview, she did two last episodes of *The Little Bachelorette*. It's been a huge success, and it's now linked to her website. Everyone loves the spin of her ending up with one of the contestants.

My sister and Aaron, in case you're wondering, are absolutely insufferable together—in the best way. They're a blissfully happy, gorgeous couple that makes other couples feel bad about themselves.

It's gross.

Because of the success of *The Little Bachelorette*, Cari's campus radio station offered her her own show. She's thinking about doing a contest on campus—one everyone will consent to this time. Aaron and I have both told her she should do it. She's also gotten more podcast sponsors and used some of that money to buy me new clothes.

I said I didn't need new stuff, but she wanted me to look good when I'm in the fashion capital of the world. I'm hoping I will be in a chef's jacket most of the time.

Right after brownies, Aunt Jay introduced me to Chef Jeanne Dumont, whom she knew from culinary school. I've video chatted and messaged with Chef Dumont, and she's willing to audition me in her well-reviewed restaurant in the heart of Paris. She was impressed by the fact that I cooked at the pop-up benefit and that Chef Matthews recommended me. I don't know if I'll get the job—there are no guarantees, because she needs to see how I perform in the kitchen—but I'm hopeful. I'm also stunned that Chef Matthews said I "had promise."

I've practiced cooking every day, to Davey's delight. He's grown a full, unfair inch this past month, and it's made him hungrier than even normal. We played restaurant at dinnertime, where my family would order from a menu I created that afternoon. My little brother went a step too far, though. He sent back a steak one day and I sent a wooden spoon flying at his head.

My extended family has also been incredibly supportive. At our grandparents' July sixth party, the family, somewhere between being sorry for what they did and happy for me, surprised me by pooling together and giving me enough money for my rent. It was too much and I didn't want to take it, but they insisted. Aunt Regina called it damages for emotional distress.

And now I'm holding the ticket Emily, June, Aaron, and Justin Michael paid for as I stand among them and my entirely too big family at the departures section of Orlando International Airport.

I already checked my giant suitcase. I'm bringing a carry-on on the plane, which has books and a change of clothes in it, in case they lose my luggage (my mom insisted).

The mob of Venturas and Yaps descends on the TSA checkpoint, and the guards are visibly alarmed. They're talking into their radios, and I'm pretty sure my family will be asked to leave.

"Well, I guess it's time to go," I say.

I start my goodbyes. This'll take a while. There are fifty of them between slaps with cousins, perfumed hugs with aunts, and waving to my dad, who, obviously, is recording this moment.

Actually, there's fifty-four with June, Emily, Justin Michael, and Aaron. Paul didn't come to the airport, but he texted and wished me a good trip. We don't talk much anymore, but it was nice that he remembered.

"Goodbye, June Bug," I say.

She wraps me in a hug and I can feel her tears on my shoulder. "I can't believe you're leaving. . . ."

"You're leaving too, don't forget," I say.

She and Justin Michael are going to drive together to college because Georgia Tech and Emory are both in Atlanta.

I've raised my eyebrows about how "close" they'll be, but she keeps shaking me off and pretending like she doesn't know what I mean.

Note: she knows what I mean.

"Get in here," I say to Emily.

We have one last Angels' hug. Emily has to leave straight from the airport to drive to LSU with her parents, but she refused to miss this.

"I love you both so much," I say.

"Obviously. We're incredible," Emily says. "You'd better be on WhatsApp all the time."

"Constantly," I say.

"I love you," she says.

It's hard to believe this is the last time I'll see them in person for a while. They've said they'll come to Paris for spring break and I can't wait. I let them go physically, but they're in my heart forever.

Emily fans her eyes to dry her makeup, and June tries to stiffen her lip. Justin comes alongside of her.

"Stardust," I say.

"I'll miss you, Candy," he says.

He wraps me in a hug and even though it's not there, I smell Cocoa Puffs and newsprint on him once more.

"Take care of yourself . . . and her for me," I whisper.

He releases me and gives me a look like, "Did you say what I think you said?" I raise my eyebrows once and glance over at June. He blushes. Actually blushes.

"I'll, um, drive safe," he says.

But his look tells me all I need to know. Maybe there will be another unexpected love match from *The Little Bachelorette* contest after all.

I slap Aaron five. "Take care of my sister or . . ."

"Or you'll come at me with a baseball bat again? Believe me, I'm terrified," he says. He spins me up into a hug. He's different now that he's dating Cari. There's less of that playboy façade and just a deeply nice guy. "Take care and come to Nashville when you're back stateside."

"I will," I say.

When he puts me down, I'm facing Aunt Jay. She's the last person I need to say goodbye to. And also the hardest. We've been cooking together during all my free time since the night she and I talked.

"I'm going to miss you, kiddo, but you're going to do great," she says.

I throw my arms around her. "Thank you again for everything you've done. Even with the pop-up . . . I couldn't have done this without—"

"You could've. And you would've done it without me," she says, shaking her head. She hands me a small box. "Open this when you get to Europe."

"What is it?"

"You'll see later," she says.

I'm thoroughly confused, but I take the small box from her and put it in my carry-on. "Okay."

"I love you, Jaz, and I'm so proud of you," she says. "You have what it takes."

Tears prick my eyes but I smile at her. "I've always been proud of you," I say.

I already said goodbye to my parents, but I hug them one more time and tell them I'll talk to them soon.

My family and friends watch me go through security, my dad taking a million pictures, until I turn for my gate. I immediately feel the loss of them, and there's still a part of me that wants to turn around and run back. But a part of me will always want to take the safest route. I just have to conquer it.

I'm going to Paris. My dream, the one I barely dared to whisper a season ago, is coming true. With the help of my family and friends, it's become real. I've been reading French books, listening to French songs, trying to immerse myself and . . . I still suck at French. But I'll try harder and get better.

I find my gate and sit down. I look at the clock and I have only . . . two hours before the plane boards.

Ugh. Mom and her ever-earliness.

I read. I eat. I do another Duolingo lesson, and I still have . . . more than an hour to go.

I sigh. With my adrenaline so high, it's hard for a book to keep my attention. I rummage through my carry-on for the other book, and the box Aunt Jay gave me tumbles out.

It was weirdly cryptic when she gave me the present, but there'd been so much emotion in saying goodbye to my family and friends that it didn't even register. It does now. It's a larger jewelry box, which is odd because Aunt Jay isn't a jewelry fan. Maybe it's something for the kitchen.

So, like Pandora before me, I open the box.

My heart stops.

Inside there's a watch. I know this watch. I remember the boy's wrist it used to decorate. I remember the boy.

Eugene already left for Europe. He flew out August 1. Not that I stalked him or anything.

Note: I totally still creep on his Instagram.

But this is his watch. Why did Aunt Jay give it to me?

I lift it up, and the back of the face is engraved. TIME TO FIND YOUR WAY.—E. B.

I shake my head. Eugene is E. M. But E. B. sounds familiar. Then it hits me: Eugene Bruin was Chef Matthews's mentor. He basically got Jack off the streets when he was addicted to drugs and introduced him to the kitchen. He must've given this to Jack, who gave it to Eugene, and now . . . he's giving it to me?

That's impossible. I'm a girl he only went on three dates with. And we haven't spoken in more than a month.

But I look closer. It's the same brand, but it's not the same worn leather. This is new. The same way his dad has a newer one. It's a replica.

Underneath the watch there's a business card. It's from Lantern & Jacks. I flip it over and there's writing.

I hope you find your way, Jasmine. And
maybe, one day, it'll lead you to me.
—E

I stare. I read it. I read it again. And again. And again. I miss him. We didn't know each other long at all—the impression was swift, but it was deep.

I put the card back in the box and place the watch on my left wrist. It's ticking, but the time is wrong. It's . . . wait, it's on Paris time.

Before I can overthink it, I grab my phone and open iMessages.

Captain Eugene Crunch

> So, if you're ever in Paris and want to look me up,
> I'll be the girl with a fancy new watch

Gray dots finally appear and I hold my breath. He's there, and at least he's trying to talk to me.

Hi, Jasmine

Are you already in Paris?

> Not yet. Waiting to board my flight

Well, I can be the guy with the matching watch who picks you up from the airport

If I were sipping water, I would've spit it out.

> Wait, are you really in France?

I can be

Okay, I am, but I sound less creepy if I claim I'm not

I can't help it. I smile.

It's the gentleman creeper thing to do

I am in France. I'm here with my mom because she wanted to do a second wine course. But also . . . because you. Jay told me you were coming

A last, parting interference from my beloved family. But just the thought of Eugene takes my breath away. I don't know where this will go. I don't know how to feel about him after everything that happened. And I don't know how it'll be to see him again. But maybe that's okay.

I'll text you when I land

And I'm still smiling when they announce boarding for my flight. It's so cheesy, but that's okay. Cheese is honest.

I grab my bag and make my way toward the plane and whatever future lies ahead.

ACKNOWLEDGMENTS

First and foremost, an enormous thank you to my long-suffering agent, Lauren Abramo, who signed me in the first ever #DVPit and has constantly believed in me, even when I doubted myself. Thank you for your wisdom and for fielding all my emails that started with "a great idea from me!" and ended in "idk what if I just became a sock puppeteer instead." I don't know where I'd be without Jennifer Ung, whose amazing guidance helped me breathe life into Jasmine and her zany family. Words can't express the value of your support in helping me shape this story and how fantastic it was to work with you.

Thank you to everyone at Simon Pulse, now Simon & Schuster Books for Young Readers, for your hard work and talents. Special thanks to Krista Vossen and Kat Goodloe for the beautiful cover and for making Jasmine so perfect. Thank you to Justin Chanda and Kendra Levin for believing in this story. Thank you Krista Vitola for all your ongoing support. Thank you also to Dainese Santos, Katrina Groover, Lynn Kavanaugh, Sara Berko, Lauren Hoffman, Chrissy Noh, Lisa Moraleda, Christina Pecorale, Victor Iannone, Emily Hutton, Michelle Leo, and Anna Jarzab for helping me turn this wild dream of writing a young adult novel into reality.

A million thanks to Beth Phelan for creating #DVPit which not only introduced me to Lauren, but allowed me to become part of the fantastic DVSquad. The community I gained remains priceless and I'm ever grateful for your selfless dedication to making publishing more inclusive. Thank you to my fantastic CPs, especially Karen McManus, who inspires me as an amazing author and an even better friend. Thank you to Jenn Dugan, for your humor and wit and murder cat stories. Thank you to Llama Jen, for your insight and counter-balance. Thank you to Gloria Chao, for sprint rush CPing with me when we thought: hey, maybe we can land agents. Thank you to Straight Justin, Karen Strong, Erin Hahn, June Tan, Caroline Richmond, Patrice Caldwell, and Fallon DeMornay for your friendship and advice. Thank you to Kiki Nyugen for your love and being the best cheerleader ever. A big thank-you to Kara Leigh Miller for teaching me so much when we were mentors together, and thank you to all my mentees for allowing me to be a small part of your journeys.

To my zany family: Thank you to my children, who were mostly good while I was "*still*" writing my book. My sunshine and heart, you are my true loves and inspirations. Thank you to my loving mom, who has always been there for me and who said maybe I should actually sell one of the books I write, and to Gregg for making the time for me to try. Thank you to my sister Jill, who is not at all feckless, for reading my first, not-good books but being kind about them, and Matt for much the same but also being my best friend. Thank you to my father, for first instilling this love of books that I've carried with me to today. Last but not least thank you, my readers, for taking this journey with me.

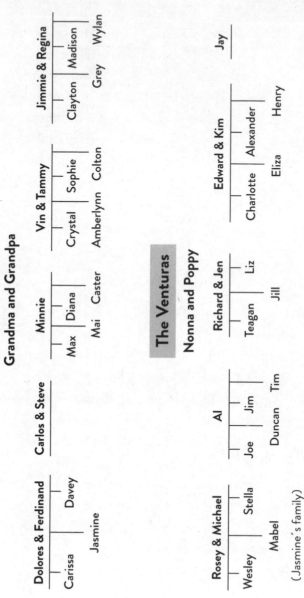

The Yaps

Grandma and Grandpa

Dolores & Ferdinand
- Carissa
- Davey

Jasmine

Carlos & Steve

Minnie
- Max
- Diana
  - Mai
  - Caster

Vin & Tammy
- Crystal
  - Amberlynn
- Sophie
- Colton

Jimmie & Regina
- Clayton
  - Grey
- Madison
  - Wylan

The Venturas

Nonna and Poppy

Rosey & Michael
- Wesley
- Stella
  - Mabel

(Jasmine's family)

Al
- Joe
  - Duncan
- Jim
  - Tim

Richard & Jen
- Teagan
  - Jill
- Liz

Edward & Kim
- Charlotte
  - Eliza
- Alexander
  - Henry

Jay